substitution cipher

edited by Kaye Chazan

Candlemark & Gleam

For information, address
Candlemark & Gleam LLC,
104 Morgan Street, Bennington, VT 05201
info@candlemarkandgleam.com

Library of Congress Cataloging-in-Publication Data
In Progress

ISBN: 978-1-936460-40-3
eISBN: 978-1-936460-39-7

Cover art and design by Kate Sullivan

Interior Graphics by Alan Caum

Book design and composition by Kate Sullivan
Typeface: Berthold Baskerville

Copyediting by Sarah LaBelle

www.candlemarkandgleam.com

substitution cipher

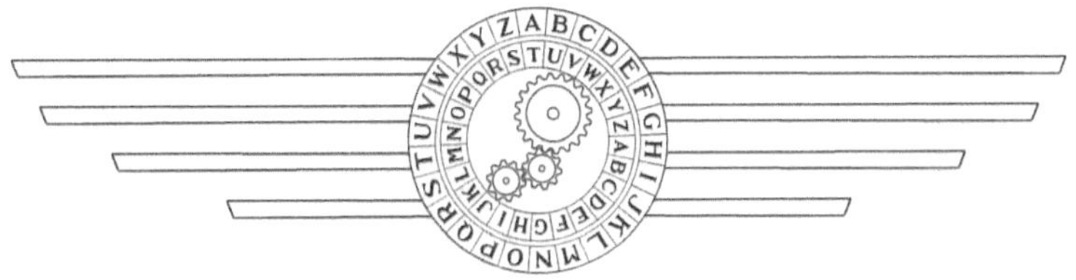

Table of Contents

Introduction

Spies cannot be usefully employed
without a certain intuitive sagacity.

Spies cannot be properly managed
without benevolence and forthrightness.

— Sun Tzu, *The Art of War*

Comedian George Carlin says that "military intelligence" is an oxymoron. It's a good joke, a great icebreaker at parties among certain crowds, but like most humorous exaggerations, the kernel of truth is just that: a kernel. War may be inherently brutal, wasteful, and occasionally downright stupid, but a great many of the people who participate in it are not. At the front lines or behind them, providing crucial information from unstable positions, intelligencers and spies make many of the wartime decisions that can end a battle on the spot–or prolong it indefinitely–and carrying such a burden takes a dedicated individual with a keen mind.

Alternate history, too, relies on those lynchpin

moments, those precarious instances where one left turn can prevent an assassination, or one turned ankle or bent horseshoe can delay vital information. Spies embody those moments, personify them, distill all the secrets and hopes of the war that employs them into one person. One choice, one *word,* and all of a sudden the July Plot succeeds, or the city-state secedes, or a well-timed riot prevents a wall from ever going up.

In short, spies make amazing protagonists. With all that knowledge concentrated in one person, they can make choices that undermine both history and fiction.

The six stories in *Substitution Cipher* call on six protagonists for whom "military intelligence" is far from a joke. In "So the Taino Call It" by M. Fenn, Rodrigo changes the course of Christopher Columbus's journey to the New World. In "Spheres of Influence" by Rebecca Rozakis, Cadenza throws a wrench into the gears of a clockwork Venice. Our two World War II-era stories couldn't be more divergent: Tyler Bugg's "From Enigma to Paradox" centers on historical personage Wilhelm Canaris, while G. Miki Hayden's "In God We Trust" turns North America inside out along with J. Edgar Hoover. C.D. Covington's "Something There Is" pits protagonist Elisabet against the Stasi with only the broken city of Berlin for her ally. My own contribution, "The Ashkenazi Candidate," offers you a spy who has a hard time keeping his name straight as he plays on both sides of a new Cold War. All of these heroes–inasmuch as some of them can be called heroes–control not only the directions of their respective stories, but history itself. They're smart, and the stories are smart—as provocative as they are entertaining.

And who knows? In any of these new histories, George Carlin might be a spy.

– Kaye Chazan

So The Taino Call It

By M. Fenn

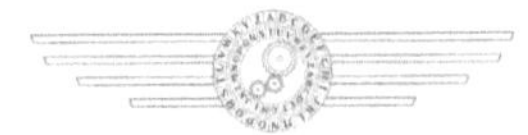

"This is a replica of the first and only European building in the entire western hemisphere."

The museum docent, a stocky woman with long salt-and-pepper hair, pointed to a haphazard-looking fort situated a few feet away from the wooden walkway she was sharing with a small group of teenagers. A nametag on the woman's mint-green uniform read "Ms. Mayagüez." The walkway led to the history museum, a large, low-slung building constructed to emulate the longhouses that the island's ancient leaders once lived in. It was made from wooden poles, woven straw, and palm leaves, but reinforced with steel and concrete.

The dozen boys and girls, in their early teens, looked down at the fort with varying degrees of interest as the woman continued.

"The Europeans built this shelter from one of their ships that ran aground. As you can see, it's not very big. Hard to believe ninety men squeezed in there, isn't it?"

"What did they come here for?" one of the boys asked. He ran his fingers through his hair, pushing it back from his angular face.

The docent smiled. "They were trying to sail to Asia."

"They didn't know that Aztlán was in the way?"

"No, they had no idea."

The children looked at each other smiling. A couple couldn't help but giggle.

"How could anybody not know that?" a small, thin girl asked, a look of disdain on her face.

"Well, it was a long time ago, Yahíma. Our people didn't know there was a Europe either."

"Did they go back home?"

"No. There was a battle further up this beach." Ms. Mayagüez pointed past the fort. "Except for a few that surrendered, our ancestors killed them all."

The children looked past the fort and down the low hill to the beach. The waves crashed into the shore; the tide was coming in.

"Why?" a quiet voice asked.

The guide's face grew solemn. "When the Europeans landed on our shores, our ancestors welcomed them and treated them as honored guests. They thought the strangers might be gods come to earth, but they were rude and violent, except for a few. You've heard of one of them in your history classes, I'm sure: Rodrigo de Escobedo. He helped us against his own people and taught us the best ways to fight against them. Our people defeated the Europeans, and Escobedo's lessons spread to the other islands, even to the mainland."

She turned away from the fort and led the students to the next exhibit. This display was closer to the walkway. The figure of a tall, pale man stood in the center of a group of people who were crafted to look at him with an admiring gaze from wherever they stood or sat on the sand. He was dressed in Spanish armor.

Next to the man stood a woman who looked like the rest of the statues in the display: her long hair in bangs and flowing behind her shoulders, and her dark skin bare, except for a small apron tied around her waist. She wore the feathered headdress of a *cacica* and rested her hand on the man's arm. Her other hand was raised with his, clasping a sword.

"This is Rodrigo de Escobedo with Anacaona, the Golden Flower, two people instrumental to our people's survival and development."

The students spent more time studying the man than they did looking at the woman or the figures around them. Bare skin was still commonplace after all these years; pink skin was not.

Escobedo's facsimile was close to six feet tall. His brown hair, flecked with grey, fell to his shoulders; his sharp chin sported a thin beard. The artist who created him also gave him a beatific smile. The docent thought it was a bit much, but museum-goers seemed to like the look.

"The artists took some liberties in their creation," Ms.

Mayagüez pointed out. "Anacaona wasn't yet *cacica* when Escobedo arrived here. And Escobedo rarely wore armor, according to the records we have. Artists, though, like a bit of flash."

"He's so pale."

"I like his eyes," one girl murmured. She pulled at her ponytail as she studied the figure.

A tall, muscular boy caught the docent's eye. "Why did he betray his own people?"

The woman smiled. "Good question, Macuya. It turns out that he was being paid to sabotage his captain's mission."

The students' expressions became puzzled. A few started questioning her at the same time.

"Why?"

"Who paid him?"

"Why did our people think they could trust him?"

"For profit," the docent responded. "The Portuguese. And they didn't know. He didn't tell them, but the journals he left behind told us."

Ms. Mayagüez walked a few more feet, reaching the last exhibit of the tour, housed inside a walled porch that was open to the ocean view. Flat-screen monitors lined the three walls. The students jostled each other as they clustered around them.

"Escobedo kept a journal from the night he set sail from Spain until the day he died. You can see pages from these books on the screens. Go ahead and touch the screens to change the pages, if you'd like to."

"What language is this?" one boy asked.

"It's Italian, Abey." She chuckled. "But even if you could read the words, you still couldn't understand what you read. It's all in code."

"Wow!"

The guide nodded. "He started using code because his work was secret, and he never stopped using it. That's also why he wrote in Italian instead of his native language, Portuguese."

"How did you figure out how to read it?"

"Our archaeologists found his cipher. It opened a new world of understanding for us. His place as one of our national heroes was assured while he was still alive, but there aren't many records from that time. Finding the cipher allowed us to meet the man behind the hero. Fascinating fellow."

The children studied the screens as the woman watched them. The girl who had liked Escobedo's eyes was focusing intently on the pages in front of her.

"What are you finding there, Ana?"

Ana shook her head. "I just wish I knew the language. I'd love to break the code." She looked at the docent. "I'd love to learn more about him."

"Well, we have a few books on Escobedo in the shop. Your school library would have them, too."

"Have the journals been published yet?"

"Not yet, no. We still have to decipher and translate the last few volumes. Hopefully in the next year, though."

Ana frowned. "A year?"

Ms. Mayagüez patted the girl's bare shoulder.

"How would you like to see translations of the first

few volumes? I think I can arrange that."

"Really?"

The woman smiled. "Sure. And any of your friends can read them, too."

She looked hopefully at the rest of the group, but Ana knew better and returned her gaze to the screen in front of her. The kids looked uncomfortable, and no one responded. Finally, Yahíma spoke up.

"No offense, but Ana's the book nerd in the group. Nice tour and all, thanks, but we have better...um..." Yahíma stopped, realizing too late that she'd put her foot in it again. She rolled her eyes at herself and looked away.

The docent pursed her lips. "I see. Well, you certainly don't have to join in."

She opened the door that led back to the main hall of the museum.

"This concludes our museum tour. I hope you enjoyed it."

Everyone hurried by her, muttering their thanks.

At least they can say "thank you," she thought. She looked up to see Ana watching her. The girl shrugged her shoulders and tried to smile.

"Sorry about them. They're really all right. Just not as interested in history. You know."

"Hm. Sadly, I do."

"Um..." Ana paused, finding herself nervous and not wanting Ms. Mayagüez to think her as rude as her friends. "When might I be able to read the journals?"

"When do you have a free day?"

Ana thought for a moment. "The day after tomorrow.

No school, and I'll be done with chores by mid-morning."

The guide patted her on the back and ushered her through the door.

"Very good. I'll make the arrangements and be in touch."

Ana grinned as she ran off to join her friends. "I can't wait!"

Two days later, Ana was rushing through her chores in the little house she shared with her father and his sister. Her father had to tell her twice to slow down before she broke something. Finally everything was done, and she stood by the front door, waiting to be released.

"You've taken your aunt her meal?"

"Yes, Papa." Ana forced herself not to roll her eyes.

"And she's taken her medicine?"

Ana sighed. "Yes, Papa. Everything's finished. Can I go?"

Her father tilted his bald head as he looked at her.

"You have your phone?"

"Yes!" Her exasperation was obvious, and her father chuckled.

"All right, then." He held her by her shoulders and kissed her forehead. "Be careful."

Ana shook her head. "'Til later, Papa."

She kissed him on the cheek and ran out the front door. She grabbed her bike, brown and in need of new tires, from where it stood in the gravel near the side of their adobe home. Her father watched her pedal away down the busy street lined with houses identical to theirs. The only difference amongst them was the color of each house's trim. The trim on Ana's was a dusty rose. Others were turquoise, yellow, or ochre.

Ana's short legs pumped the pedals of the bike as she steered it through the city's labyrinthine streets, lined with little beige houses, dingy shops, charging stations, and vast factories. She wove through traffic of electric cars and buses. The sidewalks were full of people.

And then she was at the gate, a simple checkpoint that monitored everyone entering or leaving the city. Ana pulled an ID card from a pocket in her thin shorts and slipped it into the electronic reader. She hardly took a breath before the green light blinked on and the barrier lifted, opening the road to her.

A few more miles of riding through traffic took her to the northeast tip of the island, where the museum was. She parked her bike in a long rack filled with other bikes and went inside.

Ms. Mayagüez met Ana at the information desk in the museum's main hall. The place was filled with naked children running everywhere, their parents trying to keep up and others trying to avoid colliding with them.

Ana and the docent made their way through the crowd and through a textured glass door marked NO ADMITTANCE. The girl found herself in a moderately lit hallway, the crowd noise from the other room diminished to a quiet rumble.

"Here we are."

The docent stopped at another textured glass door, this one marked ARCHIVES. She opened it, and let Ana walk through first. She stopped, her mouth dropping open a bit. Every wall was lined with books, and the room was huge. It seemed as big as her little house. From floor to ceiling on every wall were shelves that held hundreds—thousands?—of books, manuscripts, loose sheets of paper, and even rolls of parchment.

"It's quite something, isn't it?"

Ana swallowed. "Yes, ma'am."

Many tables filled the floor of the archives. Some had computers installed, but many didn't. A few people clustered at the tables, engrossed in their work.

The docent led Ana to one table near the front. Several dark blue bound books sat in a pile, looking new. A much older collection of papers lay next to them.

"These are the new translations you have permission to read." The docent patted the books. This..." She pointed to the papers. "...is the first original journal and Rodrigo de Escobedo's cipher. I thought you'd like to see them before you started reading."

"Oh, yes!" Ana held her breath as she looked at the ancient rag paper in front of her. The pages were small—much harder to read than they had been on the screen. She had to squint to see some of the inked letters. Ms. Mayagüez, wearing thin, white gloves, turned the pages for her.

"This is wonderful," Ana whispered.

"Have you started languages yet in school?"

"Oh, of course." Ana frowned. "But I've only taken

western languages. I don't think my school offers Italian."

"Maybe not. Some colleges teach it, though."

Ana sighed. "But that's so long from now. Three years!"

"Good thing we have these translations, then."

The woman gathered the original documents together and returned them to the archivist's desk, then walked back to the table.

"Well, take a seat and dig in. You can read until we close at six." She pointed to a small silver bell sitting on the table. "If you need anything, ring for the archivist. He's grumpy, but he'll help you. Now, you didn't bring a camera or anything to write with, did you?"

"No, ma'am."

"Good girl. Enjoy yourself. I hope you find Rodrigo de Escobedo as interesting as I do."

She walked away as Ana pulled the first book off the pile.

The Journal of Rodrigo de Escobedo
Volume One

was embossed in the cover. She opened the book and found herself somehow disappointed that the words were printed instead of written by hand with ink hundreds of years old. She shook her head.

"I can pretend," she muttered and closed her eyes. She called up a memory of those ancient pages she had just seen, the way the writing flowed and bumped across the rough material, the way the ink had made sharp, thin lines, and the way the paper was torn in some places from too forceful a pen stroke.

She opened her eyes and began to read.

2 Aug 1492
Palos de la Frontera

The men I drink with when I go down for dinner think I'm mad for sailing away to find Asia tomorrow. Even they know you can't go west to get to the East. I won't come back alive, some say. Sea monsters, others say.

It's hard not to laugh at those old fools. That's not why I won't be coming back. Everyone knows the world is round like a ball.

Well, not *everyone* knows, I suppose, but the real problem is that Cristóvão Colón believes it to be a much smaller ball than most men who study this sort of thing. *That's* why I–and everyone I'm sailing with–won't be coming back. We're going to die of thirst and starvation somewhere in the midst of the Ocean Sea, thousands of miles short of our goal.

Why am I doing this, then? And why am I writing my thoughts in code in this cheap, ugly inn, waiting to leave my life behind? Writing my own history, even though no one will ever read it but me?

It's my father's fault, now that I think about it.

I'm a blacksmith's son, born in the castle of the duke

my father worked for. He's Spanish, from Murcia, and followed my mother's father to Portugal on the promise of a good job and a pretty wife, the man's daughter. She died squeezing me out, leaving my father to raise me while he worked his trade. I learned all that I could to bend and forge metal. I could have taken my father's place when he died, if that had been God's will.

It wasn't.

As a child, when I wasn't working for my father, I was drawn to the chaplain of the court and the monastery that was nearby. These men were kinder to me than my father, who never forgave me for killing his wife.

The large books the priest and monks read fascinated me, and they soon taught me how to read them, too. They were excited by how quickly I learned my lessons, although they weren't the most patient of teachers. Languages came to me quickly, as they still do, and I was becoming proficient in Latin and Italian when my father put a stop to it.

I was forgetting my place, he argued. He insisted that I spend more time working with him and with the other boys living in the duke's castle. I still bear a scar on my face from his arguments.

I soon became expert in the skills that these boys had to teach: picking locks, scaling walls, and breaking into houses, among other things. My swordsmanship is lacking, but I know how to cheat to win a fight.

Breaking into the house of a wealthy merchant set me on the path I walk today.

I underestimated the villa's security (a mistake I've

never repeated) and was captured by the man's guards. Instead of killing me on the spot or turning me over to the duke or my father, he offered me a deal. If I would do some work for him, all would be forgiven. Refuse, or fail at any of my tasks, and my life was his.

Unless I wanted to fight, I had no choice in the matter. His guards were big men who seemed to prefer the idea of killing me—there'd be no opportunity for cheating—so I agreed to his offer. After that, life became a little more worth living, a lot more exciting.

Although I missed my books.

As I accomplished everything I was ordered to do, my reputation grew. Soon the man was farming me out to other minor magnates who spread the word of a young man, competent and discreet, who was willing to take on any job for a good price. My master, as I called him, took a hefty commission out of my pay. Still, there was money enough to leave my father and rent a room in the village.

I didn't realize how far up the ladder I was climbing—or that I was even climbing one—until my master arrived at my room one evening and took me to meet the duke. I returned to the castle, continuing my work of thievery and espionage at a higher level. I continued to climb that ladder, eventually reaching the top, working for King João himself.

I'm now the scrivener for Captain Colón's ridiculous voyage. My main responsibility—other than maintaining the captain's logs and writing down anything anyone needs written down—is to keep a record of the path we take across the sea to get to Asia and then to return home, either back the way I came or by the Silk Road, with that travel record. I'm also tasked with preventing Colón and his men from returning home at all.

Yes, my employers think quite a bit of my skills. I'll admit, though, that as I get older, my reflexes aren't what they used to be.

Writing down my thoughts like this could be my undoing if someone deciphers this journal. The cipher I've created is well hidden in my belongings, and I pray to God it won't be discovered. He's treated me well, the Lord has, and I'm grateful. If dying at sea while serving my king is to be my end, so be it. The Lord has a plan for all of us.

So, I'll write down my thoughts while I have the time.

It was a long journey overland from Lisboa to Palos de la Frontera on the southern coast of Spain. I was exhausted when I arrived, as was my horse. She got to rest, but I immediately set out to find Captain Colón.

I visited the inn where my sources informed me he was staying, but he was out. The innkeeper thought he might have had a meeting with his investors at their quarters near the Rábida Monastery, so I headed there next.

I was in luck. A man was just leaving through the main gate of one of the villas near the monastery as I was arriving. I thought it must be the captain. He walked like a seaman, for one thing, with a rolling gait, and he fit the description I'd been given: taller than me, with auburn hair and pox scars on his face. Also, as I drew closer, I could tell that he was speaking Genoese.

I followed the man and his entourage as they walked back through this port town. They stopped at a large inn, different from the one where Colón was staying. Not the one I've been staying at, either. Too rich for my purse. Maybe too rich for Colón's purse, as well. He pretends to be more well off than he really is, so I'm told.

Such is how you gamble with royalty and bankers, spending beyond your means in the hopes of such profit that makes your investment look puny and cheap. It's the nature of things. So, he makes an appearance at the town's fanciest inn.

I followed the men into the building and made my way to the bar as they settled around a table not far from me. The captain looked pleased with himself, and wine began to flow freely. I bought one brandy and nursed it as I watched the men get drunk.

At one point, Colón staggered to his feet and lurched away from the table and toward the door. Seeing my opportunity, I stepped away from the bar. I bumped into the bigger man, spilling my drink on the two of us. He grabbed me by my tunic and I tensed up. I'd been warned of the captain's violent temper, but he showed no anger, only drunken bemusement.

"You've spilled your drink," he said.

I began to apologize, my words slipping from Spanish into Genoese.

He cocked his head at me. "You're from Genoa?"

I nodded, pretending to look surprised. "Why, yes. Are you?"

"Of course! Cristoforo Colombo at your service."

He started a bow that might have been a disaster if I hadn't taken his arm. Once he was firmly upright again, I introduced myself.

My own bow was a little more elegant, but Colón assumed I would need help and took my arm. When I rose, I saw suspicion in his eyes and felt his grip tighten.

"That name's Spanish, not from Genoa."

I smiled. "True, indeed. My mother, she married a Spaniard. She believed the rumors, you know."

He laughed at that, clapping my shoulder hard enough to knock me back a step, and invited me to refill my glass with him and his companions. His original errand forgotten, he took my elbow and led me back to his table. He offered me a seat, yelled for more wine, and then proceeded to grill me about Genoa. He hadn't been back in more than a year and was hungry for news from home.

So, I told him about Genoa. It was a collection of lies, of course, but he enjoyed the stories, almost upsetting the table at one point when he emphasized his laughter by slamming his fists into the wood.

After a while, though, he started asking me about myself. Even in his cups, the captain's not stupid. I lied a little less this time, sharing how I could speak several languages and had experience sailing in the Mediterranean. All of that's true, as is the fact that I can read and write and know the Bible well. It pays not to lie any more than you have to.

His eyes lit up when I mentioned that I was looking for work on a ship and asked what kind of work I'd like.

I gave him a rueful smile and told him that if I could find a ship in need of a scrivener or an interpreter, I'd be pleased. (I wasn't lying when I said that I wasn't as young as I used to be.)

He nodded in sympathy as he refilled my glass. "As it happens, I've already hired an interpreter," he said. "But my ships *are* in need of a scrivener. How would you like to travel to Asia?"

I almost laughed at his offer. Finding Colón and convincing him to hire me had taken no work at all. I took a deep swallow of wine to hide my amusement, but it paid to ask questions, to not look too relaxed about the prospect he offered.

"That's a long voyage, isn't it? Around the bottom of Africa?" I asked.

Colón laughed and shook his head. He looked at the other men at the table. A couple had fallen asleep, while the rest were in the midst of a game of dice. He looked back at me.

"We're going west."

I gave him a skeptical look. "To the East?"

"Indeed. It will be a great adventure with riches at the end. Your fame will be assured."

I pondered his words. The first part, no doubt, was true. Fame and riches, though? Not likely. I looked at him with what I hope passed for sincere excitement and told him I'd be honored to join him. I also asked what the job would pay.

He grabbed the flagon of wine and filled my glass, not answering my question. He pointed vaguely to one of the other men.

"Report to the docks in the morning," he said. "My ship's master will get you sorted out."

I nodded and met his toast when he pushed his glass my way. He drained his drink and began to tell stories of his own. Other men at the table chimed in when the captain's voice lulled and the storytelling went on for hours. The evening finally ended with us all stumbling back to our rooms.

That was a week ago. The flagship's master and owner, Juan de la Cosa, a barrel-chested man with a long scar running down the side of his neck, was suspicious when I approached him the next morning, but my ability to write and copy everything he said without mistake softened his mood. After I told him that I was handy with tools and could speak Spanish and Portuguese, as well as Genoese and Italian, he became downright cheerful.

I've been working on one or another of Colón's three ships every day since. They're good ships. Small, but sound. *La Santa Maria*–the flagship–is the largest, a three-masted nao (called a carrack by the Spanish). *La Pinta* and *la Santa Clara* (nicknamed *la Niña* by its crew after its owners, Juan and Alexander Niño of Moguer) are caravels, quick in the water, although built for coastal sailing, not the adventure Colón has in mind.

I find it interesting that the caravels are both owned by different sets of brothers: *la Niña* by the two Niños, and *la Pinta* by the three Pinzóns of Palos de la Frontera.

Colón's friendship with both the Pinzón and the Niño men has been key in securing the funding the captain needs, as well as in overcoming the doubts of the sailors he's tried to recruit.

The captain's a different man when he's sober. He didn't appear to recognize me when he approached de la Cosa while the master and I were speaking. Colón nodded vaguely when de la Cosa explained who I was, but then continued to give his orders to the master while ignoring me.

At least he didn't order me off his ship. The master's happy with my work, too, it seems. A fair beginning is a blessèd thing.

When I'm not working, I've been exploring the city, discovering its charms. This may be the last Christian city I ever see. I may never see my family and friends, what few I have, again.

I must leave for confession now. The captain wants us all shriven before we set sail tomorrow.

3 Aug 1492
first day at sea

We left port this evening and have been at sea for several hours. A large crowd gave us a raucous send-off—cheering, yelling obscenities, the usual enthusiasm for men risking their lives for some ill-defined goal. Men going to sea, going to war, going to the gallows: I've found that it all tends to draw a similar reaction from people.

I should probably keep that thought to myself.

I've brought only a few things on this voyage. My belongings fit in a small shoulder bag: a small Bible, my writing materials, a few pieces of clothing, and my rosary.

One of my teachers at the monastery gave me the Bible. He remembered my love of reading and hoped the Book would turn me toward a less sinful life. I don't know if that's possible, but reading the Word of God makes me feel closer to Him.

The rosary belonged to my mother. Her father acquired it on a pilgrimage he made to Santiago when he was young. The wooden beads and cross are a deep red that seems to glow in the right light. It's well worn, and I imagine my mother's fingers caressing it as she prayed. It's the only thing of hers I own, and I'll admit to these pages alone that when I kiss the cross I think of her sometimes, and not of Our Lady.

I've also brought my own quadrant and compass and am experimenting with finding the best place on the ship to take surreptitious readings. While, as scrivener, I have access to the captain's logbooks, I wish to keep my own records as well.

6 Aug 1492
at sea

Today is the Feast of the Transfiguration, when Christ

showed His divine nature to His disciples. This was my contemplation as I prayed over my rosary this morning. I wonder what it was it like to be there and witness His true face.

In more earthly matters, one of the two smaller ships, *la Pinta*, has lost its rudder. Not completely, but it's come unhinged, and we're stuck in the water until we can get it repaired. The captain is hoping the Pinzón brother in charge of that ship can do enough to get us to the Canaries. I've heard rumors of sabotage.

I wonder if I'm the only spy on this voyage.

4 Sep 1492
San Sebastian la Gomera

We reached the Canaries nearly a month ago. Along with its crippled rudder, *la Pinta* had begun taking on water. I think everyone sighed with relief when we limped into port.

Once again on land, the men have been grumbling about returning home. Colón has strong allies on two ships, *la Santa Maria*—my ship—and *la Pinta. La Niña,* though—the Niño brothers are the loudest grumblers of any of them. I can't blame them, honestly. Good omens have been lacking since this voyage began. And now that we've reached the islands, the captain doesn't seem to want to leave.

We first dropped anchor in the port of Las Palmas. There our wounded ship was repaired, and we renewed our supplies of fresh water and wine. While making his courtesies to the governor of the island, Colón met the regent of la Gomera (a nearby smaller island), Beatriz de Bobadilla y Ossorio. She's the widow of the Spanish governor of this place. Her son inherited the position, but he's still young, so she rules in his place.

I've seen the woman. She's beautiful and tall, with incredibly pale skin. Her bearing is as regal as her clothes. I've heard rumors, too, of her cruelty. The native people here tell stories in that whistling birdsong they sing. It's eerie to listen to. I doubt, though, that she's any more cruel than the Portuguese who owned this rock before Spain. I love my king and my people, but we're all cruel. I fear it's human nature.

Now we twiddle our thumbs while the captain pays court to a woman who pays him nothing in return.

So the rumors say.

I've begun to see Colón's temper flare up, and I wonder if that's evidence that those rumors are true. He strikes out at his men when they anger him, including me, and he had to be pulled off of one of the whistling natives who offended him somehow.

When I'm not writing for the other sailors—mostly letters to send home and wills—I walk a great deal to pass the time and stay out of the captain's way. One blow from him is enough.

La Gomera is a lovely island. It's nearly round, except for the bay to the southeast, and its mountains rise up high from all sides, filling the center. The hills are covered in mist most of the time, and the thick groves of trees drip with dew.

The port of San Sebastian is small, with the bulk of the village built into the valley between two ridges that come down to the water. The harbor is a crescent bay with a broad opening to the ocean. A long dock reaches out into the water, partially blocking the bay's mouth.

This afternoon, I was hiking along a ridge that borders an eastern beach, enjoying the view of the water and the volcano that towers over the nearby island of Tenerife as I contemplated Jesus's cursing of the fig tree. Why would He do such a thing? It doesn't seem in keeping...

Well, who am I to question the Word of God?

A flash of motion or light caught my eye as I pondered, and I looked out over the waves. There I saw ships.

I sat down, hanging my legs over the edge of the ridge, and waited as the ships sailed nearer. After an hour or more, they approached near enough that I could recognize the flag the boats flew.

Portugal.

Was this King João's alternate plan? Why would he be sending three large warships–for so they were–close to Spanish territory if not to disrupt Colón's voyage?

My guess is that these ships will lie anchored there waiting for us to set sail. Once out at sea, they will attack and put an end to us.

❖

morning, 5 Sep 1492
San Sebastian la Gomera

After dinner last night, as the sun was setting, I hiked back up to that ridge, this time with a dark lantern.

In the dark grey of twilight, I wasn't sure I'd be able to see the ships, but I hoped for the best as I walked. Reaching the spot where I had relaxed earlier in the day, I squinted out to sea with no success. I'd waited too long, and it was now too dark to see any distance.

Still hopeful, I lit my lantern and flashed the Portuguese navy signal for friend.

For several minutes, I saw nothing, but then the same signal flashed back to me.

Before I could return the signal, the distant light flashed again.

Who are you?

I flashed the code for my initials, but saw no light in return for several minutes.

Hello? I flashed. Nothing again for a moment. Then:

We must meet.

Why must we meet, I wondered. I'm doing my job. Go away.

Instead, I flashed back:

When and where?

Tomorrow came back immediately. *Midday near the dock-master's hut.*

Yes, my lantern replied.

Nothing more came from the warships, so I climbed back down the hill to town and my little room.

Have I lost the king's trust or have new problems appeared?

evening, 5 Sep 1492
San Sebastian la Gomera

I hate bureaucrats. They're detestable creatures whose only joy in life is mucking about in the affairs of men who actually accomplish things.

I arrived early at the docks and wandered around eying the several ships at port with vacant curiosity while keeping a fierce watch on the port's entrance. As the appointed time drew near, I spotted a large dinghy rowed by six men approaching the docks. Three others sat in the bow of the boat.

As they rowed closer, I could see that one man was unhappy about the sea spray hitting his face and smiled at his discomfort. Not very Christian of me, but I wasn't feeling overly charitable at that moment. I approached as they secured the vessel.

The three passengers stepped onto the dock, and we studied each other before anyone spoke. Two of the men were sailors, their clothing similar to mine: linen shirts, jerkins, breeches, and low boots. The third was dressed like a courtier, his doublet and hose rich and colorful. He brushed his clothes with his hands, trying to remove the water.

I looked around the dock. At the other end of it,

men were loading sugarcane onto a caravel. In between the dock-master strolled, looking for trouble or fees to collect. He looked at my group with a questioning eye, but a smile and wave from me seemed to satisfy him. He eventually returned to his hut.

"You wanted to meet me?" I suggested, hoping to start this conversation.

The three looked at each other. One of the sailors, his hand on the hilt of the cutlass he wore at his hip, spoke first, asking if I had sent the signals the night before. I acknowledged that I had, and the courtier began to speak. I stopped him with a frown and a sharp wave of my hand.

"Not here. My shipmates might see us if we loiter here. Come."

I turned without waiting for their agreement and left the dock. Veering into a narrow alleyway, I glanced back to see that only three were following. They'd left the rowers behind. The alley was short and opened onto a path that led to the beach or up into the island's interior. I turned toward the interior.

"Sir, where are we going?" the courtier asked as the path began to climb.

"Somewhere private."

Soon we were in the mountains, and the path ended in a flat space fenced in by sharp spires of rock. A thick fog filled the air. I turned to my companions, my mood grim. I asked them who they were and why they had come here.

The courtier puffed himself up as well as he could in the dim dampness of the place. The sailor with the cutlass had drawn his weapon and was looking back down our path. The second sailor extended his hand to me and smiled, introducing himself as Captain Nunes, of the *Santa Teresa.* I shook his hand and gave him my name in return. He introduced our guard as Pedro Alcides, his master-at-arms.

The courtier interrupted Nunes then, declaring himself to be Diogo de Almeida, from the court of King João.

I shook his hand, finding it clammy and his grip too tight. I wiped my hand on my breeches, a rude gesture, but I wasn't in a generous mood. I asked again why they were here.

Almeida went on at some length, seeming to avoid answering my question just so he could continue filling the air with his voice. Finally, he summed up. "His majesty has put a lot of his trust in you, and he asked me to confirm that everything is following the plan."

He looked at me like I was an erring servant; I looked at him like he was the pompous ass I took him to be.

"It is. Other than our extended visit to this island," I responded.

He wondered how long we'd be here and I shrugged, telling him it was up to Colón. He asked what I could do to speed up our departure, and I chuckled at the thought of pushing the captain to do anything right now that didn't involve Señora Beatriz.

"Why the rush for us to return to sea?" I asked him.

The man tried to look nonchalant, but didn't carry it off well.

"No reason, really," he said. "Other than his majesty would like this resolved."

I eyed him suspiciously. "How so?" I asked. "What was your plan to be if something had taken me out of the situation?"

Almeida stumbled on his words and wouldn't meet my eye.

"Our orders were to sink Colón's fleet," Nunes admitted, confirming my guess.

The courtier coughed, waving away Nunes's words as if they gave the air a bad smell.

"But you *are* here," he said. "So that's not an issue anymore."

Something in Nunes's expression made me wonder, even as Almeida tried to gain control of the conversation, telling me that his majesty has full faith in my ability to succeed in the mission, that he'd merely asked Almeida to confirm that all was well before the long journey west begins.

I smiled, not trusting any of these men. What would the reward be for sinking Colón's fleet, I wondered.

I clasped my hands behind my back as I told the men to please return to Lisboa and tell his majesty that everything *was* well.

"Now, I should get back to town before I'm missed," I added as I turned to leave.

They all smiled and made way for me to lead them back down the path. We didn't speak again until we'd reached the main road to the dock. There we parted; I didn't want to be seen with them. They were friendly enough when they left me, and they hadn't tried to kill me on the way down the trail, but I wasn't convinced that their plans had actually changed. I went in search of Colón. Taking the risk of interrupting him as he strolled with the governor, I told him of the Portuguese ships I had seen.

6 Sep 1492
at sea

The captain took my warning seriously, and we're at sea again. The masters-at-arms of all three ships collected the crew last night with the help of the dogs they'd brought along for jobs like this. Big ugly things with vicious tempers, these dogs. The ships left port before dawn.

I feel better now that we're away. There's been no sign of the Portuguese.

4 Oct 1492
at sea

It's been four weeks since we left the Canaries. No sign of land, and everyone's nervous and quick to anger.

My quadrant readings and the captain's match closely, but both the pilot and I have noticed something wrong with the compasses. They're both off north by a noticeable degree. I heard Colón tell the pilot that he was aware of the compass discrepancy and it wasn't anything to worry about. I imagine the pilot saw the same look on my face as I did on his.

We're lost.

10 Oct 1492
at sea

Last night, I woke to shouting amongst the ships. Rising from my corner on deck, I found most of my shipmates clustered along the far rail yelling a mix of obscenities and encouragement across to one of the other ships. I approached and asked what was going on.

"Mutiny," one sailor responded. "The Niño brothers are trying to turn *Niña* around."

"We should do the same," another remarked under his breath.

I squinted into the darkness, trying to see what was happening on the other ship, but only my ears could make out anything.

Raised voices and swordplay. I recognized Vincente Pinzón's deep voice yelling for calm.

Colón appeared behind us at the rail and pushed his way through. The men groused and complained as he did so, and one was brave enough to push back. Colón raised his hand to strike him, but the anger he could see in the men closest to him made him stop.

"Men!" he yelled. "My brave men! Hear me!"

He spoke then of our duty to him and their majesties at home in Spain, how fame and riches awaited our success, how even God Himself wanted this mission to succeed.

The men studied him in silence until the sailor who had pushed back spoke.

"Our ships are lost, Captain. We should have found land before now."

This set everyone muttering in agreement, the volume increasing. Colón raised his hands.

"All right! Give me three more days. Three days!" He yelled loud enough for his voice to carry to the other ships. "If we don't sight land by the thirteenth, we'll turn for home. I promise you."

The wariness of the men didn't diminish, but enough nodded in agreement that the captain visibly relaxed. He turned to the rail and yelled for Pinzón.

"Three days, Vincente! Three days to find land, or we go home. Tell them."

Soon I could hear the chant of "Three days!" from *la Niña*. The men on *la Pinta* as well as on our ship joined in. Colón ordered an extra ration of wine for everyone and returned to his cabin.

11 Oct 1492

at sea

Flocks of birds flew over the ships this morning, their

heading more to the southwest than ours. Colón ordered a change of course to follow them. Birds must land somewhere, no?

The crew's much calmer today, but men have asked me whose side I would be on if there was a revolt. Not that bluntly, of course, but the question they ask is plain. My response has been noncommittal, although, I guess, as I'm the captain's scrivener, they assume I'll be on his side.

I might as well be. Colón's survival and arrival in Asia is an important factor of my mission. What happens after that is another matter.

12 Oct 1492
at sea

The watch of *la Pinta* got a glimpse of land early this morning. Four bells, it was. I awoke again to shouting as our watch caught sight of it, as well. Everyone wanted to climb to the crow's nest and take a look, but the captain forbade it.

"Plenty of time for that," he grumbled. "Besides, I saw lights before going to my cabin last night."

The sailors quit crowding the mast, but looked at the captain askance. The master of the ship, one of the masters-at-arms, and I were with the captain when he claimed to see lights in the distance last night. The three of us saw nothing but the moon shining on the water.

However, Queen Isabella promised ten thousand maravedís to the first man to see land.

Regardless of petty bookkeeping, land is near. Was Colón right in his figuring after all? Have we reached the East?

13 Oct 1492
anchored

We dropped anchor near an island this morning. The water is a deep, clear blue here, and I saw brightly colored fish swimming just below the surface.

The land that I can see is fairly flat, rising only slightly from where it meets the sea. There are many tall trees; most look like palms of some kind.

And there are people here. A large group of them, men and women, came out of the trees and walked to the edge of the beach. There they stood—or sat—and watched us watching them. These people have dark skin and wear very little. Several of my shipmates have felt compelled to point this out to me. There's been a lot of jostling for position at the rails.

Not that I didn't appreciate the view. Only a celibate priest wouldn't have, but I have more pressing matters to think of now that we've reached our destination, if we *have* reached our destination. The second part of my mission now begins—scuttling our little fleet and abandoning any hope I might still have had for returning home. My heart tells me I'll die on this island, for good or ill.

14 Oct 1492
San Salvador

So Colón has named the island. I was lucky enough to go ashore with him today. The Pinzón brothers were with us, as were two masters-at-arms and a few others of the crew. The captain has ordered me to record what's said and done at any meetings he has with the inhabitants of this island, so I'll observe as I did today and return to the ship to write everything down for him.

As well as for myself. If I can return home somehow, there'll be men there interested in what I've written.

Colón ordered those of us going ashore to wear our armor, so I strapped my breastplate and breeches on, as did nearly everyone else. Colón and the Pinzóns wore their full suits. The effect it had on the natives of this land was surprising. Some of them actually fell to their knees as we stepped onto the beach, as though we were royalty, if nothing else.

Colón declared that he'd discovered the land in the name of Jesus Christ and of their majesties, King Ferdinand and Queen Isabella. He then smiled an odd patronizing smile as he looked at these new people through the open visor of his helmet.

"Is there anyone here," he asked in Italian, "who can speak with me? Anyone at all?"

The interpreter asked the same question in Spanish. For a long time there was no response other than the smiles of the natives. They seemed content just to watch us. One man even approached and touched the captain's armor. He ignored the glare Colón threw at him and laughed, turning to smile at his friends.

I noticed another man walking toward us at that point. He was naked, like all the rest of the men, but wore an elaborate headdress that hung to his waist. It was made from the feathers of birds I'd never seen before. So brightly colored, so radiant. He also wore a necklace of shells and pieces of gold, and bracelets of the same materials around his knees.

He approached with a couple of other men, and they all bowed, the headdress on the one fanning out across his back. He rose and spoke, but, of course, none of us understood him.

I was wondering how this was going to play out, when one of his companions started motioning with his hands. Our interpreter picked up on this more quickly than I expected him to.

"They welcome us!" he reported, a triumphant look on his face.

And so the morning went, with the conversation a pantomime event.

The captain and Martín Pinzón did an entertaining job of acting out our voyage across the great Ocean Sea. Our hosts seemed impressed, or, at least, incredibly polite.

They're very friendly, these people. Their leader, the man with the feathers and finery, ordered that wooden platters of food be brought to us and insisted we eat right on the beach. Such sweet fruit I have never had before, so juicy and delicious. There were new vegetables and bread, as well, and meat from I don't know what animal.

They gave us fresh water to drink, as well as a fermented juice that brought a smile to everyone's face—native and stranger alike.

After we ate, the captain tried to explain our reasons for our journey: our desire for trade, for gold and spices. Our hosts continued to be polite, but we learned very little from them. They claimed to have no gold, other than the small pieces they wore as jewelry. I saw that several people wore copper in the same way.

The conversation was slow-going and my attention drifted now and then as I looked down the beach, watching a small group of shorebirds scurry around and stab their long beaks into the white sand. A loud flock of birds startled me, and I looked skyward to see several large, multicolored birds flying overhead and into the trees further inland, squawking as they flew.

I'd never seen birds like that—feathers of bright yellows and reds, greens and blues, like on the leader's headdress. They—all of these new things—have made me feel as though we've sailed to another world.

One of the native boys sitting near me smiled. He pointed at the birds and rubbed his belly. These birds are good food as well as good to look at, it seems.

Finally, the captain and the leader of the islanders agreed that there would be a feast this evening to welcome us to the island. Every crewman's invited; all the islanders will be attending, too.

Before we left to return to the ship, I asked, as well as I could, if there was someone who could teach me their language so we could communicate more easily. Colón nodded his approval, but our interpreter glared at me.

The leader and a few of the people–men and women together–spoke amongst themselves for a little while, but then turned back to me, smiling. One woman–a girl, really–stepped forward and mimed that she would be honored to be my teacher if I would teach her my language in exchange. We agreed that we should meet on the beach every noon.

Language instruction with a nude girl. This has to be a sin on some level, on several levels. I must pray for guidance, but first I need to copy what I've already written for the captain. We leave soon for the feast.

15 Oct 1492
San Salvador

I spent this afternoon in the company of a beautiful girl unashamed of her body, and all we did was stroll around this island and speak of everything and nothing.

It's hard for me to describe her. She's like the rest of her people–the Taino, she tells me, *good people*–handsome, of medium height, strongly built, skin the color of the earth, hair long and black. She paints her face, short white stripes on either cheek and her chin, and she ties her hair back with a flowering vine of some kind. Fringe covers her forehead.

She's young, maybe fourteen or so, and a daughter of the community's leader, the *cacique*.

I won't speak of the rest, except to note that some women cover themselves. Married women wear a short apron to mark their status. I wish my teacher were married, I think. A bit of clothing is better than none.

Her people don't trust me, I know. Several followed us at a discreet distance.

I can't fault them for this. While the feast last night went well over all, a few of my shipmates were less than perfect guests—treating our hosts more like servants and taking advantage of their gentleness. Some men can't hold their drink.

Other than our distant chaperones, however, I felt nothing but kindness and trust from my new teacher. Her name is Anacaona, a word that rolls off the tongue, sweet like the fruit we ate yesterday. Ana-ca-ona.

My name seems hard and unfriendly in comparison, although it sounds better when she says it.

We agreed to start by sharing basic phrases such as "hello," "goodbye," and "my name is..." As we walked around, we would also take turns pointing at things and naming them: tree (*ara*), rocks (*çiba*), those colorful birds (*higuaca*), the large huts the Taino live in (*bohio*).

At one point, she pointed to my eyes and gave her name for them (*dako*). I answered her with the Spanish (I continue to keep my true origins to myself). She then took my hand, but I had to move away, finding something else to name, anything. I may have hurt her feelings, but if we start naming body parts, I won't be able to help myself, and her people will be right in not trusting me.

16 Oct 1492
San Salvador

Our new friends gave us a tour of part of the island yesterday. This group that we've met lives in one village of many. Anacaona joined me on the tour and helped me when I showed confusion over what the guides were miming.

Our tour started on the beach and led first to our guides' village. It's a good-sized community with several bohios built of thin wooden planks with roofs of thatched palm. These houses can hold several families each; they surround a large field in the middle of the village. At the far end of the village lies the *caney*, the longhouse of the cacique and his family.

We left the village and came across fields of beans and other crops I didn't recognize planted amidst groves of palms. One field held short, broad plants laden with dense, white flowers that women were plucking with their fingers and dropping into woven sacks that hung off their shoulders. In another field, tall, thin plants stood erect like soldiers. Men were pulling large fruits from these plants and dumping them in larger sacks of the same make.

Anacaona found one of these fruits near the path and

showed it to me. She calls it *mahiz*. The skin is a papery husk of green and brown, lined with brown and yellow threads that feel like silk. The meat inside is yellow and more like grain than anything else I can think of: rows and rows of large seeds. Anacaona broke the skin of one seed with her fingernail, and milk squirted out of the wound. She laughed as she tossed the fruit to me. I caught it and followed her as we continued the tour.

At the end of the fields another village began, and we were greeted by this next community's leaders. They treated us with the same kindness and grace that the first group of natives had.

As we walked, I wondered where we could be. My knowledge of Asia is limited and is probably based more on myth than on reality.

But I expected more, well, clothing, for one thing.

Also, according to what I've heard, the Japanese and Chinese, even the people of India, have built large, elaborate temples to honor their strange gods. There's nothing like that here.

18 Oct 1492
Kuba

For the first time in a few days, Anacaona and I haven't met for our daily language lessons. The captain ordered me to accompany him and several of his men in an exploration of nearby islands. Guaybana, the cacique, told Colón of a larger island to the west, and the captain is convinced that this must be Japan, if not China itself, even though the cacique referred to it as Kuba.

This new island is indeed larger than San Salvador. Sailing around its coastline took the better part of a day. It's a beautiful land, as they all are here, with long, white beaches rising to wooded hills, taller than I've seen in the other islands we've explored.

The people living here speak Taino and appear to be of the same race. Their customs are the same, although the cacique is more aloof to the captain's introductions.

Still, the people have treated us kindly. One of the dishes they served us included meat from the *higuaca*. My young friend was right; they are delicious. Their feathers are also large and strong. I'm experimenting with one as a quill. It works quite well.

The natives told us, when Colón asked about gold and spices, that, while they have to trade for the gold they have, they mine for the copper that they use for decoration. When the captain professed his interest, the cacique offered to take us to visit the mine.

We traveled up into the hills today. It was interesting. The landscape entices me as much as it does on San Salvador, if not more so. The hills are rugged and covered in dense woodlands that are full of noisy birds, lizards, and odd-looking rodents.

The mine is small, nothing more than a depression in the ground bordered with the dirt that's been removed. Bits of copper in the dirt winked in the sunlight. Colón immediately began discussing the possibilities of it with the Pinzóns. They ignored our hosts as they contemplated the mine's expansion and forcing the natives to work it for them.

This saddens me. I think of the whistling natives of the Canary Islands and how my people and the Spanish took over their land and made them into servants. Our rulers tell us that this is the way of the world. Our priests say the same and quote Scripture as proof. Darker-skinned people have been cursed by God with the mark of Cain. Fair-skinned men like us are supposed to rule over them. It's God's will.

Christ says nothing about Cain or ruling over people like that, though, in His Gospels. He talks about loving everyone equally, and the meek inheriting the Earth. I might be blasphemous in my thinking, but could it be that Jesus might be including everyone in what he says? That's not what the Church teaches, but I don't like the idea of what could happen to these people if Colón's mission succeeds.

20 Oct 1492
San Salvador

Anacaona was happy to see me today. We met for our first lesson since my return from Kuba at a lagoon near the middle of the island. She almost threw her arms around me, but the expression on my face stopped her. Instead, she crossed her arms and tilted her head, giving me a long-suffering smile.

"You're afraid of me?" she asked in Spanish. She's been practicing.

I smiled. "Very good. But no. It's just..."

"I'm ugly?" She pouted.

"No!" I looked at the ground and then beyond her to the water. "You're...too young. It's not right for me..."

I stumbled over my words, embarrassed, and glanced at her; she wore a puzzled look. I tried again, using Spanish, Taino, and pantomime in an attempt to make my point.

"Where I come from, women are only naked with their husbands, not just anyone. It's God's law." I pointed to the sky, to heaven beyond.

She raised an eyebrow. "God's law?" She pointed upward, as well. "God?"

I nodded, but she gave her head a slight shake. After a moment, she motioned for me to follow her.

We left the lagoon, following a path that took us into thick woods, palms and cedars rising tall, the ground heavy with brush and vines. We reached a stony hill that the path cut into. The path, open to the sky, delved into the hill for several paces until it ended at an opening in the rock. We stopped, and I peered inside.

The hole was about my height and twice as wide. The air smelled damp—moss trimmed the rocks—and I could hear water dripping within.

"What is this place?" I asked.

Tied bundles of grass coated with a dark waxy substance were piled next to the entrance. Next to them lay a few small, flat stones. Anacaona knelt and moved one of the bundles away from the others, ignoring my question. She reached for two stones—they must be flint of some kind—and hit them against each other several times until a spark caught hold in the bundle. Blowing on it gently, she smiled in triumph and rose to her feet as the flame grew. She started inside, but I hesitated.

"What's in here?"

She turned and smiled at me. "God."

Cautiously, I followed her out of the bright sun and into the dark. I could only see what her small torch could illuminate; everything outside of that was black as night.

I stepped back in surprise when the torch showed a stone face staring back at me. It looked as startled as I felt, its eyes large holes in the rock and its lipless mouth wide open.

"Mácocael," my teacher said, pretending to pluck her eyelids away. "No Eyelids, we call him. Long ago, the sun ordered him to guard this entrance, but he left his post. The sun caught him, and now he guards it always."

With that cautionary tale, we walked further down the shadowy tunnel. I glimpsed other carvings in the damp walls, but Anacaona didn't think them worth mentioning.

I could feel before I saw that we had walked into a larger space. The air was colder and our footsteps echoed more richly. Anacaona led me to the center of a space, as large as one of the bohios in her village.

A stone pedestal stood there, level with my hips. A depression had been hammered into the middle of it and a greenish residue discolored the sides and bottom. The bowl smelled sweet and sour in the same breath, pleasant and unpleasant all at once.

Stone tools sat on the edge of the shallow bowl. One had to be the pestle that was used to grind the substance that remained in this mortar. More sticky remains clung to its round end.

A thin hollow tube rested alongside the pestle, as did a strange carved object. As long as my hand, the thing was as thin as my dagger but tapered at both ends. In the center, a hideous, tiny creature grinned at me. I picked it up to find it felt like bone.

"What is this?" I asked her.

She took it from me and mimicked sliding it into her throat and then vomiting.

"To speak with God, the priest must be empty."

"Then what?"

"Cohoba."

She took the tube and pretended to inhale the residue, the cohoba, from the bowl.

"If the priest is open, God enters here." She patted her chest. "And then..."

Anacaona held the torch higher and walked closer to the walls. They were covered in pictures, charcoal drawings of a man smoking a pipe, or perhaps using the tube as my teacher had shown me; frogs and fish; giant birds chasing stick figures of men; and other images too disturbing to mention.

I was bewildered and asked her how she knew these came from God. Her uncle told her, she said. He was her village's priest and healer and was training her to take his place. She patted one of the walls.

"Taino came from these caves into the sunlight. Our ancestors' spirits, our gods, still live here, guiding us."

I fingered the rosary in my pocket as we left the cave. My priest would tell me that this girl's gods were demons, especially if he saw the creature on the vomit stick. I remained silent as we walked, and Anacaona left me to my thoughts. Instead of returning to the lagoon, she led me to the beach.

We sat and ate the food she'd brought: bread, fruit, and dried meat. Not knowing what to say about the cave, I asked her what she'd been doing while I was gone.

She pondered the question, but was distracted by the crunch of footsteps back along the path we'd taken to get here. Luis, Colón's interpreter, was passing by. He saw me and waved, walking toward us until he saw Anacaona sitting next to me. He stopped and laughed, nodding approvingly.

"Good luck!" he shouted and walked away.

I turned to see my teacher hugging her knees to her chest.

"What's wrong?"

"He touched me."

I frowned. "How? What do you mean?"

She met my eye with a look I couldn't read. It felt like she was figuring my worth, whether she could trust me. Suddenly, she reached forward and grabbed my tunic, squeezing and pulling on the fabric.

"Like that and..." She reached for my groin, but I caught her hand.

"...like that."

"What did you do?"

She bared her teeth at me and brought her hands up, her fingers bent like claws.

She'd fought.

"Are you all right?"

Anacaona nodded, but the sadness didn't leave her eyes.

"One of our servants, he hurt her. His friends, too."

I didn't want to believe her, but I knew better. I doubt she and her servants are the only ones who've been hurt, either.

21 Oct 1492
San Salvador

La Santa Maria ran aground today, no thanks to me. Colón had ordered another exploratory trip; one of the Taino had told him there might be gold on a larger island to the northwest. Something went wrong, though, and the pilot ran the ship onto the reef that encircles the north side.

The hull splintered apart where it ran into the reef, and the ship sits lodged against the coral, jutting out from the water. The waves smash into it, slowly tearing the boat apart. The crew, including me, escaped with no injury, but the gallant *Maria* will sail no more. I'd consider this a victory, but Colón wants us to salvage the wood to build a fort. He plans to leave men here when he returns for Spain. And he plans to leave soon, sometime next month.

22 Oct 1492
San Salvador

Anacaona wasn't waiting for me on the beach today. I found her in a bohio with her uncle, the priest. I rapped my knuckles on the door frame, and she looked up from a low table where she knelt, her hands full of herbs. More herbs hung from the rafters above. Even with large open windows that allowed the sea breezes to blow through the room, the smell of them was strong.

She whispered my name, but looked at me the same way she had looked at Luis, afraid. I asked her what was wrong, but she only shook her head and returned her attention to the herbs.

I stepped into the room and saw her uncle, who folded his arms and gave me a wary look. He's a bigger man than I, an intimidating figure, made more so by my recent visit to the cave.

I tried again. "What's wrong?"

She glared at me and then started chopping the herbs with a small stone blade.

"You want to kidnap me!" She scowled at me, pointing the blade in my direction. "To take me back to your Spain. Is this your god's law, too?"

My eyes narrowed in surprise. "What? No!"

"No?" Cautious hope filled her eyes. "Do you promise?"

"Yes!" I walked to her and sat on the ground across from her. "Why did you think I would do this?"

"Your leader, Colombo. I heard him talking. He wants to go home and take some of us with him."

"Are you sure? You're learning Spanish quickly, but..."

"Tell me I'm mistaken, then."

She folded her hands in front of her and told me how that morning she and her friends had been preparing cassava by chopping it and rolling it in a *batea* (a long wooden tray). Colón and a few other men had been walking through the village, and they stopped to watch the girls.

"He said, 'These girls good to take queen to show. With us we take.'"

Her grammar was off, but there was no mistaking what Colón said. My face showed as much.

"But you won't do what Colombo wants? Your cacique?"

"I won't let him take you or your friends away."

It was an easy promise to make. It's my intention (and command) that Colón and his men never leave this island. But the smile that lit up her face made the promise feel different, more binding to her than to a king on a throne an ocean away.

23 Oct 1492
San Salvador

The sailors have harvested as much wood as they can from the corpse of *la Santa Maria*, and building has begun. It's an awkward-looking square taking shape on the beach, just above the high-water line. I'm trying to picture the men from three ships fitting into the bones of one, and I wonder. What's the point of this, other than to mark Colón's claim on this land, on this people?

I took a bold step today and asked him what his plans were. He gave me a calculating look as he smiled over his logbook.

"We've found a beautiful land here, scrivener."

I nodded, watching him, but saying nothing.

"Their majesties will be pleased, I think. There's gold here. Well, near to here, anyway. The people of these islands will make excellent servants, they're so malleable. I plan on bringing some of them home with us to show to their majesties. Does that trouble you?"

"Me? Of course not. Did you think it would?"

He smiled. "Well, that girl you're teaching Spanish to. You're fond of her, yes?"

I shrugged. "She's nice enough."

He chuckled. "I can imagine."

I said nothing, letting him think what he would.

"Do you think we've reached the East, scrivener?"

His question startled me, but I answered him honestly.

"I don't think so, sir."

Colón nodded, a look of disappointment crossing his face.

"I agree, but the discovery of a new land could be worth even more."

He stood, a look of calculation replacing that quick glance at his vulnerability.

"Don't get attached to these people, scrivener. They're just in the way."

24 Oct 1492
Guanahani
so the Taino call this island

Anacaona came upon my people at their worst today. Their rudeness at the feast was brushed aside somewhat through the captain's apologies and the payment of what, to him, are trinkets. So it's been with the molestation of some women in the lower classes. Not much different than back home.

For this, though, I don't know what the cost will be.

We'd stopped at the lagoon again early this afternoon. Anacaona was teaching me the names of the fish that swam there. She pointed to a fish as it came near us to eat the crumbs she threw in the water. She said its name, and I repeated what she said. The trick came when the fish swam away. When it returned, she expected me to remember the name she'd given.

She refrained from laughing when I failed; only a small smile crossed her lips. The monks weren't so kind with their corrections, as I recall. Her fear of me has faded as well. I hope she trusts me again.

On our way back to the beach we heard noises nearby: men's laughter and someone crying. Anacaona's eyes widened, and I caught a Taino word I knew: *stop*. It came from a young voice, pleading.

"Bohechio!" She cried as she tried to push past me, but I grabbed her arm.

"Wait," I whispered. "Let me."

She nodded, frowning, and waved her hand at me.

"Hurry."

I pushed through the undergrowth enough to see what was going on. Two men I only vaguely recognized were standing and laughing as their companion—another man I didn't know—buggered a Taino boy, the boy who had recommended the *higuaca*. Anacaona's brother. None of the men were armed.

Anacaona had followed me and saw, too. She tried to push past me again, but I held her back. I shook my head and clapped my hand to my chest.

"No. Me," I told her.

I stepped into the clearing. The two stopped laughing when they saw me. I drew my sword and pointed it at the man on his knees.

"Stop."

He glared at me and grunted, "I'll stop when I'm finished."

My sword was at his throat in one quick step.

"You'll stop *now*."

He snarled a curse at me, but withdrew from the boy, who crawled quickly behind me.

"These people are our hosts, and this is the respect you show them?" I asked. "This is their leader's son, not some serving girl."

He smiled at me, an evil grin, as he stood. "I've had their serving girls, too," he said.

He disgusted me. "Cover yourself and pray for forgiveness," I demanded.

His companions chuckled, and he snorted as he pulled up his hose, reminding me that the captain had allowed us to do what we liked with these people and that I ought to remember whose side I was on.

One of the other men laughed at me. "Now I recognize you," he said. "Too busy with your pens and Bible to behave like you should." He pointed his finger at me. "There's no priest in this crew. Quit acting like one, if you don't want your throat cut."

I pointed my sword at the three of them and told them to stay out of my way. I helped the boy to his feet, never losing eye contact with the men, and we backed out of the clearing. When we reached Anacaona, she took her brother in her arms. He collapsed against her.

"Can he walk?"

She asked him if he could, but he shook his head. I reached for him to pick him up, but she beat me to it, easily lifting him and holding him against her chest. His head fell against her shoulder, his eyes closed.

Her eyes were open wide and wet with tears. This wasn't a matter of honor or respect to her. These men had injured her brother.

We walked back to the village in silence. I kept my

sword drawn and looked around constantly for signs that we were being followed. The penalty for killing me would be worse than for hurting a native boy, but I expected an ambush every step of the way.

Anacaona and Bohechio's parents were outside their longhouse when we arrived. The woman ran to Anacaona when she saw her. Anacaona explained what had happened, and her mother took the boy from her and carried him inside. The father, the cacique, gestured at me and said a word I didn't quite understand. It was a curse or challenge of some kind, as my teacher quickly came to my defense. She spoke quickly, telling him what had happened.

Guaybana studied me for a long moment and then nodded. He offered his hand, and I took it in mine, surprised that he used my people's gesture in this moment. I shook his hand firmly and gave him my thanks in Taino. Now it was his turn to be surprised, and he even smiled before going to his son.

25 Oct 1492
Guanahani

Bohechio died early this morning.

Guaybana and his wife, Yahíma, invited me in while the medicine man—Yahíma's brother, I've learned—treated the boy. He lay on a low table in the center of the main room of the caney. My teacher assisted her uncle as he examined Bohechio.

There was a bowl of water sitting next to him, and Anacaona dipped a sponge into it, using it to clean the blood and shit off of her brother's legs and backside. The smell, though, that combination of smells, worried me. That smell means death to me. It reminds me of the diseased dogs I've seen in Lisboa, either crawling away to die or already dead in the alleys.

Once he was clean, and they'd packed moss between his legs and up against his buttocks, the shaman carried the boy to his *hamaca* and laid him down. Anacaona followed and gave him a strong-smelling cup to drink from.

Bohechio spoke to her, and she nodded, her voice reassuring as she responded.

"Finish."

The boy smiled and drained the cup dry. Anacaona took it from him and kissed him on his forehead and his lips. He lay back and closed his eyes.

His sister and uncle moved the table against the wall, and then the man began to dance—a slow, steady raising of his feet while he shook a heavy stick in the air. He chanted, as well, and was joined by Anacaona as she lit a thick sheaf of bound grasses and waved them over her brother. The odor was strong, almost canceling out the smell of death, but not quite.

I sat on the ground to the side, praying over my rosary, fingering the wooden beads, whispering the prayers for each one as it rolled past.

The boy lingered for hours, but there was nothing to be done. Something inside was torn, and the blood kept seeping out. They had to change the moss twice as it became saturated. I doubted that their gods would answer their ritual. Unless the Holy Mother chose to intercede for him, his life was lost.

Right before dawn, the boy woke and cried out. Everyone ran to him—except for his mother, who was already at his side—and I hovered in the background. He saw me and smiled. I returned his smile, but he'd already closed his eyes. Not long after that, he gave a shuddering sigh and was gone.

27 Oct 1492
Guanahani

The captain decided that the best way to deal with the death of the cacique's son and the complaints against his men was to lift anchor and explore the surrounding waters once more. Many smaller islands that we haven't visited lie near Guanahani. Larger ones can be seen in the distance.

Colón talked to himself as he paced the deck while we were sailing. What little I could overhear concerned presenting this new land to their majesties, nothing about the boy or the other Taino injured. Any time he saw me near him, he moved, so I could catch little else.

But the voyage was pleasant enough. It cleared my head in many ways.

Before discovering this new land, my goal was simple: scuttle the ships and find my way home, leaving my shipmates to their own fate.

Guanahani has complicated that plan. Scuttling the ships I can still do. However, I don't know how to find my way home from here; there's no overland route, and there's no other ship to use, if I destroy the two we have. Colón claims to know the winds well enough to bring us home, but I don't, and I haven't found anything that the captain's written down that could help me. He keeps the secrets in his head.

Further confusing the issue is this: if I were to strand the rest of the crew here, the natives would be at their mercy. These gracious and patient people don't deserve that. They've tolerated our appearance on their shores and our treatment of them with saintly fortitude. When I compare their behavior to our ugly, violent ways, to the captain's plans, I wonder who the Saved truly are. We behave like criminals evicted from Eden for our sin and disobedience, while these people act as though the Lord never asked them to leave.

Even though I don't understand their ways, I look around this paradise and am beginning to think He never did. I read His Word and pray to His Mother relentlessly, hoping for guidance as to what my next steps should be.

28 Oct 1492
Guanahani

Colón tried to pay off the complaints like he had with

the party: with apologies and trinkets. The cacique took them, but his expression and the way he stood showed his true feelings.

I caught up with him and his wife when they had left the captain's sight and apologized for what happened to their son and the captain's attitude.

Guaybana looked at me. "We must talk."

I nodded. "When?"

"Tonight. Don't go back to your ship. We'll meet you on the beach."

They hurried away and I returned to Colón and my crewmates. Now I sit on the beach writing by the light of a dying fire. Colón didn't question my staying behind. He merely laughed and slapped my shoulder, thinking he understood my intent.

29 Oct 1492
Guanahani

I remember when my father discovered that his only son was a thief and a sneak. He told me I had no morals and no shame. I only thought of myself, he said.

I took pleasure in reminding him that if he'd left me to the monks, I would probably be a sinless cleric with my life sworn to God, not the worldly criminal standing before him. It was his decision, not mine, that brought shame on the family. He responded with a swift hand to my ear.

That was the last time I saw him.

I think he may have been right, though. Until coming to this new world, I've rarely thought of the needs of other people. Only mine seemed important.

Anacaona met me at the fire last night, and we walked to the field at the center of the village. This field is where the Taino hold ceremonies and play an exciting ball game they call *batey*. The ball, while not large, is heavy and bounces. I don't know what it's made of, but the way it moves seems magical. Last night, the field was full of people, with more sitting or standing around the edge.

"Everyone is angry."

I nodded. "What do we do?"

My teacher started to speak quickly, her own anger getting the better of her. She stopped when she saw the puzzled look on my face as I tried to follow her words. She tried again, speaking as simply as she could.

"We must make plans. Gifts and apologies aren't enough."

I nodded again and touched her hand. I hoped she'd know from my gesture that I not only understood, but I agreed.

She smiled. "We need your help."

We sat down near the field just as the cacique began to speak. He was the first of many, talking about the death of his son, the other troubles the Spaniards had caused since their arrival, and demanding a solution.

Anacaona explained this to me as best she could.

An older woman, her hair white, rose next and spoke of the men who held her while another ripped out the gold rings she wore in her ears. She turned so everyone could see the jagged tears in her earlobes.

Several people called out that the sailors had stolen their jewelry and other things, too.

The next man rose and told how two sailors had set the ship's dogs on his wife and daughters, laughing as they had tried to fend them off. He'd tried to stop the men, but they'd struck him, knocking him out. He woke to find his women crying, in pain and bleeding, and his youngest daughter cowering under a hamaca, her face torn open.

Anacaona stood and spoke for several minutes, her voice strong as she told her story and that of her brother. As she finished speaking, I saw her uncle enter the field. His face was grim as he strode through the crowd and pulled the cacique aside. I could see Guaybana becoming angry as the priest spoke. He motioned for the big man to tell everyone his news. Anacaona stopped translating for me and looked at her uncle in shock.

What had happened, I wondered, and I touched her arm. She turned on me with such a look of anger and grief, I stepped back from her.

"Your people have found the sacred cave. They have destroyed Mácocael. They have defiled our ancestors!"

And then everyone was looking at me. I wondered, then, if the Taino would take revenge on me for what the Spanish had done. I wouldn't have blamed them. I started to speak, trying to find the words to apologize, but Guaybana bid me silent with a wave of his hand.

Anacaona looked at me, her expression softening, and

asked the question everyone wanted me to answer.

"Are you with us?"

I looked at her and then out at the people of the village.

"Will you help us?" she added.

I nodded. "Yes," I responded in Taino.

So much for the son my father thought he knew.

31 Oct 1492
Guanahani

I've taken to living on the island now. Several of us have, either camping on the beach or staying in the village. Two of the Taino women have taken sailors as their lovers, which surprises me.

I live in a small hut near the caney Anacaona shares with her family. Her parents explained to me that since I rescued their son, I'm their responsibility now.

Colón suspects me, I think. Not of being a traitor so much as going native more than he would like. The idea of taking a Taino (to him, *indios*) woman, as he thinks I've done, is much to his liking—he's taken a few—but I think he puzzles over my comfort with many of the people in the community, especially the cacique. They've given me their trust more readily than they've given it to him. This bothers him, understandably.

Other than my friendships with the Taino, though, I profess to be nothing other than Colón's servant, as I always have.

To his face.

When I'm not serving as the captain's scribe, I've been meeting with my new friends, discussing what steps we should take to remove the Spanish from Guanahani.

Initially, the leaders of the community only wanted to force Colón and his men to leave. It took a lot to convince them that my people don't frighten easily, especially when we're armed. I also had to explain that we'd only return with more ships and bigger weapons.

It may be the language barrier, but I don't think the Taino believe my descriptions of the people and the land I come from. Why would they? Stone castles and cannons seem like a twisted fantasy in this place.

Horses interest them, though.

A lot has been said by many people at these meetings. Everyone has a voice here, even if the caciques are the ones to make the final decisions. Anacaona is at my side for every meeting, translating—her Spanish develops as quickly as my Taino does, perhaps more so—and sharing her own story.

I think that's what's turned the tide in deciding what to do: the sharing of stories. The number of people who have come forward to tell of their experiences of violation, theft, violence, or just simple rudeness surprised me, and I think it surprised the cacique, too. We've been here less than a month.

So we agreed that something must be done to eliminate Colón and his men entirely. Many of the young men supported a direct attack. Several even brought *macana* (war clubs) to one meeting, ready to fight that day. One of the women suggested that surprise might work to our advantage and several people, including me, agreed.

But the weapons are what concern me. The clubs are made of wood and are thinner than my wrist. The edges are sharpened, though, and the wood is dense. They can inflict damage, but compared to steel swords? Even surprised, the crew will fight hard, and Taino will die.

And even if they win this battle, there'll be more, when the Spanish, the Portuguese, or someone else sails this way again.

One battle at a time. I hope surprise will be enough to bring us victory.

2 Nov 1492
Guanahani

It's difficult for me to write this morning. Two of my fingers are broken.

I hiked around the island yesterday following the path that runs between the fields and the grove of palms. I walked along it for a while, letting my mind drift, until I spotted one of the other villages on the island.

I studied the village for a while. From where I stood, I could watch a batey game in progress and I was enthralled by the magic of that ball flying around, and the strong men chasing after it and bouncing it off their chests.

The game ended, so I turned to go. I didn't get far.

Someone's fist slammed into my face and knocked me down. I looked up to see my friends from the other day. Today, they were armed.

Two of the men grabbed my arms and dragged me up to my feet. The other—the one I'd interrupted—held a sword and an untrustworthy smile.

I didn't want to wait around to see what he did with either of them, so I tried an old trick from my youth. I threw all my weight to one side, hoping even that simple move would be unexpected. It was. Too much so, in fact. Instead of the man I leaned away from losing his balance and losing his grip on my arm, he only lost his balance, and we both fell into the man who had my other arm. We all went down.

My hand hit a large, smooth rock in the dirt, and I felt the last two fingers of my right hand snap. I may have screamed with the pain, but I don't remember. The fall loosened everyone's grip, and I rolled away from my attackers. I came up running, scrambling back down the road, cradling my hand against my chest.

They were close behind me, though. I expected one of them to reach out and pull me down at any minute.

It was Anacaona who saved me.

I'd reached the outskirts of the village when she saw me and my predicament. She ran into the village, yelling for help.

One of the men chasing me hit me in the back and I fell, sliding forward on the rough dirt. I rolled over to see him raising his sword to run me through, but he never got the chance. Three Taino men knocked him to the ground, and I witnessed how effective Taino war clubs actually are. Dense wood with a sharp edge wielded by a strong man cleaves easily through a sailor's skull. The warrior pulled the club out with a wet noise as his friends rained their own blows on my attacker's body, crushing his throat and hacking a deep wound into the arm he'd raised to protect himself. Three more knocked the other down, and inflicted similar wounds. The remaining sailor looked at his friends dead on the ground and then glared at me as I struggled to my feet. He spat and cursed, but ran off, back to the beach and the safety of his ship.

My rescuers wanted to follow him, but I argued against it. If there were more sailors on the beach, they'd be killed, I said. With two of my assailants dead, they were already running the risk of Colón ordering the murder of every Taino on this island in retribution.

Anacaona and the men took me back to my hut, and helped me into my hamaca. My teacher handed me a deep cup of *uica*, a fermented juice made from the yucca plant. It smelled strong, like the drink she'd given Bohechio, but I took a long swallow.

"All of it," she said as she took my hand in hers, sitting down on a low wooden chair. I took another drink as I watched her stroke my hand. The pain even seemed to lessen until, with a quick twist, she pulled my broken fingers straight.

I gasped as fresh pain and surprise coursed through me, but she gave me a comforting smile as she reached for a couple of flat pieces of wood and some leaves she had set out nearby.

She easily set my fingers, wrapping the leaves around them to hold the splints in place. She looked at me as she tied the last knot.

"Your fingers will heal well now," she said.

I thanked her, and she told me to finish drinking the uica.

I tried to smile at her as I emptied the cup. She took it from me and patted my hand gently as she laid it on my chest. She stood and seemed to tower over me, lying in my hamaca not far off the ground.

My eyelids closed, and I was nearly asleep before she finished wishing me a good night's rest. Her gentle voice came as if in a dream.

"Rest now. The pain will start to fade soon."

3 Nov 1492
Guanahani

The master-at-arms came for me after I'd finished writing yesterday. Two sailors were dead, and he wanted to know what I knew about it.

I asked if he was accusing me of their deaths.

"No," he said, giving my bandaged hand a curious look. "No. We think it was some of the indios. Another man saw you there, so I wanted to talk to you."

"Another man?" I asked with a derisive snort. "Friend of the deceased, I'm guessing."

I was making the man uncomfortable, but I didn't

care. My hand hurt.

"Those men attacked me," I snapped at him. "The Taino prevented them from hurting me." I waved my wounded hand at him. "More than they did, anyway. They were set on killing me."

He was surprised by that news, but brushed it aside. He was more interested in who the natives were who had killed his men. He would have to make an example of them.

"What do you mean by 'example'?" I asked.

"They'll be executed, of course. We can't have these savages getting the notion that we're fair game for those sticks they carry around." He demanded I tell him who the men were.

I stood and looked at him, angrier than I remember being in a long time.

I was not going to sacrifice the men that had saved my life. I ordered him out.

The master-at-arms looked at me as if I'd sprouted horns, and his hand moved to the hilt of his sword.

"You're being unreasonable. What do these people mean to you?"

I looked at him but said nothing. Nothing I said would make any difference.

"You know what I'll do if you don't tell me, don't you?" He asked as he turned to leave. "I'll just pick anybody to execute. They don't have to be guilty of anything."

Of course they don't.

I stopped him in the doorway.

"Do you know what'll happen if you make a show of executing anyone?" I asked him.

"What?"

"The whole island will rise against us. There are thousands of Taino living here. How many of us? Eighty-five? Ninety?"

From the way his brow furrowed, it was obvious he hadn't thought about it quite that way before now.

"They'll crush us," I added.

"What do you suggest?"

I smiled a little and suggested that he meet with the cacique.

"Explain the situation," I told him. "He's a reasonable man. He may even bring up the idea of giving you the men's lives himself. But if he approves of it and allows it, the people will be much less likely to seek revenge."

The master-at-arms nodded, pondering my words.

"I'll have to speak with the captain."

I patted him on the back and wished him luck as I walked with him outside. After he was out of sight, I went to find Anacaona and we sought out the cacique.

5 Nov 1492
Guanahani

So much bloodshed last night.

It's now dawn, and I sit on the beach watching the sun rise, looking east to a home I'll never see again.

Later this morning, we'll be loading the non-Taino bodies onto one of our ships and taking them out to sea. The Taino don't want them, and burial at sea seems appropriate. The few sailors who didn't join the Spanish in the fight will man the ship.

But last night.

The cacique decided, after hearing my news and after visiting Mácocael's cave with the priest, that there would be another feast to which the Spanish would be invited to as an apology for the deaths of the sailors. The killers would be surrendered to Colón after the feast. The entire crew came, eighty-nine of them compared to the hundreds of Taino, who still showed nothing but kindness and generosity.

But the drink served was a stronger blend, and soon the sailors were singing and arguing with each other. The man I'd found with Bohechio grabbed one of the Taino women, and the signal was given.

The woman pushed the sailor away, still smiling, and he stumbled into a couple of Taino men who were also grinning. I watched as they beat the man to the ground, their clubs wooshing through the air as they struck and rose to strike again, their smiles never fading.

At the beginning, it looked as though the Taino would have an easy victory, with maybe a third of the enemy falling fast. But Colón and the Pinzón brothers hadn't had as much to drink as their companions and they quickly mounted a counter-attack.

If it hadn't been for the sheer difference in numbers, they might have cut their way to victory, but we could afford to lose more men than they could.

Soon, the Spanish only had twenty men standing. They were all in a circle, their blades facing us, surrounded by ten times that number. The rest of the crew lay dead, and there were that many Taino lying with them.

Colón saw me in the light of the bonfire and pointed his sword at me. "Traitor!"

I laughed when he said that. I'm a traitor twice over now.

"No!" I yelled back. "I'm Portuguese. King João sends his greetings."

I should have kept my mouth shut. My mockery infuriated the captain, and he lunged out at me. I fumbled for my sword, handicapped by my broken fingers, and then he was on me. Our swords clashed, but the battle was horribly one-sided, as I had no dexterity to go on the offensive. I was lucky enough to prevent him from killing me straightaway.

Colón should have defeated me. He was by far the better swordsman, and I could hardly hold my sword, let alone wield it.

I stumbled and fell to my knees at one point. Before I could rise, I felt his blade on my neck.

"Why?" His voice was gruff. "Tell me before I end you."

I couldn't see his face from my position, but I could see his legs in front of me. His hose were torn and covered in blood. I heaved myself forward and knocked him over, his sword biting my neck as it flew out of his hand.

My sword was out of reach, too, but I still had my dagger. I pulled it out of my jerkin with my left hand and thrust it into his gut, tearing his insides.

He rolled away from me, blood pouring from his mouth and his stomach. Seeing their captain bleeding his life out convinced a few of the Spaniards to cast their swords away and fall to their knees in surrender. The rest, apparently not fearing death, at least not if they could take some of us with them, broke out of their circle of defense, swinging their swords as they came. Luis, the interpreter, headed straight for me, but Guaybana struck him down before he reached me. The Spaniards killed one more Taino and wounded several before they, too, were killed.

The beach reeked of death, women were crying over their dead men, and the men still standing looked over the scene with dazed expressions on their faces. I imagine my face looked the same. I know I felt, and still feel, stunned.

Colón died with his question unanswered. I don't think he would have understood.

I only vaguely understand, myself. With this battle won, I've done my duty to King João. Spain won't succeed in finding a western route to Asia this time. I end my duty there. I don't want any explorer to sail west now to hurt the Taino or any other people who live on these islands or the mainland they say lies near.

We have two ships and four-score swords. That's a start.

I wish I had my father's tools. But we'll make do somehow. If we can find tin and trade for copper from Kuba, I can teach the good people how to make bronze.

And if we can find iron!

I've shared with Anacaona my ideas of finding ore to forge more weapons, to build more ships, to learn more of the other people who live in this new world, to form alliances so when the next fleet from the east arrives, there's no welcome.

She agrees that my ideas are sound, but she's more interested, at least for now, in the writing I do. She's watching me write these words, in fact. The Taino don't write down their thoughts, and Anacaona wants me to teach her how it's done.

I think of all these plans and wonder. Will this knowledge throw these people out of Eden, too? I've tried to explain this dilemma of mine to my teacher, and she shakes her head at me. Whether she's confused by my words, or simply disagrees, she won't say. She only smiles that amused grin she gets when I've called a bird a toad or asked her how many palm trees she has in her hut.

I have a lot to learn, too.

"It's time."

Ana looked up to see the docent smiling at her. For a moment, she didn't understand.

"What?"

Ms. Mayagüez chuckled. "Did I interrupt you in a good spot? The museum will be closing soon."

Ana tried to smile. "Oh, I'm sorry, I..." She looked back down at the book and touched the page she was reading. "Heh. It took hold of me. Can I come back to read more?"

"Of course. But I have to send you home now. Come."

Ana closed the book, regretting it as the pages fell together, and stood to follow the docent. They left the archives and walked back down the hallway.

When they reached the door that opened onto the main hall, Ana met the docent's eye.

"I didn't realize that Anacaona was so young when all this happened. She was..."

The docent smiled. "Your age. That's right. You're named after her, aren't you?"

Ana nodded. "I guess, yeah. Two of my cousins are, too."

"Ah."

"And three other girls in my class."

Ms. Mayagüez smiled. "It's always been a popular name." She crossed her arms, watching the other visitors leaving. "What do you think of Rodrigo?"

A puzzled look crossed Ana's face. "I don't know. He had strange ideas about things."

"He lived a long time ago."

"Hm. And I've just started his story, haven't I?"

Ms. Mayagüez nodded. "It's not just his story, either." She opened her arms. "It's our story, too. Escobedo raised the alarm and was a teacher, but he was only one man, a man with his own motives, as you'll learn as you read further."

The docent opened the door and ushered Ana through the thinning crowd and out the front door.

Ana smiled. "I do want to read more. You'll let me know when I can visit again?"

"I promise. Now get along home."

"Yes, ma'am. Thank you."

Ana walked down the short sidewalk to the rack of bicycles and backed hers out. She looked back at the front door, but the docent had already left the entrance.

She shrugged and mounted her bike, heading out of the museum's parking lot and onto the wide, busy road that would take her home. Electric cars and bikes passed by her in both directions as she pedaled along.

While the island was still as flat as it had been when Escobedo first saw it, the road did run over a few small hills. Ana crested one of these and stopped, dazzled by the light the setting sun behind her cast on the cityscape of the capital at twilight.

The lights of the city were just starting to glow, so it was the video billboards that stood out, broadcasting their message to any who would look, advertising the merits of taking one drug over another, the importance of being attractive and what you needed to achieve that, plus special bulletins about the war.

Ana was still too far away from town to get the full effect of the billboards, but she could appreciate the panorama laid out in front of her, from the multitude of small houses like the one she lived in beginning at the bottom of the hill to the boards and the outlines of the skyscrapers in the distance .

Beyond the human-made view, the great Ocean Sea rolled on, unfazed by human history.

Ana breathed a deep sigh and continued her journey home.

Spheres of Influence

by Rebecca Rozakis

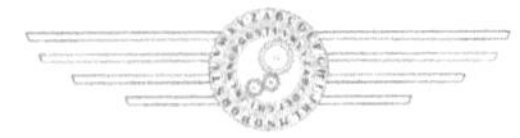

Cadenza Orseolo slipped through the night, black cloak clutched tight against the November fog rising from the canal. A catcall echoed off the stone walls, some foreign sailor clearly having mistaken her for one of the Republic's legendary courtesans. She smiled behind her mask. He would be quite surprised if he'd known whom he had propositioned.

But that was the ostensible purpose of the masks, was it not? To foster an illusion of equality between the classes, however temporarily. Although, in Venice, the citizens wore masks out of doors for the better part of the year. The fact that it made secrets and rendezvous, whether between lovers, merchants, or spies, all the easier certainly had nothing to do with the custom.

Venice wrapped herself in a cloak of mystery and

then invited all the world in.

Beneath her feet, Cadenza could feel the grinding of the great pumps that kept the city afloat. They were an engineering marvel, Venice's greatest defense against invasion and simultaneously, its greatest threat. Two generations before, they had held off Napoleon himself. But should the pumps fail, they would suffer more than the occasional flooding *acqua alta* the residents were accustomed to. The wreckage of the Campanile would barely break the waves with St. Mark's piazza at the bottom of the lagoon.

The heels of her shoes clicked against the folding joints of the tiny bridge, which lay quietly waiting for the next invasion. There would always be a next invasion. She shivered in damp chill.

It was a simple enough assignment, although she was not so inexperienced as to think that simple assignments would ever stay simple. She had heard enough of her father's stories. But the complications were not yet apparent. Meet the contact, reacquire the stolen item, and report back. Why this required a nobly born agent, Cadenza was not sure. Perhaps it was a test of her abilities.

She had wanted this, she reminded herself. Asked for it, begged for it, even. She had been proud to receive the summons to the Doge's Palace. They had directed her not to the public rooms, with their grand painted walls, but to the narrow, wood-paneled offices that lay hidden behind those walls. She had not needed to be told where the secret doors lay—she had played in many of those rooms as a child. But it was the first time she had been summoned in her own right. The chamber of the Secret Chancery was lined with cabinets filled with records from the Venetian intelligence networks for generations. Cadenza thought them infinitely more appealing than the fine paintings in the chamber of the Council of Ten.

It should have been her father, she knew. Or her brother. But the latter was dead and the former...was no longer the man she remembered. And if she wanted to uphold the Orseolo family tradition of service to the Republic, then this was up to her.

Well, if it was a test, she would not fail. She peered through the mist, lit hazily by irregular lanterns whose glow reflected off the canal and the wet stones. Nobly born or not, her father had ensured she knew every *riva* and *calle* in each of the six *sestieri*. She only hoped her contact had not wandered out and gotten lost.

She edged her way through the iron gate of the *pensione*, careful not to catch her skirts, despite the crinoline beneath them. Gardens were a rarity in Venice, with so little space available. But the tiny fountain burbled next to a small tree. In the summer, oleander would blossom, repelling the mosquitoes. Such a sweet scent for so poisonous a flower. But now, the evening dew wet the remaining leaves on the branches.

A silhouette stepped out of the deeper shadows by the wall. To Cadenza's surprise, it mirrored her own bell-shaped outline. She immediately chastised herself for leaping to conclusions–that her contact was a man, or that this was her contact at all.

"There's a high tide tonight," she ventured, hoping

that the woman would respond with the appropriate phrase and not merely demand to know what Cadenza was doing in her garden.

"The wind ruffles the waters," came the reply, slightly muffled and with a faint accent. Her voice was young, its speaker perhaps the same age as Cadenza herself. The woman drew close enough for Cadenza to see that she too wore a mask, the butterfly-shaped *volto.*

"The fish do not mind," she said, completing the sequence. She scanned the garden surreptitiously for any observers.

"Oh, thank heavens," her contact replied, pulling off her mask. "I don't understand how you Venetians can wear these all the time."

Cadenza blinked. It was like looking at a younger version of her mother. Or one of her infrequently visited cousins. Adelaide Orseolo had begun life as an Austrian countess, married to a Venetian noble in one of endless attempts to strengthen peaceful ties between the tiny maritime republic and the massive empire of the Hapsburgs. The only trace of Adelaide's legendarily delicate beauty in her daughter was a pair of startlingly blue eyes. Cadenza had inherited her father's dark hair, bronze skin, and stubbornly masculine jaw.

This young woman had the same eyes. But she had the milky skin and flaxen hair to go with them, with an adorable, saucily upturned nose to add insult to injury. Cadenza repressed a sigh.

The girl held out a hand. "I'm Maria."

Amateur. And shockingly intimate. But then, they

were hiding in the garden of the girl's hotel, which was not quite the normal setting for a proper introduction. Unfortunately, there was no way the girl would trust her unless she reciprocated now. She almost gave a false name. But if she did need to call on official authority, it might become embarrassing. Better to just leave off the surname until necessary. She reluctantly removed her mask. "Cadenza."

Maria smiled, showing perfect white teeth. At least Cadenza could place the accent now. She had to admit, the Austrian's Italian was quite good.

"So you are to help me, then?" Maria turned big eyes on her new benefactor.

She would need to hide a lot of sighs, Cadenza realized. "I understand that your orrery has gone missing?"

Maria nodded. "It's glass, you see. It seemed like such a clever gift—my uncle loves astrological models, and we ordered one made of glass instead of the usual brass. It was supposed to have been shipped here from Murano this afternoon, but it never arrived."

The great glassworks for which Venice was famous had been sequestered on the outlying island of Murano for generations, for fear of an accident setting the crowded city afire. It was a non-mobile island; the exquisite products were priceless results of trade secrets, but nothing an invading army would be interested in.

Cadenza nodded, caught herself, and continued nodding as if nothing had happened. An Austrian personally picking up a gift for an uncle, with fine manners and a well-bred air that reminded her of her own noble cousins. The girl's cloak pin confirmed it—the double-headed eagle of the Hapsburgs winked in the moonlight. No wonder the Council of Ten was concerned—this gift was intended for a member of the royal family of the Austro-Hungarian Empire itself. She felt a warm glow that they had trusted her with so delicate an assignment right before her blood ran cold. Everyone knew that Napoleon had only attacked the Republic in order to turn it over as a courting gift to the Hapsburgs. Venice, its onetime naval empire nearly erased by the Portuguese to the west and the Songhai to the south, feared their Imperial neighbors far more than they ever had the French. A diplomatic incident could always tip the scales against them, and all the strategic marriages in the world would not save them.

The question, of course, was how subtle a creature was smiling at her at this moment. Was the pin an oversight or a warning? Or intended to be taken as an oversight? Cadenza halted the spiral in its tracks. She could almost hear her father's voice—when one could only guess at a motive, it was time to gather more evidence.

So she smiled back at the lovely Maria. "Tell me: who was supposed to deliver your orrery?"

The other girl fished through her reticule and produced a handwritten address. Cadenza glanced at it, impressed despite herself. It was the home of the most renowned master glassblower in Venice. But then, if this toy was intended for the person she suspected, it should not surprise her in the least.

"Well, then I suppose we ought to pay a visit." She pulled her mask back on and the Austrian followed her lead with a sigh. She gestured for Maria to precede her, giving herself a moment to look again for any other witnesses. She saw no one. But the darkened windows of the house above could conceal anything.

There was no reason to think that this was anything out of the ordinary yet. It could be a simple theft, or even a badly concealed accident, as easily as some kind of diplomatic incident. But the hairs on her neck still rose as she turned her back on those windows.

Maria hesitated outside the garden walls, but she was facing the correct direction for the Barovier family's residence. Cadenza briefly considered guiding her to where her personal gondola waited. She had chosen to arrive on foot to be inconspicuous, but it always made sense to have transportation on hand. But gondolas implied wealth, which attracted attention.

So they made their way back through the fog on foot. It was thicker now, the irregularly placed lanterns a dull glow here and there, good more for ruining night vision than lighting much of anything. Their footfalls were muffled. Cadenza had a peculiar feeling of privacy, as if she and the Austrian were the only two people in the world and no one could interrupt or overhear them.

"I expected some sort of a policeman," Maria confessed in a low voice. She glanced around at the empty street.

"I think perhaps the council thought you might be more comfortable with a guide," she answered. If Maria was not going to bring up the diplomatic ramifications, neither was she. "Someone similar to yourself." As she said it, she realized that Maria might have no idea that

Cadenza was of noble birth at all. As far as the young woman knew, Cadenza might as well be the courtesan she had been thinking about earlier.

"A guide?" Maria snorted. "Then why so many passwords? Admit it—you Venetians are so in love with intrigue that you cannot resist complicating everything."

Cadenza smiled, despite herself. It *was* a bit ridiculous. "Ah, but that is our charm, is it not?"

"That may work on the men, but it won't work on me!" Maria laughed. The fog deadened the echoes, so her voice sounded more like they were in a small room. "But really, not to be terribly rude, why are you involved?"

Cadenza's feelings were slightly hurt, but she could understand. And how could she explain? "For the same reason they sent you to pick up the orrery in the first place, I suppose—because sometimes a young woman can get farther than a man."

Maria laughed again. "I think we shall be friends, you and I," she said, linking her arm with Cadenza's.

It startled her, enough that she did not immediately pull away. Friends were not something she was quite used to considering. Allies, yes, and pawns. Her father had trained her well to maneuver, determined that even when she married out, his daughter would not be useless to her family, or helpless. And when her brother, the Orseolo heir, had died, she had done her best to step up to maintain the family honor and traditions. It left very little time for friends. And an Austrian might well be the most dangerous friend possible. But—she could not quite help herself—she liked the bubbly young woman.

"We'll get your orrery back safe and sound," she promised, patting Maria's hand.

"I know you will," Maria declared with great confidence that Cadenza hoped was not misplaced.

It was rather after polite visiting hours when they arrived at the Barovier residence. Surely he would be dining with his family or perhaps some guests. But a quiet word with a footman and a flash of a dagger pommel emblazoned with the winged lion of St. Mark gained them admittance. Cadenza remained unsure of how much her new friend was aware. She might not have caught all of the Italian, low and hurried. But had she seen the dagger that Cadenza had produced from and returned to her sleeve? She must know that Cadenza was attached to the government somehow, of course. Yet she was still not sure of the extent of Maria's understanding. And there seemed no graceful way to ask. Something, perhaps merely a lifetime's habit of secrecy, kept her from wanting to reveal too much.

Master Barovier came in looking annoyed, but as soon as he caught sight of them with their masks in their hands, his expression smoothed out into one of willingness to please. "Ladies, welcome. What brings you here so late?"

Cadenza knew that he must have been told that an agent of the Council was here. But she didn't know if he had recognized who she was. Her father, most significant people recognized on sight. And she knew all too well how perfectly her own features duplicated his. Someday, she vowed, she would be well known enough to be unmistakable, like he had been. But for now, she watched him carefully. His eyes were mostly caught by Maria, however. Had she placed the order personally, then?

"Oh, Master Barovier," Maria said, a little more breathlessly than seemed quite necessary. But Barovier did not seem to mind. "The orrery never arrived this afternoon."

He looked genuinely surprised. "I don't understand—it left the glassworks. I supervised the packing this morning myself."

Cadenza kept her own voice cold. "Perhaps you should have supervised the delivery as well."

His lips thinned slightly. "I entrusted it to my most senior apprentice. There was no reason to think that there would be any problems."

"And you have witnesses to the packing?" she challenged.

"Of course, the entire workshop was there," he said, looking affronted.

"What could possibly have happened to it?" Maria interrupted, her eyes wide.

"I don't know, my dear lady," he assured her. His words were calm, but his voice had begun to tighten with nervousness. "But we'll figure it all out in the morning, I promise. It's probably just a minor misunderstanding. I'm sure it's sitting in its crate in the wrong one of our warehouses. There is no reason to worry your head."

Maria bit her lip. "But I need to catch an airship from the mainland tomorrow. If we do not leave first thing in the morning, then I'll never make it."

His forehead knit in concern.

"Can you tell us where to find this apprentice?" Cadenza asked.

"Raul usually sleeps here, with my family and the rest of the apprentices," he said slowly. "But his mother is ill and I gave him permission to go home for the night."

"And she is...?" Cadenza said with exaggerated patience. If Maria was going to play sweetness and light, then she would be the aggressive one.

He did not look pleased. She raised an eyebrow, a maneuver she had practiced in the mirror until she could perform it with suitable elegance. Her cold stare reminded him how little the Council was known for its patience. He scribbled out an address.

Behind his back, Maria gave her the barest hint of a wink.

She inclined her head slightly, thanks without warmth. He should have been more forthcoming, late at night or no. Maria was more effusive in her thanks. And then they were out of the warm light and back into the damp evening.

"Well, that's a start," Maria said matter-of-factly. "We work well together."

Her respect for the other girl rose a notch. She had not been sure how much of the flightiness had been an act. But Maria seemed to have an excellent sense of her effect on men. It was a pity it was a tactic that Cadenza herself could never apply so well. Still, Maria was right— they were a good team.

Naturally, the address was in the Giudecca, the

sestiere on the far side of the city. Cadenza gave up on any pretense at subtlety. They backtracked to where her gondolier sat patiently waiting. Stefano had always seemed to have boundless patience. Maria glanced at where a family crest would normally be located and shot Cadenza a significant glance at its absence. Cadenza shrugged slightly. Removing it had seemed prudent at the time.

Echoes traveled strangely along the *rios*, the tiny side canals. They soon gave up conversation and listened only to the soft splash of the oar. Maria seemed fascinated. The front doors of Venice opened to the water—it was the back doors that were accessible by foot. Golden light spilled from the lobbies of restaurants and hotels only a few steps up from the waterline. Their reflections shivered in the choppy surface, jarred always by the steady thrum of the pumps below.

Maria was staring at the ripples. "Do the islands really move?"

Her voice was hushed, but it was still enough to make Cadenza jump. She tried to pass off her disorientation as consideration of the question. Details about the pumps were Venice's most closely guarded secret. But the Great Retreat was in the history books, even outside the Republic. It couldn't hurt to confirm what was just common knowledge, could it? "Yes, they do."

Maria stared down into the inky water as if she could see the workings below. "So we really are on feet, then?"

She dodged the question. "No, we're on water."

Maria smiled ruefully. "I'm sorry, I'm stepping

beyond my bounds, aren't I. But still—did the city really crawl across the Lido?"

"It did," Cadenza confirmed. During the Napoleonic Wars, the legendary builders of the Arsenal had performed what was later toasted across Europe as the greatest feat of engineering ever accomplished. Long ago, they had built an entire warship during the course of a banquet to impress a visiting French king. When his many-generations-later successor arrived without an invitation, they replaced the wooden pilings holding up the island city with pumps and clockwork legs, floating the city across the lagoon and crawling over the barrier island to escape to the safety of the ocean. Under the leadership of her own grandfather, the tiny nation had kept the *Grand Armée* at bay. Only Russia with its winter and Britain with its fearsome fleet had managed similar.

Maria looked at the houses looming above them with distrust. "But what if they fail?"

"It's perfectly safe," Cadenza assured her. It wasn't, of course. With Venice squatting back in its traditional location, the Republic paid for its mobility and its freedom with constant vigilance. They were nimble, but so very fragile. Cadenza knew it was worse than even most residents believed. But she was certainly not going to tell the young Austrian anything of the sort, no matter how friendly she might be.

Fortunately, Maria seemed once more engrossed in watching the world glide by. Cadenza found herself drifting into a trance, lulled by the sound of the oar. The little craft nosed its way through the tangled neighborhoods, across the expanse of the Grand Canal, and back into the labyrinth. She jolted out only when she heard the creak of Stefano shifting his weight to tie them up to the landing.

It was late, nearly midnight by her wrist chronometer. All this for a toy? But if the Austrians wanted a toy, they would have it. If they wanted an excuse, they would not. She left quiet instructions with Stefano. He had worked in far stranger circumstances for her father for fifteen years—he understood his part. They knocked on the door of the small building quietly. If need be, she would come back with a force of armed men. But it would be better for everyone if this could be resolved with some decorum.

The door creaked open and a young boy's face peered out sleepily.

"I need to speak with Raul immediately," Cadenza said. When he hesitated, she added, "By order of the Council."

He looked more confused than impressed, but he let them in. "Mama is already in bed," he said in an undertone. "Should I wake her?"

"I don't think that's necessary at the moment," she replied softly. "Raul is your brother?"

He nodded.

"Then just bring Raul down."

He scurried up the rickety staircase, leaving them alone with a smoky fire. Maria ducked her head to avoid a clump of onions hanging from the ceiling. Above, they heard footsteps. Only two sets, one much lighter. Good. Cadenza had feared that there would be others in the house–this would be easier if she did not have to worry about being ambushed.

Raul crept down the stairs, careful not to make too much noise. He looked puzzled and annoyed, an expression Cadenza was getting used to. When he saw that his visitors were two young women, his expression lightened. Then he got a better look at Maria. The blood drained from his face.

"I trust you know why we are here, then?" Cadenza kept her voice low, but her tone was cold.

He paused and then started to back up the stairs towards who knew what. "The Council will hear of this."

"I *am* the Council," she said, pulling the dagger from her sleeve and slamming it point down into the scarred wooden table. He jumped. The crest glinted in the firelight. "Get down here."

He edged down the rest of the stairs, his eyes wide. She pointed at the bench. He stayed with his back against the wall. She raised her eyebrows. He swallowed hard and sat where she pointed.

"There is no reason this needs to become unpleasant," she said, leaving the dagger embedded in the table for the moment. There was another, unmarked for anonymity, in her other sleeve, anyway. "Where is the orrery?"

He glanced at Maria and then back to Cadenza wildly. "You don't understand..."

"You're right, I don't," she said, her voice still soft. "By all accounts, Master Barovier is an excellent master. I don't know why you would steal something that took him months to make. I don't know how you could think it would go unnoticed. And I don't know what you were expecting to do with it." She leaned in and dropped her voice even lower. "But I do know that you will tell me, or you will regret it to the end of your very short days."

"But..." he stuttered. "You don't realize. It's going to the Austrians. It's going to the Archduke himself!"

She paused to allow the idiocy of that statement sink in. Was *that* what this was all about? Some kind of misguided sense of patriotism? "I know that," she said, once more with exaggerated patience. She ignored Maria's speculative glance. "Did you really think we would miss something like that?"

He looked dumbfounded. "The Council knew?"

"Of course," she said. "Which is why it needs to be returned. Immediately."

He shot another fearful look at Maria. A horrible thought occurred to her.

"You didn't dump it in the lagoon, did you?" she demanded.

His jaw dropped in shock. "A masterpiece? Never!"

She tried not to show just how relieved she felt. "Then where is it?"

He swallowed. " I put it back."

Cadenza and Maria exchanged confused looks.

"I came back to the workshop and hid the crate after everyone had left," he explained, anxious at her confusion. "I didn't know what else to do with it."

She raised an eyebrow. "And it never occurred to you to report any of this? There are Lion's Mouths in every *sestiere*." The stone statues had collected secrets and anonymous tips for the government's perusal for generations. "If you had shoved a note in, someone would have come and dealt with this by the end of the day. And we all could have skipped this farce."

She hadn't believed he could wilt further, but he did. "I was going to do it tomorrow. My mother–" He gestured upstairs.

Cadenza pursed her lips. Of all the insignificant chains of events to make a diplomatic incident out of, this was one of the more ridiculous she had heard of. She could have smacked the boy. He was probably not much younger than she was, but she felt infinitely old in her weariness and exasperation. He cringed, clearly reading the displeasure on her face. She sighed. "Well, then I suppose we're all going to take a long, cold ride in the dark."

She extricated her dagger with slightly more force than she'd expected. Pounding it in had seemed like a good dramatic gesture, but it was harder to get out than she had anticipated. She did her best to keep her face neutral, as if she'd meant to do it.

"Stay in front, and no sudden moves," she cautioned him, nearly pushing him out the door into the quiet street.

"We're going all the way out to Murano tonight?" Maria whispered, looking concerned.

"If you want your orrery in time, I think we have to," she replied, equally quietly.

"Are we going to get a bigger boat?" Maria eyed the gondola as they approached. The tiny boat bobbed gently in the rippling water.

Cadenza shook her head. It was more time than she wanted to take. While it was unlikely anything would happen, she could not help feel that every minute the orrery was out of Maria's sight, there was a possibility for disaster. And she did not want to be blamed for it. Better to get the orrery to Maria and let it be her problem. "The gondola can make the crossing easily enough. It's still in the lagoon, not out on the open ocean."

Maria nodded but did not look completely convinced. Still, she climbed in after Raul.

As Stefano guided them back through the nearest canal and out towards the open lagoon, the boat fell into silence once more. But now Cadenza could feel a difference in the quality of the silence. Before, with just Maria, it had been companionable, almost relaxing. There was a charge now, though, between Raul and Maria. He kept glancing at her nervously, clearly uncomfortable with a foreigner. She watched him with annoyance and distaste, irritated at the hoops his actions were now forcing her to jump through. Cadenza repressed a sigh. It was going to be a long boat ride.

The little gondola slipped out of the tangled canals and onto the open water of the lagoon. This was not the Grand Canal—there were no welcoming lights on the other side. Behind them, Venice glittered on the water. But around them were a darkness and a silence only broken by the lapping of the water against the sides of the boat. The fog quickly dimmed what light there was. She had not expected to leave the city and had not wanted to be noticed—they had no lantern, whether kerosene or one of the newfangled battery-powered ones. It was like sailing into an abyss.

Stefano knew how to guide them, though. After an eternity, Cadenza was relieved to see an enormous shape rear up in front of them. Maria gasped when she realized there was something there, and then made out the outlines and laughed, embarrassed. Her voice echoed across the water.

"It's an island—is that Murano?" she asked.

"No," Cadenza said, regretfully. The wind along the water was freezing and her hands were nearly numb. She would have liked it to be their destination. "We're only halfway there. That's San Michele."

"Why aren't there any lights?" Maria rubbed her hands together and blew on them. She sounded disappointed.

Tension broken somewhat, it was Raul who answered. "It's the cemetery, my lady."

Maria paused. Cadenza could not see her face. "The entire island?"

"We've been here for centuries," Cadenza reminded her. "It's getting quite crowded, by now."

"I see," Maria replied, doubt shading her voice. Black-on-black outlines of cypress trees loomed at them from over black walls. "Isn't it a bit...unnerving, to have an island of the dead staring at you from across the lagoon every day?"

"I think I've always found it somewhat comforting," Cadenza said thoughtfully.

Maria turned to face her. She could barely see the other girl's face, but she could tell by her posture she was inquisitive.

"Venetians are always very aware of where they come from," Cadenza explained. "The city and its history—it's in our blood. And there's something reassuring about knowing where you are going *to*. Times change fast these days, it seems. But I know that someday, I'll end up with my forefathers. It's good to feel like there's at least some bit of the future one can foresee."

Maria made a contemplative noise. "I always preferred to think I made my own future."

Cadenza laughed. "Oh, I didn't say I was going to give up on trying to do that."

As they rounded the island, the hazy lights of Murano leapt into view. It was a welcome sight. Dimmer by far than Venice, but an end to the oppressive darkness. Leaving the quiet shelter of San Michele meant that they lost their windbreak, though. Soon, Cadenza's teeth were chattering, despite her cloak. She hoped that they would find the orrery in good condition so she could commandeer a bigger boat and get them all safely back to the city in short order. She badly wanted a soft bed with a hot water bottle tucked inside. She supposed Maria must be used to colder temperatures, being from farther north and higher up. But she was glad that snow was a rarity in Venice—the November night was quite cold enough for her.

They had nearly reached Murano when disaster struck. Having seen no other boats during their late-night crossing, the occupants of the gondola were shocked when a steam-powered ship roared up out of the fog behind them. That ship, too, was running without lights. Cadenza had barely enough time to compose a stern warning in her head to the captain before the gondola was caught in its wake.

The boat nearly keeled over, despite Stefano's frantic efforts. Cadenza scrambled out of her seat as the gondola turned nearly on its side. Her chair splashed into the lagoon, cold water slapping up at her face. She grabbed Maria's crinoline, frantically trying to keep the other girl from falling out. Spring steel creaked her in her hands. Just as quickly, the boat snapped to the other side. Already off balance, Cadenza was hurled into the inky depths.

She spluttered to the surface immediately. Her father had always insisted that, however improper or even unsanitary swimming near the city might be, drowning was an incredibly foolish way for a Venetian to die. The heavy skirts and corset did not make swimming easy, though, and the cold stabbed at the very marrow in her bones. She frantically shrugged off what she could, kicking all the while. Gone were the mask and heavy cloak, gone were the shoes. She spat out a mouthful of brackish water, trying not to gasp more in.

Stefano had righted the gondola as the last of the waves passed. It was Maria who leaned over, plunging her arms into the cold water to try to drag Cadenza back aboard. The gondola tipped dangerously at Cadenza's waterlogged weight. Raul leaned in to help, and all of them nearly toppled into the water on top of her.

"Don't!" Cadenza cried as Stefano once again tried to

stabilize the craft. "We're almost there. Just get us to the island."

"I'll hold on to you," Maria promised. Her hands were warm through Cadenza's wet sleeves.

It only took a few more minutes to cross the remaining distance, but that distance seemed to last a lifetime. Cadenza's feet were numbing quickly. She tried to move them to keep the blood circulating, but that only caused the gondola to wobble alarmingly, so she stopped. She bit her lip at the ache in her bones. Maria looked into her face worriedly, harsh shadows cast across her features by the gaslights on the shore.

"Talk to me," Maria begged. "About anything. It doesn't matter."

Cadenza wracked her brain for something to discuss that would not tell more than she wanted to give away. What did unworried young ladies discuss in ballrooms when they did not have to worry about politics and freezing to death in the lagoon? Her mind was nearly blank.

"Opera!" Maria cried. "I love going to the opera when I'm home in Vienna. Aren't Italians supposed to like the opera, too?"

Cadenza knew it was bait, but she rose to it eagerly. With her haughtiest voice, she declared, "My dear, we *invented* opera." Her chattering teeth did ruin the effect somewhat. "The first opera house in the world is in Venice."

"Perhaps you did, but everyone knows that modern form is best displayed in Vienna," Maria declared.

"Copies, merely," she replied dismissively.

They continued to banter, Cadenza increasingly breathless, until Stefano finally pulled up to the dock. Raul swarmed onto the pier, tying them off clumsily. It took all three of them to pull Cadenza first from the water into the boat, and then up onto the dock.

She staggered when she tried to climb to her feet, her toes completely numb. Maria caught her. The Austrian waved off the men. "I'm already damp, there's no point in all of us ending up wet. Is there somewhere we can warm her up?"

"But your orrery," Cadenza protested weakly.

"Has waited this long and can wait a few minutes longer," Maria said. "I doubt I'll sleep tonight regardless. I can sleep on the airship." She turned to Raul. "Surely you know someone who lives here who can loan her some dry clothes?"

Cadenza found herself bundled into a house a few minutes' walk away. Each step brought pricks of pain in her feet that made her eyes water. She was glad— dead flesh felt no pain. The mistress of the house looked understandably annoyed at being awoken, but her face softened when she saw the condition Cadenza was in. Maria relinquished her hold, giving Cadenza's hand a squeeze of support. In no time at all, Cadenza was whisked into another room and stripped of her wet clothes. Her hostess' eyes widened at the sheaths strapped beneath her sleeves and to one leg, but the woman said nothing. Cadenza wiggled her toes experimentally. The skin was an angry red, rather than white, which was another good sign. The new garments were of considerably lower quality than she was accustomed to, but warm and dry.

"Thank you," she said sincerely. "I'll have these returned in the morning, I promise."

The woman nodded, her face softening another fraction. They might well be the only spare clothes she had, and Cadenza wondered if she had not thought to see them again. She made a mental note to include a gift along with the returned clothes.

Maria nodded approvingly to see Cadenza in dry things. She reached out tentatively and tucked an escaped tendril of hair back into Cadenza's ragged bun. Cadenza gave her a rueful smile, which she returned.

The rest of the party wanted to wait for her to warm up fully, but Cadenza insisted on heading straight to the workshop. She just wanted this assignment to be over at this point. Her hair was still dripping icy rivulets down her back, and her feet rattled around in shoes that had been made for someone with very differently sized feet.

When they approached the workshop, Cadenza was alarmed to see that the lights were ablaze. Who would be there at this time of night? The party exchanged worried looks and hastened towards the entrance. Raul fumbled with the key in his nervousness, but the door finally swung open.

The workshop was a disaster, with crates upended and furniture pulled away from the walls. They paused in the doorway, staring. What immediately struck Cadenza was that the there was no broken glass. Each of the pieces being worked upon had been set carefully out of the way, while all the rest was chaos.

Was someone else searching for the orrery? She could not imagine why, unless someone was trying to create tensions with Austria. All the more important that they find it quickly, then. She glanced at Raul.

"Where did you put it?" she asked.

"That's exactly what I want to know," roared someone from the back of the workshop.

They whirled to face the intruder.

Master Barovier stomped out from behind a kiln and then stopped short at the sight of the three of them together. His face was paler than Cadenza remembered and a sweat broke out on his forehead. Then the skin reddened. "You! You traitor!" he spat, pointing at Raul.

"*I'm* the traitor?" Raul exclaimed. "You–" He glanced at Cadenza and cut off.

Barovier shut his mouth abruptly and waited to hear what Cadenza would say. Maria watched curiously. Cadenza sighed.

"Just show us where you put it," she said, not bothering to hide the weariness in her voice.

"Back through here," Raul said meekly.

As they followed him, Stefano caught her eye. She nodded, and he slipped back out the front door.

Raul led them through the wreckage of the workshop. Cadenza glanced at the master glassblower, who seemed to have brought himself back under control.

"And what brings you here this late at night?" she said lightly.

"Couldn't stop worrying about that girl's order," he muttered gruffly. "Months of work. Wasn't about to see it ruined by some fool apprentice. I gave up and rushed myself back."

"You knew he brought it back?" Her voice was dangerously soft.

He shrugged. "Had no idea. It seemed a long shot, at best. But I didn't have any better ideas, and I couldn't just sit fretting."

She suddenly gave him a suspicious glare. "Was that your boat that came in with no lights?"

His eyebrows knitted. "I suppose. I didn't want to wake anyone."

"We are going to have words," she said, her voice suddenly hard. "Later."

He swallowed.

Raul led them out the back door into the alley. Cadenza grabbed a lantern, checked to make sure the door remained unlatched, and followed him out.

The chest was barely disguised—the rubbish heaped on top did little to obscure the name. Clearly, this had not been a well-thought out plan. Barovier glanced back at his ransacked workshop and looked disgusted.

"Open it," she demanded.

His hands fumbled with the clasps. The lid trembled slightly as he lifted it. The two women leaned over his shoulder.

It truly was a marvel. A twisty, tufted Sun of glass lay in the center, mounted on a thin golden spike. Tracks of gold wire mapped the orbits of the planets around the sun, and the orbits of the moons around the planets. Beneath it all, interlocking gears of glass shimmered, ready to drive the entire mechanism. Each planet was a ball of swirled colors. The Earth had tiny continents, as precise as any globe, with clouds dotting the surface. The Sun's tendrils looped wildly, strands of gold dust sparkling in the uncertain light. Each of the glass gears was inscribed with delicate abstract patterns. It might have been one of the most beautiful things Cadenza had ever seen.

"Is everything here?" she asked Maria.

The Austrian leaned over, counting moons. She carefully removed one of the gears, holding it up and peering through the patterns to the candle. She studied the pattern, checking for chips. Nodding, she clicked it back into its place. A gentle push of the Earth moved the rest the same way that pushing the minute hand of a clock might move the second and hour hands. The Moon spun around the Earth, Mercury and Venus proceeding in their orbits quickly, Jupiter so slowly as to be barely noticeable. Even Saturn had a thin glass ring that turned.

Maria looked up, smiling. "It's all here."

Cadenza felt muscles in her stomach she had not realized were tense unclench. Barovier stopped twisting his hands.

Towards the front of the workshop, she heard a commotion. Police burst through the back door, looking about the alley wildly. She caught the eye of the officer in charge and nodded towards Raul. The bewildered apprentice found himself pressed face against the wall. Cadenza beckoned the officer over.

"Him to the Palace. And if you would be so kind, an escort for Miss Maria and her crate here back to her hotel." She helped Maria gently repack the hay around the delicate glass.

"I'll accompany her, if you don't mind," Barovier said. "I don't think I will sleep until that crate is safely out of the city."

Cadenza nodded, sympathizing.

Behind her, the police secured Raul's hands in clockwork mechanisms. Only a magistrate or a jailer would be able to release him now.

"But I showed you...you said the Council knew..." Raul sounded more hurt and confused than afraid. That would change.

"And it's up to the Council now to decide what to do with you," she replied briskly as the police bundled him back through the workshop. She fought back any wave of sympathy—he was a thief who had put the Republic at risk. Maria looked away.

They bundled the lot back onto Barovier's ship, with the gondola dragged behind. Cadenza insisted on lighting the fog lamps this time. By the time they reached the city proper and docked on the outer edge, she and Maria were both stumbling with weariness. They made their goodbyes, and heartfelt inarticulate thank yous, and promised to keep in touch. As Cadenza slid onto the remaining chair in the gondola, she wondered absently if perhaps it was time to make another visit to her mother's relatives.

The great clock in the piazza showed it to be nearly three in the morning when she finally returned to the palace. The Scala d'Oro glowed like sunshine even by candlelight. The gold leaf had been intended to overwhelm visitors in the Republic's heyday; to Cadenza, it felt like a warm welcome. She sat on a bench only for a moment.

Sunlight streamed through the windows when someone shook her awake.

"Where is the orrery?" Foscarini was one of the *capi,* the three leaders of the Council of Ten. He had been terse but relaxed enough the day before when he had given her the assignment. Now, he looked nearly panicked.

She blinked, trying to get her brain to work. "It's fine, they returned it last night. She should be safely on the way out of the city by now."

He swore loudly enough to make her blush as he looked wildly for a clock. "They must be stopped!"

"What?" She stood, shaking out her borrowed skirts and rolling her neck, trying to gather her wits and make herself presentable at the same time. She had to scramble to catch up when he stormed out of the room.

"The apprentice stole the orrery to keep it from the Austrians," Foscarini explained as they hurried down the grand marble staircase to the courtyard.

"I know, very thoughtful but rather poorly thought out," she said impatiently.

"No, he was right," Foscarini replied, equally impatient. "It's not a toy."

"I beg your pardon?"

He stopped and looked her full in the face. "Apparently, hidden inside are the plans for the pumps."

She opened her mouth to declare that that was impossible. And then she remembered the inscriptions on the gears, and Maria's intense scrutiny. Her stomach plummeted. The plans for the elaborate pumps and walking mechanisms were one of the closest guarded secrets in a city built of secrets. With that information, a saboteur could slip over any canal edge and swim to the best places to cripple the entire system. With a diving bell, they might even be able to walk along the lagoon bed from a ship or any point on the shore. They could pin down Venice like a butterfly to a board.

"But how?" Her legs started moving again under their own volition to catch up with Foscarini as he strode ahead. Her mind was still stunned.

"Barovier," he said grimly. "Apparently the man has both a brother in the engineering corps and a great number of gambling debts."

Suddenly a number of factors snapped into place. Barovier's cold sweat, Raul's inarticulate accusations, the unlit steamship. Her stomach, only just beginning to crawl back to its normal position, fell once more, and she wondered if she was going to be sick. "Did we catch him?"

"Of course," Foscarini's expression promised that one master glassblower would have trouble walking across the Bridge of Sighs when the interrogators finished with him. "At her *pensione*, right after she had left. But that does not solve our problem."

Cadenza's lips tightened. "We have to stop her before

she leaves the city."

They hurried through the twin pillars at the edge of the piazza, between which the traitors of the Republic were traditionally executed. A function for which they would soon again be employed. She shivered despite herself. A small steamship waited for them. Ordinarily, powered craft were banned from within the city's canals to reduce waves that the pumps would have to deal with. But the Council had its own craft for emergencies. And it was only this that could save them now.

They chugged through the twists of the Grand Canal, billowing smoke, their wake sending smaller craft bobbing adrift. The pilots took one look at the winged lion flying from the mast and looked meekly away. Cadenza gripped the railing, her knuckles white. If they missed them at the dock, perhaps they could catch them as they made their way up the Brenta canal, which wound its way from the lagoon inland. Or telegraph ahead the field to have them stopped before they could board the airship. The landing field was situated well inland for security reasons, and Cadenza had never been more grateful. If they made it to the airship, however, it would be almost impossible to legally stop them. Venice had agents in Austria, of course, but those she knew of were not particularly well suited to this kind of endeavor. Most likely, it would simply destroy their carefully built covers without actually recovering the inscribed gears.

When she found herself mentally rehearsing the telegraph to send from the office at the end of the harbor for the fourth time, she wrenched her mind away from the subject. Which left her little to do but to think about Maria. She chastised herself for not seeing through the other girl. Was it because she was female? Cadenza herself should have known better. She had noticed that the Austrian was smarter than she let on to some of the people they had talked to. Had she really been so naïve as to think she had found a friend? She should have known that anyone capable of being a peer must automatically be a rival. Years of carefully distancing herself from her potentially treacherous Austrian relatives only to fall for one well-timed wink, like a lovestruck schoolboy. Maria had so obviously been playing the others that it hadn't even occurred to Cadenza that she herself was being played. She felt her ears burning, even in the brisk wind.

The boat puttered to a halt at the customs house on the far side of the lagoon and she and Foscarini nearly leapt ashore. Any foreigners leaving or entering the city were required to go through the queue. A quick check with the door official established that Maria and her party had not yet finished with their paperwork. Cadenza nearly sagged with relief. Instead, she and Foscarini strode through the office, awed clerks falling back in their wake. They approached the little knot of officials clustered around the orrery box and conversation quieted. Cadenza became suddenly very much aware of the assorted lower-level officials and foreigners who now gave them their full attention.

The box was open, straw carefully set in a pile on the floor to be replaced. Maria looked lovely and innocent in her smart peach traveling dress. She had opted not for the circle crinoline that Cadenza herself wore, but for one of the new collapsible bustles instead. Her flat front and the cascade of ruffles projecting out behind her would have made Cadenza feel outdated and a bit frumpy even in her best attire. The gently nodding ostrich feathers from the top of her hat completed the look. How had she managed to look so smart and put together, in the shockingly latest style, while Cadenza herself was rumpled and baggy-eyed?

"Is everything all right, sir?" the customs officer asked Foscarini worriedly. He kept his voice low, glancing around at the audience they had acquired. "Her papers are all in order..."

Foscarini pursed his lips. He evidently had come to the same conclusion that Cadenza herself had. There were far too many people watching to admit that priceless information was in the process of being smuggled out of the city. "I had wanted to see the orrery myself before it left," he said casually, waving his hand in imitation of a bored and useless aristocrat. Cadenza knew better, but there was no reason to think anyone else would.

They strolled over to the open crate. Maria did not startle upon seeing Cadenza. She merely gave her a blandly pleasant smile. It was that smile that confirmed Cadenza's suspicions. From the sweet and flirty young woman she had met the night before, she would have expected surprise. Maria reminded her far too much of someone trying to conceal surprise. Her heart sank, despite herself. She realized that somehow she had hoped that a mistake had been made. That professional, undismayed face merely reminded her of how stupid she had been.

They peered in and Cadenza had to control her own features. The globes of the orrery were the same as she remembered. But the elaborately inscribed gears were blank, merely clear glass. She blinked, hard, wondering if her tired eyes were deceiving her. She glanced up at Maria, who merely tilted her head questioningly.

"Good morning. Is something the matter?" Maria asked.

Cadenza looked down again, wondering if somehow she had misremembered. It had been dark and she had been tired. She had not gotten that good a look, and then all the police had burst through. Had she imagined the inscriptions? No. She remembered how intently Maria had looked at them. They had to have been there. They had to have been.

She smiled back up at Maria, equally bland. "Oh, I can't believe so. This will take just a moment, surely."

Foscarini poked at one globe, setting it turning for a moment. He walked around to the other side of the crate, taking the opportunity to hiss in Cadenza's ear. "Where are the inscriptions?"

She guided him away, smiling, but shot a hard glare at the customs agent. He swallowed and produced paperwork that he set Maria and her porters puzzling over before hurrying over to his superiors.

"They must have switched them during the night," she said in a low tone.

"But where are the originals?" Foscarini asked, his

face composed but his voice tense. He turned to the agent. "How long will that paperwork take?"

"At least another five minutes," the man answered. "And then we have to process it. Which, if we lose the stamps, could take as much time as you want."

"But her airship leaves soon, so she will start getting suspicious in a few minutes," Cadenza reminded him.

"And we have no hard evidence without the gears," Foscarini continued for her. "And if we delay the delivery and we're wrong, it could be a major diplomatic incident."

"They have to have them. There's no way they would risk leaving them, not after all of this," Cadenza said, frustrated.

"Did you check the rest of their luggage?" Foscarini asked the customs agent.

"There wasn't anything unusual," the man replied, looking back and forth between the two of them, bewildered.

"Could they be in the lining of her personal trunk or some such nonsense?"

Cadenza shook her head. "There are too many—you'd need at least a square foot of space to fit them all."

"We could demand a search of her personal items," Foscarini mused.

"But it would be a major insult if we didn't find anything," Cadenza said, watching the elegantly attired woman in her cutting-edge gown bend over the paperwork. She thought about how easily she herself had been fooled. "And it seems too simple. It's too easy to find, if we went searching. She'd never risk it—better to embarrass us sorting through her underthings and come up with nothing."

Foscarini looked doubtful. "We have to take the risk."

They crossed back to the crate as Maria finished with the forms. Cadenza glanced at her, and back at Foscarini, whose mouth had set in a grim line. He was not going to find anything, she knew. Even if she had not been too subtle for that, Cadenza could not believe Maria would let those gears ever be loaded onto an airship with the rest of her luggage, out of her control. And suddenly, she knew where they were hidden.

With a radiant smile, she linked her arm with Maria's. "These men, they'll be fussing for the next fifteen minutes," she said, guiding the girl towards the wall. "Let's just get out of their way. We can make plans for the next time you're visiting."

She wheeled her around so they could watch the proceedings. And then suddenly, without warning, she sat on the bench behind them, pulling Maria's arm hard enough to force the girl to sit down, too.

The clever bustle collapsed, just as it was designed to. But Cadenza was sure that the crunching sound was not part of the design. Maria went white as a sheet. A tiny whimper escaped despite her obvious attempt not to allow her face to shift.

"Why, Maria, whatever could be wrong?" Cadenza asked innocently. "You weren't trying to smuggle some of our glass out without paying tariffs, were you?"

The Austrian shot her a look so full of loathing that Cadenza fancied she could feel the impact.

"Oh dear," she continued. "I'm afraid you're going to miss your airship after all. You really shouldn't have tried to take undeclared merchandise out of the city. You know the Austrian border patrol frowns on such things. And we would never want to upset our dear friends in the Imperial government."

She smiled sweetly. Maria continued to stare at her, lips pinched tight. She relented a hair. "I'm afraid you look just terrible–do you need a doctor?"

She had ended up holding the poor girl's hand as the surgeon removed the shards of glass from the back of her legs. The remnants of the inscribed gears had, of course, been spirited away to be "properly disposed of." The plain gears that Barovier had swapped in were judged to be harmless. By the end, Cadenza had pitied Maria. It had been a clever plan and a valiant effort. Her admiration only partially covered her bitterness.

Ordinarily, someone with such an injury would have never been allowed on an airship, but everyone agreed that the brave young lady, who uttered not one word of complaint about her mishap, would want to be home as soon as physically possible. Maria and her orrery, minus any incriminating information, were loaded onto the night ship under the cover of darkness.

"I'm afraid that we will not be able to make those plans after all. I think, perhaps, it would be better if you did not return to Venice," Cadenza said softly. Expulsion was the best they could do to a foreign noble—especially one related to the Imperial family.

"That would be best," Maria agreed groggily. She had been given quite a few drugs for the pain.

Cadenza watched as the porters carried her up the stairs. At the top, Maria looked back. The Austrian touched her forehead, giving Cadenza a hint of a salute, only marred by the fact that her eyes were completely unfocused. Cadenza nodded in return anyway. A worthy foe deserved the recognition.

Foscarini stood in the shadows on the platform, waiting for her. "In the bustle."

Cadenza shrugged. "It was a daring look for her. I don't know why else she would be traveling with both a bustle and a crinoline."

"You're not at all like your father," he noted.

Her heart sank.

"But then, she was not at all like your father's rivals. We seem to have a new day dawning," he continued.

"The Orseolos have always served the Republic faithfully," she reminded him.

He gave her a considering look. "And continue to do so."

She nodded, once. And turned her back on the departing airship, doing her best to squash any impulse to watch as it carried Maria away. It was a victory, she reminded herself firmly. Her eyes prickled. A victory.

From Enigma to Paradox

by Tyler Bugg

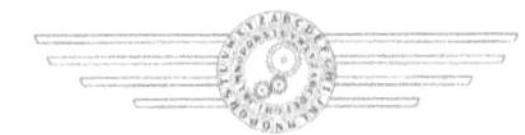

The rumble of Panzer engines still echoed in the distance and the stench of burning oil, gasoline, and human bodies still hung in the air as a sleek black command car pulled to a halt beside the shattered row of vehicles; a small French flag still bravely flew from the front of one wreck. Birds in the trees above still shrilled in annoyance at the smell and smoke, fluttering from branch to branch in anger and trying to get out of the stinking black clouds.

Hauptmann Hans Jageur stepped out of the car as it pulled to a halt, ignoring the sounds of the wildlife railing at the humans that disturbed their carefree lives. The tall, lean man straightened the peaked cap on his head, touching the brim of the Schirmmütze with the delicate grace of a man who was more likely to be seen playing a piano or giving lectures on Ancient Rome than in the middle of a battlefield. The grey uniform he wore gave him a commanding presence—though almost every person wearing the Third Reich's colors could give off a commanding aura, from a lowly private to the Führer himself. His sharp eyes darted among the trees of the back country lane, peaceful until the moment that a couple of low-flying Luftwaffe fighters had noticed the vehicles rolling down this stretch of road.

Men—both in the dark blue tunics of the French and in the feldgrau that he himself wore—were lying on the ground, fit for nothing more than a brief service at the side of this road and another entry in the casualty lists of the conflict. Others, wounded, were being cared for by the few medics present; the serious cases were to be carted back to a hospital behind the lines. A few soldiers who had thus far survived the series of battles into the Low Countries, then into France itself, were running over the dead bodies of the French soldiers, picking up packages of cigarettes and other supplies and goods that the British blockade of the North Sea had cut off from the Reich. Without good tobacco, German cigarettes had gone from bad to worse since the conflict started, and these lucky men could now enjoy some of the contraband they'd been denied since September of last year.

The German officer walked briskly up to a gaggle of men surrounding the vehicles. They all turned and gave off a brisk salute to their superior, who graciously returned it.

"Where is your commanding officer?" he asked, his melodious voice better suited to an intellectual than a military man. And, indeed, Jageur *was* an intellectual—a teacher of Latin and Greek at Munster University, though now simply a reservist called to arms. Fortunately, though, that ability to decipher dead languages had allowed him to skip going to fight at the front this time. Instead, when the conflict with Poland began, he was invited to join the Abwehr: the Reich's military intelligence agency. Since most of his students had already been called to the flag, he agreed. His university seemed pleased enough; one less person they would have to pay at a time when very few students were attending.

An older sergeant, who must have seen battle in the trenches over twenty years before, nodded to a young man who was still peering into one of the massive trucks in the convoy. "Leutnant Karlz is over there, sir," he said with a voice that no officer could miss, but couldn't quite claim was insubordinate—that of an old soldier having to rein in a young man not far removed from being a boy, who had yet to see the truly awful aspects of war. Jageur nodded knowingly to the sergeant before walking over to where Karlz was standing, trying to do his best to feign interest in whatever was inside the truck.

Before Jageur could say anything, though, the young Leutnant surprised him with an about-face; he snapped his right arm to attention and bellowed a "*Sieg Heil!*" that startled what few birds were left in the nearby trees. Jageur returned the salute, though he refrained from barking like the young man did.

"Why did you send for me?" Jageur asked, relaxing a bit now that the formalities were over. The rigidity of military life just didn't come naturally to him.

"Sir, my men stumbled across this convoy as we continued the advance for the victory of the Fatherland!" Karlz bellowed, making Jageur understand why the sergeant felt the way he did about his superior. He was too steeped in the propaganda of the Reich, blind to the realization that this advance could be halted at any moment by a successful counter-attack by the Allies. He believed that Germany was triumphant over all, and they deserved to master all that opposed them.

In other words, a perfect follower of Hitler and the National Socialist Movement.

Jageur personally did not care what others thought. He was a historian and teacher of ancient languages, more at home in a lecture hall than on a battlefield. The Nazis had done well since taking power, he'd admit; they'd righted the wrongs of the Treaty of Versailles, punished the Poles and Czechs for mistreating Germans, and now handed one defeat after another to the French and British for foolishly declaring war on them. However, he was a bit repelled by their treatment of the Jews—many of his colleagues before 1933 had been Jewish and not one still held his post. Some had managed to get out of Germany, but others now lived in the slums, working as simple laborers for the Nazis.

But he would never admit that he hadn't voted them in. He was a nationalist, yes. But not like the men running Germany now, and not like the people their educational efforts were churning out. And he damn well knew he never would be.

Jageur sighed softly and turned his thoughts back to the work at hand, since Karlz still hadn't told him why he was here in the first place. He glanced at the charred wreckage of the convoy truck and was about to turn around and hop back in the car to return to his other duties when he noticed a half-burnt wooden box inside. Curious, he stepped closer, gingerly reaching in to pick up the wooden case and carefully trying to withdraw it from the wrecked hulk of the French vehicle.

"A lot of the French swine had tried to hold us back from here, but the brave Aryan soldiers of the Reich prevailed, as they always shall!" Karlz continued, extolling the virtues of Germany's soldiers in a way that would make Goebbels proud.

"Though I have to wonder," he mused, "How come so many were defending this useless pile of scrap metal? This convoy only carried boxes of papers, most of them destroyed, but we still had to call for an intelligence officer to deal with them. Sir."

Jageur finally managed to get his hands on the wooden box, and tugged it out of the wreck. The front of his jacket was now covered in black soot marks, but he was more concerned about the box in his hand. It was heavy, about the weight of a typewriter, and it still seemed to be intact.

A loud crack dispelled the theory that it was, indeed, undamaged. Both Jageur and Karlz leaped out of the way as the insides of the box tumbled out, nearly crushing the reservist's toes in the process.

Jageur muttered something so vile that even the sergeant he talked to before might have gaped. He bent down to look at the object that had fallen out and stopped, his hands inches from the device.

"It's a good thing you called," Jageur gasped, his fingers twitching.

"What is that?" Karlz asked.

"Our secret weapon," the older officer replied, his voice quiet and trembling. "The one weapon that could make or break the war for the Reich: the Enigma Machine."

Hans Jageur stood outside a pair of massive oak doors after coming down the length of the largest hallway ever, dwarfing the Hall of Mirrors in the Palace of Versailles three times over, or so he was told. He had never dreamed he would be standing inside the massive Chancellery Building that Albert Speer had built for the Führer, and yet... He took a deep breath, trying to do his best to not show his apprehension and nervousness. Never in all his life had he such an important lecture to give.

A lecture to Adolf Hitler himself, to tell him that the Allies had managed to break into the German military's secret codes before he even came to power. He wondered if being the messenger would save him or if he would simply vanish, erased like so many had been since Hitler became Chancellor.

He looked over to the man standing beside him,

Admiral Wilhelm Canaris, his superior, and head of the Abwehr. He seemed calm, his face an impassive mask that didn't betray a single thought. After all, any spymaster who couldn't keep a secret would never have become a spymaster. Jageur knew he was not an expert on the psychology of the human mind, and so he didn't even try to guess what might be going through Canaris's mind. Would he be having the same doubts? Jageur highly doubted it. He would no doubt be used to such meetings, such lectures. After all, the admiral's job was to give all the news, good and bad, to the high command so they could make the decisions with which to run the war and the nation.

Canaris craned his neck around to look at his subordinate. "Feeling all right, Jageur?" he asked.

The professor-turned-spy nodded quickly before returning to his thoughts.

Canaris chuckled. "I wouldn't worry too much about this. The Führer may well start ranting and going on after you tell him; of that, there is little doubt. However, he may also see the advantage in this opportunity. It's a way to make sure that our enemies are led in the wrong direction until the right moment, when we shall strike and annihilate them."

Jageur's mind suddenly clicked back into gear again, the nervousness replaced with the curiosity that his intellectual side was born of. "I thought you weren't a Nazi, Admiral."

"I'm not. Nor will I most likely ever be. But I'm a German, and a German I will remain."

Before Jageur could respond, the two doors were opened by two black-shirted SS officers, standing at ramrod attention. It was time.

The two officers marched into the massive office, turning to face the Führer. They saluted at the same time; Jageur in the modern salute of the Army, Canaris in the traditional Navy style. "Heil Hitler!" Jageur called.

Adolf Hitler—Reichskanzler, Führer—was sitting behind his desk, wearing a simple brown uniform that was adorned with only the Iron Cross he had won in the trenches of the last war. His hair was immaculately combed to the side, and despite sitting at a desk doing paperwork like an ordinary office clerk, the man radiated an air of power, triumph, and victory.

He looked up to the two, and his eyes bored straight into Jageur, making him feel as if the Führer was looking straight into his soul. The professor wavered for a moment, his breath caught in his throat from having the leader of the Reich stare at him with the unblinking, hypnotic eyes that he was famous for.

"Heil," he said simply, motionless behind the massive battleship of a desk he worked at. With that, both of his visitors dropped their salutes, but Jageur was damned if he was going to relax.

"Mein Führer," Canaris started, "we have a matter of most pressing importance to bring to you."

Hitler reached for his glasses, sitting atop a pile of papers on his desk. He perched them on his nose as he started to read through the sheaf, giving only the slightest attention to the two Abwher men. "Go on, then."

There was silence for a moment, before at last Canaris nudged Jageur to give him his cue to start. "Mein Führer," he said, doing his best not to stumble, "I was called to the scene of a Luftwaffe strafing run and skirmish, due to the contents of a disabled convoy, which the commanding officer correctly assumed was full of important papers that would be of immense value to both the Allies and the Reich's war-making capabilities."

Hitler paused halfway through his reading and glanced back up to Jageur; his eyes drilled into the scholar again, making him freeze. "What is it, hmm?"

"Mein Führer, we discovered that the Allies have broken the Enigma code, the code we use for all our top-secret messages. Since December 1932, the Polish, and now the French and British, have managed to decipher our codes with varying degrees of success. Our secrets are no longer so."

The silent room seemed to turn even quieter as Jageur finished. Hitler simply gazed at the captain for a few moments. His left arm twitched slightly and he took off his glasses, settling them onto the paper he'd been reading as he rose.

"They told me the code was unbreakable. They told me the machine was the most secure device in the world," he started, his harsh, Austrian-accented voice a low rumble. "But they have been lying to me? Can it be true? Was the Enigma code indeed broken by the incompetent, inferior Poles? Have they managed to break through the best German technology of the present?"

Jageur gasped slightly at the sudden hurricane of

fury and anger rising in his leader. Canaris himself straightened, as if bracing for the inevitable storm surge that could level entire towns.

"The fools of the General Staff lied to me! How could they not notice that their messages were being read? How could they dare believe that the Enigma was perfect if the English and the French were reading the messages *from before I came to lead the Reich?"* he roared. Jageur could feel himself cowering, shrinking smaller and smaller as Hitler continued his tirade, his body seeming to grow with the anger that was fueling him.

"Canaris! How could you not know they'd broken Enigma? You call yourself an intelligence agent? How could you not have noticed that they had already cracked the code? How many plans of ours have already been handed to our enemies on a silver platter? How long will it take until that imbecile Churchill can take advantage of this? Because, damn it, he will! He will find any way to get back at us! He despises the Reich, and that we managed to escape from that arrogant Treaty of Versailles that he himself helped write to make sure that he and his lackeys came to dominate the world!"

Hitler, his calm composure long gone, panted as he loomed over the desk. "Well, Canaris," he spat out, "what do you say about this?"

Canaris took a deep breath. "From our records, it appears that the Poles managed to break Enigma by finding a worker to replicate the inner workings of the machine; they used him to make a copy. The French, thanks to an agent in the Cipher Office, managed to get their hands on the key changes, with which the Poles were able to continue reading our messages. However, we have since found the identity of the man responsible, and with help from the SS, we have already tracked him down. We had no way of knowing that they had broken the codes, mein Führer, since they never captured an actual device–they made their own. We lost nothing, and so did not know we had anything to lose."

Hitler sat down, still angry, but at last calmer. "So, what do you expect us to do?"

Hesitating only slightly, the admiral set his briefcase on the corner of the desk, then retrieved a piece of paper and handed it to Hitler. The Führer grabbed the page with one hand, his glasses with the other, and started reading.

"From our records, it appears that the British do not yet know what has transpired. They don't know that the convoy was stopped. I recommend that we give them clues suggesting that the convoy was completely destroyed, but that nothing of value could be recovered. They will believe that their secret is safe, and that we don't know they've broken Enigma. Then we can play them to our wishes, giving them useless information, interlaced with some that is real, to mislead them about our true intentions. This way, we can direct the war in such a way to make sure that we retain the element of surprise, and ultimately force the British to fail."

Hitler listened and read intently before, at last, nodding. "A clever idea, Admiral," he admitted. "How soon do you think that this can be underway?"

"Once you give the order, mein Führer, we can start."

"Who will you put in charge of this operation?"

"Hauptmann Hans Jageur," Canaris declared, making Jageur, silent until this moment, squawk in surprise.

Hitler looked over to the startled professor, then nodded. "Very well. I trust you know what best to do, Admiral Canaris."

Canaris nodded, and made to reach for his briefcase, still on the desk. "Excuse me, but may we get that in writing? A direct order from you, to ensure cooperation from everyone?"

Hitler sighed, but pulled out a piece of paper emblazoned with the outstretched eagle clasping a swastika, and scribbled his directive on the page before at last signing it and handing it over to Jageur.

"Um... excuse me, mein <u>Führer</u>," Jageur mumbled, reading the order. "It says 'to entrust under the directive of *Major* Hans Jageur...'"

"That is correct, Major. On my order, you are now promoted. You have done the Reich a great service for uncovering this. You deserve a higher rank."

Jageur was stunned. He had been surprised when he was offered a job with the Abwehr as a captain, having only been a lieutenant at the end of 1918, but now he was jumping all the way to major? "*Jawohl*, mein Führer!" he barked, giving his best salute to his leader.

Hitler nodded curtly before at last returning to the work before him, though the flames of his anger still stirred and crackled in the background. Canaris had already closed his briefcase and turned to go, motioning to Jageur to follow.

They left the office of the Führer, the most powerful man in Europe, and the wooden doors closed behind them. The two men walked a few steps before Canaris started chuckling again.

"What's so funny?" asked Jageur, unaware if he was party to a joke that went over his head.

"You don't realize how important you have become, do you?" the admiral asked. "You're going to be going head to head with MI6, one of the best intelligence services in the world. And, hopefully, misleading them and the entire British army into doing what we want. We'll make them our puppets."

Jageur stopped, suddenly understanding what had just happened. "Oh my God," he croaked, the dizzying responsibility catching up with him.

Canaris turned around to look at Jageur. "Don't worry. With some help, you should be able to help us find a way to win the war and ensure a righteous and proper peace afterwards."

Jageur gulped. As they walked out of the massive Chancellery building, he began to wonder how he was going to explain this to a tailor when he got his uniform upgraded…

Paradox. Operation Paradox. It simply explained what Jageur was doing, and how he was going to do it, while at the same time confusing those that might hear of it outside of its proper context.

Not that the context for it would make sense, in any case. It was simply, really: issue a bunch of orders through the Enigma machine in the next few months to refocus British attention. "With the Battle of France over, now the Battle of Britain begins," as Churchill said on the radio. And Germany must make sure it won this battle now.

Major Jageur set to work almost the moment he got settled into an office at Abwehr headquarters in Berlin. Jageur's living style had changed so often in the past few months, the only thing missing was sleeping in a cave like Barbarossa from legend; then he could say he'd lived in every manner he thought possible. Going from a constantly moving camp during the invasion of France to a rented room in the capital was a sudden shift, but not as bad as the shock he'd had before. He'd locked and bolted his apartment in Munster and then gone to the roving camps of the front, leaving a steady existence for one that promised destruction at every instant. He had been convinced he would never get used to sleeping under canvas with complete strangers in a different place every night, but was surprised to find that he adapted quickly. It almost reminded him of the camping trips he took with his family to the Black Forest long before the Great War had started. But now the bed of his new apartment seemed too comfortable after a cot under a tent, and having privacy—or as much as you could have in the Third Reich—was a strange sensation after weeks spent without it.

He could, however, live without being shot, bombed, or fired upon ever again.

But his work was much more important. Now, he was basically writing a massive script that the entire German war machine must play out in order to trick the British in the upcoming fight, the Luftwaffe most of all.

Jageur was to work directly with the Oberkommando der Wehrmacht, the high command, as they planned how to destroy the RAF as a precursor to Operation Seelöwe, the invasion of Britain. But almost from the beginning, he noticed that the generals and admirals in charge did seem to have much hope in them; they were going through the motions, as Hitler ordered the attack, but they knew their chances of success weren't good. Most were sure that the Royal Navy was too strong to face directly, and the Kreigsmarine too weak to protect the barges as they crossed the choppy English Channel. The attack on Norway had already laid bare the faults of the Kreigsmarine for all to see, but nothing could be done about it now. They were certain the Luftwaffe would not be able to protect the escorts properly, but alas, Germany did not possess the large surface fleet they thought would do the job. They thought that the failure to prevent the evacuation of Dunkirk was the greatest flaw in the stratagem. Had the professional British Army been destroyed on the continent, they would not be available to repel any invasion. But they were now in England: almost weaponless and impotent, but still there.

Jageur was not directly involved with the planning. He wasn't a career military officer and the pervasive Prussian snobbishness of the office didn't do a thing to distance him from that fact. The generals in charge of planning, who had done so well in Poland, in Norway, in the Low Countries, and most recently in France, felt that they knew precisely what to do and how to do it. They did not like the idea of a campaign of false information against the British; they thought that a decisive battle of engagement was the best course to take. No tricks, no cunning schemes—nothing could dissuade them. Some thought that secret tactics were for a division to use as a bit of skullduggery, not for the entire military to try to follow. They had already gasped in shock at Jageur's plans and had come back from meeting after meeting with Hitler deflated and resigned to helping the major. A few officers began to see the value of the secret operation after discussions with Jageur, but only a few.

They didn't trust him, either. Besides the fact that he was not a career military man, he had brought them the bad news that Enigma had been cracked. The generals all ranted and raged at Jageur, as if blaming him for the codes being broken.

But Jageur was going to push through anyway. Hitler had approved Paradox, and Paradox was his, so therefore, Hitler had approved of him. At the moment, he was more powerful than any of these generals, though he was more interested in trying to write a mystery around their textbooks than in making their textbooks conform to his mystery. He wasn't going to force them to like his plans, but he needed to make sure that what he did would hold up when the actual events took place.

The plans for Operation Seelöwe were well underway and the Luftwaffe was already flying sorties over England in order to lure the RAF out and destroy it. Jageur decided that was the most important tactic right now: they would try to trick the RAF into a series of decisive battles and destroy its power.

The first battles were taking place over the Channel, attacking the convoys that carried materials, supplies, and goods from port to port. Little could be done about that, as it was already winding down after neither side gained a decisive edge. But the next stage, set to begin on August 10, was already being planned. Called "Eagle Day," it was supposed to be the first big attack on the English coast. And this was where Jageur was going to put his tactics to the test.

"I still see no use in this," a colonel mumbled as he guided Jageur around a Luftwaffe command room. "I'm still sure we should be able to knock down anything that the damned British send up."

"Well, certainly, Herr Oberst," Jageur said calmly, glancing between the clock and the clipboard with him as they walked. "But what if you are wrong?"

Before the colonel could sputter out an indignant remark, Jageur walked toward a radio operator, who was hurriedly tapping out messages on the exposed Enigma. He'd planned very carefully. Every so often, the radio operators would be instructed to send messages throughout the Luftwaffe command. Those messages would mean nothing to the Germans, but they could—no, *would*—be misinterpreted by the British. All of it would explain why the messages that he had sent earlier in the day failed to detail the plans for the upcoming attack, which the British might be expecting to happen.

He watched as enlisted men wearing massive headphones moved markers showing squadrons of planes, and read the reports on the British forces they were facing. It was a carefully orchestrated ballet at the beginning, two different troupes performing at the same time with different choreography and different scripts. But starting from the first times that they clashed, the ballet was thrown off: the British and German fighters would have to move in different directions based on the result of the smaller battles.

As Jageur continued to walk between the different Enigma operators, he stole glances at the board and began to grin like a schoolboy. He could see that the British fighters were gathering more over the cities, and especially London, as Operation Paradox had urged them to do. They weren't taking up positions in the south to deal with the German bombers and fighters. His plan was already starting to blossom.

His Luftwaffe escort was amazed. "So it *did* work."

Jageur nodded. "It is also proving that they have deciphered Enigma, and they trust it. However, we must make sure that they continue to do so, no matter the cost."

The Luftwaffe officer, one of the many who claimed that the Enigma Machine could not be broken and that Jageur was insane for believing it, flushed red at the declaration. He turned on his heels and left, barking some mundane order at an unfortunate adjutant.

Jageur merely shrugged and turned back to the Enigma operators, who were still sending both the real and fake messages that allowed the German Army to function and confuse the British at the same time. A few more battles like this one, he was sure, and the RAF would be no more, and the Wehrmacht would be able to cross the Channel with minimal difficulty.

What would it be like to walk in Occupied London, with the swastika flying in the place of the Union Jack? Jageur secretly hoped to see it, but what would the cost be beforehand? Were the generals right? Was Hitler demanding the impossible? When would they find out who was right?

And would it be too late? Would Germany be set to lose its second war in thirty years?

Being summoned to Admiral Canaris's office was always an interesting experience; the organized chaos within never failed to make an impression. Though Jageur did not have to make the trek that often, he was still nervous about it, like a young child being sent to the headmaster for something that he may or may not have done.

Canaris was a gracious host, pouring cups of tea for both himself and Jageur, who accepted it with nary a comment. Although he preferred coffee, he wouldn't refuse tea if his superior offered it. The admiral was in his naval uniform and clearly felt quite comfortable in it. A model of the *Dresden*, a plucky little cruiser of the first war, sat on his desk. It was the only survivor of the Battle of the Falkland Islands, after it helped to destroy a British squadron a few weeks before at Coronel. Canaris had been the intelligence officer on the *Dresden* and managed to survive both battles, before the ship was scuttled at an island off the coast of Chile. He had heard the tale of Canaris making his way through South America and back to Germany after the *Dresden* went down, despite being hunted by the British intelligence services. It was an entertaining war story over midnight drinks, and one that Canaris had told Jageur at least once before.

But rehashing naval history was not the reason that Jageur had been called to his office, he was sure. Still, he couldn't very well prompt the man. So they exchanged pleasantries and polite conversation as they drank their tea and ate some French pastries.

At last Canaris sat up, leaning over his desk. "How well do you think Paradox worked, Jageur?" he asked softly.

Jageur finished his tea and set the cup on the desk. "Well enough, sir. We managed to trick the British long enough to severely cripple the Royal Air Force; the Luftwaffe has air superiority over the Channel and most of southern England now." He paused. "Although it's fairly obvious that they know now. They know that *we* know they've broken Enigma. We shouldn't have started hand-delivering the actual attack plans, instead of sending them over Enigma. When we did that, all hopes for Paradox to work were dashed."

Canaris nodded. "At a meeting with the high command, I tried to convince the Führer to keep using Enigma for actual communication along with the fake messages, but Goering said he would have none of it, and Himmler agreed with him for once." The admiral sighed. "If the generals said they didn't like it, it still could have been done. But if Goering and Himmler said it was a bad idea—well, that overrules everything else, and so we have it. It was more a matter of politics and carving out fiefdoms than actual military policy, frankly."

Jageur didn't say anything, unsure where Canaris was going with this. Was he trying to root out disloyal members of the Abwehr? Was he trying to find people opposed to the government to use them? What was his motive?

Canaris chuckled softly and leaned back in his chair again. "My friend, I realize you're worried. Suspicious. Maybe even a bit paranoid. You have doubts about speaking and answering me truthfully, and I can't blame you. This is a dangerous time to live in, believe me, and you never know who to trust."

Jageur nodded slightly. "I really do wish I was back in Munster, preparing lectures on the use of Latin and Roman history. I was prepared to do my part for the Fatherland and then hopefully go back to being a civilian. But this war is going on longer than anyone said it would, and I don't know if I will ever be able to."

Canaris waved his hand toward the massive bookshelf in the room. "But this is only the first part of Hitler's plan. Have you read *Mein Kampf?*" he asked.

Jageur swallowed. "I have started to, yes, since I've been in the military. Nothing else I felt I could read safely."

"Well, the way it is working out is that this is only the first part of his plan: Russia is his main goal, and it's plain to anyone who has read his book." Canaris paused. "And that's what I'm most afraid about."

"You don't want the Nazis to succeed?"

Canaris drummed his fingers on the desk. "A German defeat in this war would be catastrophic. But Hitler winning is a much worse proposition." He hesitated. "That is why he must not be allowed to see this through."

"You want the Führer to fail?" Jageur was incredulous. "You can't possibly…"

"Not exactly," Canaris said, his teeth worrying the corner of his lower lip. "The Fatherland cannot lose. Therefore…"

What Jageur was then told—while confusing at first, then dizzying in its possibilities and outcomes, and sobering in its perils and dangers—convinced him then and there to follow the admiral, no matter what. No plans were ready yet, he was told. Other conspirators had tried to stop Hitler over the Sudetenland in September of 1938, but had only been stalled by the British surrender there. They couldn't do anything yet.

But once the time came, Jageur was more than willing to do whatever he could to help. Even if that meant sharing a funeral plot with Admiral Canaris.

The thud of jackboots echoed through the narrow, winding streets. They stomped up and down in unison as the soldiers marched down The Mall toward Buckingham Palace. The massive stone facade so recognizable to any visitor or citizen of London had seen the effects of modern artillery and bombs: the entire north end of the building was reduced to rubble, and a shell hole was now in the place of the famous balcony where the British monarchs would watch the throngs below in times of triumph or chaos.

To Oberstleutnant Hans Jageur—promoted for Operation Paradox, as thanks for its initial success—setting foot in London was the culmination of his plan. After the British were tricked so thoroughly by his decoy messages, they were in no place to try to mount a coordinated attack afterwards and the RAF planes were chopped to pieces by the Messerschmitt Bf 109s whenever they did get off the ground.

The invasion was more difficult, of course. The Royal Navy did indeed try to sweep in and shoot up the invasion craft on the third day of Operation Seelöwe. They managed to do a bit of damage, but the Luftwaffe and the U-boats managed to sink some of their attackers, including the battleship HMS *Hood*, and the aircraft carrier *Ark Royal*, while many other destroyers and cruisers were damaged or sunk. After that, the U-boats harried the Royal Navy, preventing them from interfering too badly with the battle, and the Stuka dive bombers and Junker's bombers went back to the land battle.

And Churchill was right; they did fight on the beaches and landing zones, and in the fields and streets. It cost Germany dearly; the battles they had fought since 1939 up to France had seen somewhat minor casualties, but Britain would prove to be the most deadly conflict of the war. Many soldiers were starting to call it the "British Front," the old veterans fearing they had walked back into the trenches of twenty years before.

But this time there was a difference. An important one. No matter what, the British could not hold off the Germans. They had little artillery, and fewer Panzers. The men were armed with nothing more than rifles and whatever they could salvage from the wreck and rubble of their nation.

But the people were worse. The men and women continued to fight, even after the front advanced north. Potshots, booby traps, and poisonings were common, and the bastards came up with the "Churchill Cocktail," a glass bottle filled with gasoline, set on fire with a rag, and then thrown at a Panzer. If it landed over the rear vents, the engines would catch fire and explode, leaving the Panzer crews as sitting ducks.

The SS had already "pacified" many towns, usually with a liberal application of bullets, and the Luftwaffe visited death and destruction on Canterbury and Manchester to try to get the British to give up. However, the Wehrmacht still had to carry on; they were still fighting at this moment along the border of Scotland with the few surviving military units left. Some of the big Royal Navy ships were said to have fled to Canada with the king and queen on board.

But Churchill was captured. The truck convoy he was in had been shot up by the Luftwaffe fighters—much like the Enigma convoy had been in France, to Jageur's amusement—and soldiers managed to catch up and drag

Churchill out. They brought him back to some of the new concentration camps set up. He was most likely going to be tried for war crimes, especially over the attack on Berlin by RAF bombers a few weeks ago. Though the damage hadn't been especially bad, many civilians had been injured, and Germany had *mostly* refrained from attacking cities; Rotterdam, Canterbury, and Manchester being the exceptions, of course.

None of that was of any concern to Jageur now. He stood on the reviewing stand with the leaders of the Nazi party, Army commanders, and Oswald Mosley and his Fascists, the men who were being installed as the new leaders of Britain. The Duke of Windsor was currently being offered the opportunity to reclaim his title as King Edward VIII, as his brother had fled abroad, but in the meantime, men who could be controlled, if not trusted, would run the nation. Hitler stood in front, saluting the soldiers as they marched by in perfect goosestep, down to the ruined Buckingham Palace, flanked by Himmler, Goering, and his architect, Albert Speer, who stood a bit behind.

Jageur had seen the pictures of Hitler in Paris; had seen how, despite his almost permanent scowl in the pictures, his eyes brimmed with joy and satisfaction at defeating an enemy that would desire to see nothing more than the utter destruction of Germany and Germans. This time, there was the feeling that Hitler regretted this attack, despite its success. He was an admirer of the British Empire, according to *Mein Kampf,* and thought there was no reason why the British and Germans couldn't rule

Eurasia together.

But ruling Eurasia also meant Russia. The Soviets were presently allied with Germany, as per the deal von Ribbentrop got together in 1939 with Molotov—whose name almost sounded better with the infernal partisan anti-Panzer weapon than Churchill's, Jageur thought. But Hitler said that the Slavs who lived and ruled in the east were Untermenschen, and that the land belonged to the Reich as Lebensraum. Conflict was, indeed, inevitable.

Jageur shuddered, remembering that meeting with Canaris. He knew Russia could not be underestimated, Communist or not. He knew his history, and knew that the dreams of many empires had died in Russia. He hoped that the Third Reich wouldn't be another. Was Canaris right? Was Hitler now finishing the battles he could win, and heading for the battles he couldn't?

Jageur took a deep breath and forced himself to watch the soldiers march by. They would be the men sent to war in Russia. Not one of them could, or would, refuse. They believed in Hitler and his ability to achieve victory. They would follow him wherever he led them: Russia, China, India. America. Hell. They would gladly do it, shouting *"Heil Hitler!"* and goosestepping off to fight.

Jageur twitched, thinking about it. He couldn't in good conscience let that happen. His hand slowly slipped alongside the leather holster of his Luger P08. He paused, feeling the tanned hide and oiled steel against his fingers before he pulled away. No. Not now.

He looked to his left, toward the surprisingly intact Big Ben. Although the Houses of Parliament were nearly a gutted ruin now, the famous clock tower still stood, and was still wound up every day to be used. It was just a few minutes to two. Jageur checked his watch, and nodded to himself. It must be so then.

Smoke still curled up against the grey, cloudy sky from all around him. It would most likely start raining soon enough, Jageur thought. He continued to watch as the soldiers in grey marched by, victorious martial music filling the air with the feeling of triumph. The *Deutschlandlied*, one of the few symbols of Germany Hitler kept after the Weimer Republic, blared out for the ten-thousandth time that day, and timed almost perfectly with the ringing of the bells of Big Ben naming the hour.

Deutschland, Deutschland über alles,
Über alles in der Welt!

A series of gunshots rang out against the anthem; Jageur threw himself flat onto the hastily erected viewing stand, acting on instinct drilled into him first in 1918, and then again, here in 1940, and automatically reached for the pistol, pulling it out of its holster and searching the street for something to aim at. He was far from the only one to have done so. Cries and screams and curses went up, as the band trailed off in confusion. The soldiers marched a couple more steps before the carefully orchestrated lines fell into anarchy as well, some soldiers trying to get away from the bullets that might still be coming, while others raced up to the viewing stand to try to help.

Seeing no attacker close to hand, Jageur pulled himself together and looked around him. He nearly lost his lavish lunch, the extravagant meal prepared for the Führer and his closest ministers that he had been privileged to share.

Hitler was dead. A bullet through the head could mean nothing else. Himmler was thrashing around, his glasses shattered beyond use, and the corpulent Goering was lying still, the pool of blood around his body growing steadily. Speer, alone of the four top party members there, was uninjured, though blood spatter now covered his uniform, and he was shaking violently from his brush with death.

Some generals had also been hit, and it looked like Alfred Jodl was down with a serious wound to the leg. General Guderian and Gerd von Rundstedt were alive, as was the young Erwin Rommel, and all three flailing to do something to help the others.

Jageur sat up and looked around. From his short time at the front, he realized that it wasn't the work of a single machine gun, but a bunch of rifles. Did the British resistance do this? Or...

"Canaris..." he whispered to himself, thinking of what the admiral had told him. Did he organize this? He had contacts with MI6, of course, but did he tell the English that Hitler was coming? He might have, or British Intelligence might have found out themselves.

Either way, Hitler was dead, and Goering. Himmler was most likely going to be dead soon. Goebbels and other Nazi leaders were still alive, but would they be able to take control? Or was this part of Canaris's plan?

Jageur holstered his gun like an American cowboy from the cinema. At least he wouldn't have to use it today. All he knew was that, despite the death and destruction here in Britain, he was feeling lucky not to be in Berlin right now. It would be worse there, for sure.

Would the war be over now, with Hitler's death? Only his successor knew the answer.

"And that is all for today," the professor stated. The students in the lecture hall poured out of their seats, hurriedly scrambling their papers together to get out as quickly as they could. Others made their way up to Hans Jageur, who dutifully answered every question related to the lecture that was thrown at him. He grinned as he did, finally feeling back at home once more, though his students must have thought he was losing it. *Let them think what they want,* Jageur thought. *I'm just glad to no longer be fighting a war.*

Twenty minutes later, he finally arrived back at his office. With practiced motions, he opened the door and walked in before stopping suddenly.

"Admiral Canaris!" Jageur exclaimed, surprised to see the spymaster sitting calmly in his office, flipping through one of the many books that lined the walls. The one Canaris had picked looked like the well-thumbed copy of *Julius Caesar* that Jageur had looked through many times for his personal enjoyment.

Canaris looked up at the professor, dressed in a dark blue suit, tie loosened and coat open. He himself was in uniform, and pristine as ever. He chuckled, amused at having come out of nowhere to surprise his former underling. He looked back at the book, and began to read from it:

"Cowards die many times before their deaths;
The valiant never taste of death but once.
Of all the wonders that I yet have heard,
It seems to me most strange that men should fear;
Seeing that death, a necessary end,
Will come when it will come."

Jageur nodded solemnly, taking his place behind his desk, even more cluttered with papers than Canaris's desk at the Abwehr headquarters was. "But what happened a few months ago wasn't cowardice, was it? Nor simply a British Resistance atrocity."

Canaris looked up from the book. "It must have been, my dear Hans. The SS concluded it was, and found the shooters and the planners, and they were punished." Jageur was about to argue when Canaris subtly winked and returned to the book, cutting the argument short.

Jageur shuffled some papers in a futile effort to organize his desk, and his thoughts. He should really work on that article and get that published soon... "How about the peace negotiations? How is that going?"

Canaris looked up again. "Fine, fine. The Fascist government installed by Hitler will not be supported; new elections will be held. We will do our best to help rebuild England—for the small price of returning the German colonies from the Second Reich, along with the Belgian Congo. France and the Low Countries will be reformed, but we keep Alsace-Lorraine, Luxemburg, Wallonia, and some Dutch territory, as well as ports on the English

Channel. Ah, and Poland will be recreated, though we keep the land that belonged to the Empire before. Austria and the Sudetenland will remain, with Bohemia and Moravia being given independence."

Jageur bowed thoughtfully at the list of concessions and demands. "And how about the rumors of inviting a new Kaiser back?"

"More than just rumors, truth be told. We have asked the Crown Prince, and he's thinking about it. A shame Wilhelm II passed away a few weeks ago."

Jageur sighed. "It will be wonderful to return to normalcy again. Haven't had that since 1914, frankly."

Canaris shook his head. "The world will never be the same again. British and French power has been destroyed, possibly for good, and Germany and the Soviet Union will have to fill in that gap. Meanwhile, Japan and America are growing more powerful by the day."

Jageur sighed again. "Well, at least the symbol of the old order will be there. All you can ask for now."

They both looked at their reading for a moment, Jageur at his papers and Canaris at his book. Then Jageur glanced up. "But you didn't come here to chat about how Europe has changed. Why *are* you here?"

Canaris at last set down the book. "Germany is in dire straits. The Nazis are a broken force, and Goebbels can't do much to try to restore the country. Hitler was the only thing holding the rotten structure together, purely through force of will. The new government needs help, but people are not sure what to do."

"And you want me to help?"

"We need people who would want to help rebuild our country. Acting Chancellor Beck has called elections for March, with all parties allowed to participate. But we cannot allow the Nazis to win. If they do, then it is all for naught."

Jageur was surprised by the offer, if that was, indeed, what it was. He didn't expect to be asked to run for office. He had done work for the Social Democrats in the 1920s, but that was all.

Well, he might as well. Germany did need the help, and he sure as hell wasn't going to let the Nazis come back to power. Not after dragging Germany to the edge of the abyss.

"Very well, then. I will run." Canaris grinned and reached across the table to shake hands.

"I look forward to working with you, you know," Canaris said as he grabbed his peaked cap, and with a light touch, straightened it on his head. The spymaster walked out of the office, much like the shadow he made himself out to be. He was the true spymaster: a puzzle wrapped in a riddle inside a mystery that no one, not even the man who dealt with them in war, could decipher.

And frankly, that is the way Jageur wanted to keep it.

In God We Trust

by G. Miki Hayden

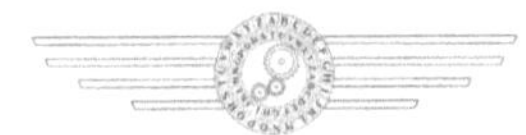

General Warashi Thundertalk stood on a narrow watchtower promenade forty feet in the air, binoculars in hand. His ancestors had climbed the nearby red sandstone cliffs herding their goats and sheep up from the plains to summer in the hills. Now, he looked out across the barbed wire fencing that divided New Mexico—held by the United Tribes—from Old Mexico—to which the Francspanics clung stubbornly despite two hundred years of intermittent UT efforts to oust them from this continent.

Thundertalk could easily make out the Francspanic patrol along the other side of the border, three bearded men whose ammunition belts crisscrossed their well-muscled torsos. The general pulled the field glasses away from his face. "Nothing unusual then?" he asked his lieutenant.

"Since the tanks on maneuvers three days ago? Not a thing."

Thundertalk grunted. Air recon had come up with nothing in particular, either. "The videotapes flown in from New Paris are rather disturbing," he commented.

"Yes," said Lieutenant Hitachi. "It's a full-scale famine. Any warlike posturing on their part might be an attempt to divert the attention of their people. But they'll need a pretty big distraction to take away the focus on that." He shook his head glumly.

"*Warui*," sighed General Thundertalk. The footage of malnourished youngsters who could barely raise their heads to gawk at their American visitors had kept him up most of the night.

He didn't like standing across an artificial divide from these people, imagining their youth drying up like grass under a blazing sun. With three little ones at home and a clan of fifteen more children and seventeen adults under his direct care, the vision nagged at his conscience. Sad.

"Do you think the Americans will help them?" asked Hitachi.

Thundertalk nodded. "I think they'll try to. If they can get Chief Nakasone to sign on to a humanitarian mission."

"And Nakasone? What's his intention?"

Thundertalk shrugged. "We go into the sweat lodge tonight to pray. Whatever the Holy People mandate, that's what Nakasone is committed to carry out."

Hitachi looked at Thundertalk without speaking, each

of them wondering if Nakasone still held the favor of the Holy People; that is, if he ever had. And the general speculating, not knowing if Hitachi thought the same about his superior—if he, Thundertalk, might soon assume the post of Chief Over All the Tribes, or if he even wanted to. From such a seizure of power as he was on the verge of, only death, death, and more death was ever known to emerge.

In the year of Jesus Christ, 1949, as the prevailing European-American calendar designated it, the general wasn't certain that he wanted death to be the heritage he left his house.

U.S. President Eleanor Roosevelt stood by her telex machine and read line by line the report that slowly rose up, so eager was she to determine how the situation stood on the Old/New Mexican border. Her emissaries had returned late last night from deep inside Old Mexico and the pictures they had brought her were heartrending in their pathos. The Francspanic Empire was on the verge of utter collapse. A series of unfortunate weather-related catastrophes had destroyed another year's crops, and all the empire's limited resources—those few that remained—took the form of added troops on the perimeter that separated Maximillian IX's holdings from his neighbors.

The telex message was from the president's ambassador to the United Tribes, which held the vast wastelands west of the Mississippi/Arkansas borders.

Thank God, the proposed Louisiana Purchase had fallen through more than two hundred years before. Otherwise, Eleanor herself might have inherited the responsibility for the whole western portion of the continent, a burden that now rested in the hands of Chief Nakasone, his generals, and the United Tribes' long-time Far Western allies, the Japanese Empire—a sovereignty that stretched from the Kurile Islands down to the great land mass of Australia and its smaller neighbor, South Nippon, and across to the utmost northwestern shores of this Newer World.

The news from J. Adger Hoover was more non-committal than discouraging. Nakasone had gone into a mighty vision quest with his advisors. The border between the other two Middle American powers was quiet.

Eleanor hoped against hope that Nakasone would allow the United States to drop aid into the neighboring regions without his declaring war and riding to battle against the densely populated, stronger, yet more vulnerable country: her own.

"Inshallah," she muttered to herself. God willing! Her faith in Allah, the one God, was strong.

Anjo Black Wolf, shaman of the Bitter Water clan, entered the hospital hogan just prior to dusk. It reassured his patients to see him here at this period of the evening. The slipping away of daylight was a fearsome time to some whose illnesses were powerful, and whose faith in the Holy People was weak. Seeing their shaman go about his healing work with a quiet chant to Spider Woman or Corn Boy lifted their spirits and kept them from too quickly departing this Middle World.

A death in the hogan would be unfortunate, requiring a long chantway to purify the entire 70,000-square-foot building. The last time it had happened—two months before—they'd had to call in fourteen shamans from as far away as the Badlands to participate. In the meantime, there had been near riots among the families of the ill. They feared the ghosts of the dead more than the physical illnesses of their relatives. And something in the *hitali/* physician had shuddered in empathy.

Most of the time, Anjo and his staff managed to heal the patients who came for their help. And those who didn't get better over time were brought out to the Sacred Places to prepare for their deaths.

Anjo's mouth sang the chantways given to the People, his people, the Navajo, so many centuries before, but his mind was elsewhere. He drifted toward the private wing of the hogan where his special patients lay. Anjo was bent on advancing the curative arts well beyond the horizons of those who preceded him. When he had first returned to New Mexico from his studies in East Tokyo—a series of seven volcanic islands halfway between French California and Japan—Nakasone had been encouraging of the new sciences that Anjo brought with him. But as Nakasone grew older, and bitter at his lack of success in several areas where he longed to leave his mark, the chief became more protective of the old ways. Anjo's new sciences remained under debate.

"There you are, Little Manchild. I thought I'd find you at home this evening."

The reclining teenager smiled up at the singer. He adjusted himself, and his liquid-filled petroleum-spun mattress shifted with him. This was just one of the many wonders Anjo had imported for his patients from the Far West.

"Comfortable, are you?" Anjo inquired.

"Changing Woman has given me comfort and much more. I know that because you are here, Black Wolf, I will be healed."

Three weeks before, Little Manchild had been climbing in the old cliff dwellings and a ladder had suddenly come undone, pitching him directly down the steep, sharp rocks. With each skid against the stone—and there were many—a bone was broken. In the end, the young man's left leg was so badly pulverized that the shaman in his village had chosen to amputate. Little Manchild's hold on life had been so tenuous at that point that the youngster had been airlifted onto the roof of Black Wolf's hogan. There, the shaman had stabilized his patient, and one week later had applied an experimental technique.

Now, he unwrapped Little Manchild's bandaged leg stub to have a look. "Very nice," he proclaimed approvingly. He nodded at Little Manchild. "I'm entirely optimistic," he added, grinning broadly. "I told you that I'd seen them do this several times in Honolulu. I just wasn't sure if I could duplicate it."

Doctor and patient gazed down at the stump. The flesh at the end showed up baby pink and budding. The stub was extending into what it remembered itself to really be: a leg. A new leg had begun to descend from the already formed root.

"Yes, it's working. I know it is. I can feel it growing, minute by minute."

Anjo soaked some fresh bandages in the DNA-stimulating solution he had brought into the room. Then he chanted the ancient words as he renewed the dressing on the amputation site. The Holy People would grant their strength to the boy.

Tired as Anjo was by the time he left the hospital, he had more, much more, work to accomplish. Tonight, he was "officiating" at the sweat lodge convened by Chief Nakasone. The question facing the United Tribes was whether to allow the Americans to fly supplies into Francspanic territories without reprisal. The UT treaties with the Americans were longstanding and the border between the two great Middle American nations had been stable ever since the Second French and Indian War. The "civilized" Americans frankly wanted nothing to do with this wilderness that belonged to the nomadic Tribes, just as the UT scorned the constraints laid down by the rigidly structured, overcrowded country to the east.

As much as Nakasone and some of his Samurai Raiders might love to see the downfall of Old Mexico and other lands to the south—even through the starvation of every last elder, woman, and child, not to mention soldier (who were the only ones now being fed more than a daily mouthful)—it would not be pragmatic to offend the American Easterners, Anjo believed.

Stretched thin enough at their boundaries to the south and west, the UT had no need to be squeezed in between *two* enemies. Surely Nakasone knew that. But the question that came immediately after that was: did Nakasone, that old fool, really care? A lot like the fabled Louis the Fourteenth, Nakasone seemed on the verge of declaring to himself, *Apres moi, le deluge.*

Anjo smiled faintly at the thought. Like many things that were taught in the tribal colleges, that little "fact" of history might have been quite distorted by the UT historians. It was beyond him that anyone could be expected to know all these years later what had really gone before, to be able to untangle fiction from fact when it came to the past.

Finding himself on the banks of the clear-flowing, icy Rio Grande, near which stood the structure of the fresh pine sweat lodge, Anjo stuck his head into the lodge and spoke to the attendant, a Samurai Guard, one Mitsuo by name, whom Anjo knew well. Anjo then disrobed down to his loincloth and, in the glow of a campfire, walked the path to the river to cleanse himself before preparing the prayer space. He brought up a dipperful of water and splashed himself, shivering.

Heedless of the unpleasant sensation of the cold water against his skin, Anjo plunged the wooden container into the swift current again and again until he'd vanquished the bodily sweat and mental pollutions of the day. Then he walked back up the planking to the fire, where he prepared to heat the large stones for the sweat house. His upper body was chilled by the night, but the heat from the brush that burned alongside him warmed his legs and hips almost to the point of singeing the flesh. He carried the first stones in a metal-lined wooden bucket and brought them into the lodge.

"Mighty Gila, hear my prayer. Lend the chief your knowledge and wisdom. Let peace remain on the land of the Tribes. And save, if you will, the children of the Francspanic." He hoped that the Gila Monster would look favorably upon his request. Science, even medical science, which would be badly needed in the midst of carnage, rarely prospered during war.

Ambassador Hoover, headed toward his quarters in the guest house, accosted Chief Nakasone, who was on his way down to the sweat lodge. Nakasone gestured to his Samurai Guardsman to step aside so that he and Hoover could talk privately.

"I'm hoping I will get the answer that I want tonight," remarked Hoover, a smile on his face belying cautious eyes that peered about, searching for whatever he was used to trying to avoid, most likely prying ears.

Nakasone smiled politely at Hoover in acknowledgement. "I think that the Holy People will side with your ambitions. By tomorrow morning, I should be able to announce that we will regard the giving of American aid to the Francspanics as an act of war." He nodded at Hoover.

Hoover relaxed, satisfied in the answer given him. "Then I'll return immediately to Potomac City and a crisis in my government that will shake President Roosevelt from her almighty perch."

"Good," Nakasone said curtly. "All I ask is neutrality when we march southward. In their weakened state, the Francspanics will snap like twigs, and we will have hold of the Gulf of Mexico and an entré to the Southern Pacific."

"The American forces will take Florida all the way to Louisiana," Hoover reminded him.

Nakasone nodded to Hoover that he concurred. On this provision of their secret treaty, however, he was not content. Having the Francspanics to the east of Old Mexico had provided something of a buffer from the same head-to-head juxtaposition of the UT and U.S. that existed elsewhere along the Continental Cutline. Still, the UT couldn't take hold in more than Louisiana at this time or the Tribes would be separated entirely from the trunk of their resources. Nor could the UT army split itself in two, one half going south, the other east, without a serious diminution of Nakasone's ability to rule.

One step at a time, the chief told himself. He would be the visionary who led the way to a regaining of the Tribal Dominion.

After preparing the space, Anjo waited outside in the cool evening air for the more influential members of the party. As he forced his mind from his own tiredness, his keen eyes wandered to Nakasone's temporary headquarters. Temporary! True to their traditions by half, the UTs called everything they set up temporary, but how much of it was? The hospital complex itself, filled with sophisticated devices as well as mystical machineries, could not be broken down and dragged away solely by a group of energetic ponies.

Some of this encampment, certainly, was meant to hold no future, but other buildings were solid and intended to serve over a considerable time. Circumstances and a pragmatic reaction to them had changed the Tribesmen's nature over the last couple of hundred years or so. For better or for worse, the UT emulated the Europeans in many ways—the worse being that the shaman's people refused to own up to it—except for some of the scholars and a few forward-thinking politicians. Anjo's country had developed under European influence as well as Japanese, while clinging to the old traditions—and not just of one tribe, but of hundreds.

General Thundertalk approached the lodge. "Nakasone not here yet?" he asked.

Anjo Black Wolf was momentarily flustered. Thundertalk, of Arapaho descent, commanded all the armies of this region and Anjo had never before spoken to the man face to face.

"No, General. His party appears to be a little late."

Thundertalk grunted, his hand reflexively grasping at his sword, as if he believed something amiss. Then he relaxed and his arm fell back at his side. He scrutinized

Anjo. "What do you think, Shaman? Should we allow the Americans to aid the Francspanics unmolested?"

"I'm a healer," Anjo answered, perhaps impulsively. "I could not say no."

"If we have no humanitarian considerations, what are we worth as a people?" mused Thundertalk quietly, thus encouraged.

"That is what the Holy People have made clear to me," said Anjo. "Generosity of spirit is always repaid."

Their high-minded discussion was interrupted by a party of warriors approaching on the path, Nakasone at its head. Anjo and the general stood aside as the chief and a single guard swept in. The other soldiers took up posts along the perimeter. With a bow to Anjo a moment later, Thundertalk followed his leader into the lodge. Anjo prayed in his heart for peace and compassion.

As if by prearranged signal, the other chiefs began to arrive and enter a dressing area of the lodge, shedding all clothing but a simple loincloth. Not only was it too hot for more than a brief covering, the nakedness of all would show that none carried weapons, an assurance that there would be no treachery.

In Potomac City, President Roosevelt had just finished conferring with her National Security Council. The advice she had received was that unless the UTs acceded, to aid the Francspanics overtly would mean unrestricted conflict. She would have to concede on the surface if the

UTs denied her country the right to deliver food and medicines to the stricken southern nation.

On the other hand, there might be a means of more secretly supplying the Francspanics by ship around the cape of Florida. Naturally, some danger lurked there, for surely the United Tribes had a corps of long-entrenched spies in Old Mexico. The question was whether Nakasone would act on what he then learned. But Roosevelt had her spies, too, in the heart of UT territory, and they would have reported by now to Ambassador Hoover, who was due to return to Potomac City soon.

Putting her worries behind her for a while, Roosevelt departed the Oval Office and headed toward her separate living quarters. She nodded pleasantly at the young woman who served as one of her chief security officers and who smiled in turn.

Ulah Whitney, of mixed British and Arabic ancestry, watched as the president entered her private apartment. She pitied Mrs. Roosevelt, really–pitied her for the crippled husband who waited behind the door for his wife.

Sometimes it seemed a shame to Ulah that the state of health technologies wasn't equivalent coast to coast. She had heard that UT medical science was far more advanced than American, that the UT could cure almost any illness through the use of special spiritual powers practiced by their shamans. As a Moslem, she believed in nothing so much as the power of God, and how could God's power as practiced by the Apache and Shoshone be essentially different from the godly power of her ancestors? Surely U.S. scientists could learn from the UT. "There is no God but God," she declared. Her heart swelled.

Ulah's piety was momentary, however, and she caught her thoughts wandering to her career. She ought to be more focused on Allah and forget about her worldly affairs, she chided herself, then allowed the bit of self-indulgence. She was pretty pleased with her position and rapid movement up the ranks.

Serving President Roosevelt was in itself a coup, but tomorrow Ulah would take on an assignment giving her even more responsibility. She would head the security contingent that flew into UT territory to bring Mr. Hoover back to the White House to report. This was nothing too taxing, of course—a routine matter, yet one that promised more in terms of her future role.

Ulah was happy that her country was egalitarian when it came to the roles of women in all areas of life. Funny, too, because it wasn't until after she was in her twenties that she'd found out that women in entirely Moslem countries wore a veil to hide their faces. That wasn't the American way at all.

Ulah felt especially thankful for the early American women, such as the first Postmistress General Betsy Ross—later secretary of state under General Washington—and others like the Adams women, Sarah Adams and Joan Quincy Adams, both heroes of the Revolution and later presidents. But more than that, the historians suggested, the pressure of a small community locked into the eastern coast of a tremendous continent and surrounded by enemies had forced the Americans to use all their resources at hand–including the talent and potential of their female citizens.

The sense of that was so evident that Ulah couldn't envision it any other way.

For her, she believed, money and power would come– God willing. And at some time in the future, she'd be able to make a pilgrimage to Mecca. Hajji Ulah, wouldn't that be something.

Flying in the Grumman six-seater Wildcat the next day, Ulah was a little disconcerted. No, it wasn't being in the fighter plane that made her nervous. The worry that she felt came as a result of the White House having received no message from Ambassador Hoover. The secretary for war, Henry Stimson, sent down word that Ulah was to lead her detail into UT territory and fetch Hoover home, regardless.

Oh, Stimson didn't call on Ulah by name, by any means. He had no idea who was in charge of this mission. And as for "detail," because this was a routine, if unusual, rendezvous with a diplomat on an errand of peace, the force that Ulah led consisted of a second Secret Service officer only, a man, along with the Air Force pilot at the stick.

Ulah was uneasy, but she would have been anyway,

even if Hoover had made that shortwave call. She simply didn't want to screw up this mission. Spontaneously and silently, she repeated to herself, "There is no God but God! And Mohammed is His prophet" to quiet her jitters.

Finally, after a droning hour frittered away by Ulah and her single subordinate, the warplane soared over a broad, brown body of water stretching forever north and south. Somewhat jerkily, then with a bounce, the aircraft touched down on the UT runway. Ulah yanked at the bottom of her red-tan uniform jacket, trying to remove the wrinkles, and once the Wildcat had cruised to the end of the runway with barely a foot of leeway ahead, she jumped from her seat and brushed off her pants.

"Christ," shouted the pilot as the big bird quieted. "That was damn close."

Ulah frowned at the profanity. She really ought not to let that sort of thing upset her, though. She glanced furtively at the other Secret Service officer, Peterson.

"The UTs have developed planes that don't require runways, but can take off and come down with only a landing pad," she commented.

"Right," said the pilot. "Their terrain is so wild..."

Ulah didn't know what that had to do with it.

The pilot reached over and pulled open the door latch, then let down the stairs. Ulah and Peterson descended onto the tarmac.

Three men ran toward them like inmates just let out of an insane asylum. They couldn't be a greeting committee, could they? Ulah felt for her sidearm, but as per the directive, she hadn't been allowed to wear it here.

The theory was that if the UT were going to be hostile, you were a goner, anyway, and if they weren't, wearing a revolver would be an insult to them.

"Quick," shouted one of the maniac figures as he reached the Secret Service officers. "We have to get out of here." When Ulah didn't budge, he went around her and ascended the stairs rapidly, followed by the other strange UTs, who pushed both her and Peterson aside. Ulah was so completely stunned that it didn't even occur to her to grapple with them. Peterson looked to his superior for direction. She stomped back up the steps and Peterson followed.

"You men are violating the diplomatic space of an official American aircraft," Ulah declared, glaring at them. Two were looking around the plane, while the first, who had urged their departure, was trying to get the pilot to take off.

"If you're here to pick up Hoover, he's dead," said one, sinking into a seat. He gave her a glance that was overly familiar for an infidel who had just invaded another country's military transport. She oughtn't to call him an infidel, though. It was wrong. Slowly, it dawned on her what he had just said–Hoover was dead.

Hoover, dead! She had failed in her duty in every way imaginable.

"I have no reason to believe you," she answered calmly. Now she had a moment to take the three of them in. Two were Native and one was a Samurai. Naked to the waist, with two swords sheathed at his side, his torso was completely covered with tattoos of writhing snakes, some coiled around cherry blossoms. Ulah blinked. How barbaric!

"I suggest that we simply take off and quarrel over the fine points later on," said the seated Indian with some authority. He called in UTlingo to the man who was arguing with the pilot, and his companion meekly took the seat behind him. The Samurai settled himself as well.

"Sorry," Ulah snapped. "But we're going nowhere until I've retrieved Ambassador Hoover."

The second Indian sat up, staring out the window, and Ulah's eyes followed his. A phalanx of Samurai with their swords drawn rushed toward the runway. Perhaps now was not the moment for debate.

"Take off, Flyboy," she ordered abruptly. "Head for the closest American airbase. I think there's one in Little Rock."

The pilot didn't move his hand to the throttle. "I can't just take off again," he protested, nervously. "The plane might need servicing and I could use some fuel. Not to mention that I'm backward on the runway."

"So wheel around and take off," she instructed, watching the Samurai horde in growing alarm.

"Christ," swore the pilot again, starting the engine.

Ulah winced as if the curse had been a gunshot. Her eyes met those of the man who had been arguing with the pilot. She blushed. Except for the long black hair, which didn't strike her as quite manly, she found his mahogany skin and chiseled features awfully handsome. He was young, too, in his late twenties as she was. Or maybe that wasn't young for the UT.

"Allow us to introduce ourselves," said the arrogant leader of the three, forcing Ulah to turn away from the attractive face she was studying.

"I'm General Warashi Thundertalk. This is my lieutenant, Kenzo Hitachi, and my young friend, the shaman..." Thundertalk searched for the young man's name.

"Anjo Black Wolf," Anjo replied helpfully. His own attention remained on Ulah's face and figure.

The plane lurched, and all of those on it looked out at the runway. The pilot had managed to wheel the great beast around, racing toward liftoff. Ulah's heart jolted as the metal dragon leaped into the air. Unconsciously, she issued forth a prayer to Allah.

What she heard then was not the prayer that came out of her own mouth, but rather a twin supplication to the Four Winds that Anjo cried. The meaning of the two petitions seemed not at all dissimilar.

Adger Hoover was not, in fact, dead; the corpse was Chief Nakasone. Hoover, now a prisoner of Nakasone's assassin, was being dragged along with him further and further into the woods surrounding the UT stronghold.

"You can't do this to me," Hoover puffed, out of shape as diplomats often are, and out of breath. "I'm an American emissary. An ambassador."

"Some emissary," sneered the killer, prodding Hoover in the back to make him move. "Plotting against your own duly elected government."

Nakasone's murderer, Claude Monet, was the perfect representation of a UT Tribesman—an Ute, in fact, which his grandmere had been. Then Grandmere had met a handsome Francspanic, and the rest had followed quite naturally. Now, some years down the line, her descendent was able to play spy with a Ute accent instead of a Francspanic one.

Claude was resourceful and hadn't hesitated to slit Nakasone's throat during Nakasone's private, early-morning meeting with Hoover, who was packing his bag at the guest house for his departure. Claude, called Hunting Fortune at the time, brought the men the makings for two or more cups of green tea, set the tray down politely, and promptly turned on Nakasone, slaughtering him. Nakasone's Samurai sentry was outside the room. Claude quickly gagged and tied Hoover, went into the hall and whispered to the guard that Nakasone wanted him to fetch General Thundertalk and the closest shaman. When the guard obediently trotted off, Claude put the tip of his knife to Hoover's back, urging him on.

Claude could have killed J. Adger Hoover, perhaps, but he didn't dare. On the contrary—Claude's most ardent wish was to return Hoover unharmed to President Roosevelt. The spy would hardly dream of handling it any other way. Not only did Hoover deserve a trial for treason, but if Claude had simply killed the diplomat out of hand, the Americans might not help his desperately starving people.

And so the spy now struggled along with the recalcitrant ambassador, whom he had reluctantly untied and ungagged. Claude fervently hoped that Hoover wasn't going to have a heart attack ascending the hills to where a helicopter would pick the two of them up. Well, going to pick *him* up, and, coincidentally, Hoover. But the status of Hoover's health was one of the risks of the game. Claude was certainly not going to leave the man to make up some story against the Francspanics for the UT, who might decide to declare war on the Mexican Empire. That would be *just* what Claude's country needed now.

"Who are you?" demanded Hoover with what little breath he could still muster.

"I'm a tribal dissident," the infiltrator lied. If he was killed and Hoover should get away, it was best that Hoover never know the truth. Naturally, Claude wanted to shake Hoover and snarl, "I'm a Francspanic spy and you are a filthy dog who would let the women and children of my people starve."

A quick glance down the slope showed no obvious pursuers. Claude's luck was turning out to be magnificent.

They sat in an airplane hanger at the Little Rock airbase. Ulah had armed herself and was keeping an eye on the three foreigners as she waited for new orders from her bureau boss. Rumor over the radio waves was that both Hoover and the UT chief Nakasone had been assassinated. She tried to rationalize away her part of what had happened to her mission, but she knew her career was virtually done after today. She might as well pack up and go home to Bayonne, New Jersey. She pictured herself as a cop walking the local beat. That was about the sum of what lay ahead for her.

Anjo had been looking at Ulah again, but from time to time, he also looked at the coffee machine in the corner of the shed where they stood. Not having American money was undoubtedly the first of many barriers that would face him, wherever he was headed. One minute he had been secure in his world, a man of some stature and with a future. No more than two hours later, he was a stranger in a strange land, as well as a wanted criminal in his own country. What a drama! Strong proof that only the Great Spirit rules the life of a man.

"Sit down," the girl said to them, indicating some chairs.

"I'm going to the washroom," said General Thundertalk with a slight smile. "Anyone else? Oh yes, miss, in the meantime, my lieutenant needs a shirt, you know. He's a bit hot-blooded, but not impervious."

Ulah frowned and called to the soldier at the perimeter. It hadn't been her intention to babysit three barbarians. No, she mustn't think of them in that way, she really must not. As a sworn officer of the law—and as a Moslem—she must have respect for all those over whom she had authority.

Yet the society in which she had grown up regarded the United Tribesman with some disdain, even though most had never met someone from the other country at all. History had shown that the Indians were savages. They were cruel and untrustworthy and, frankly, no one knew if they had changed in the last two hundred or so years.

"Hoover, dead?" Secretary of War Stimson screamed into the telephone. "I don't believe it. Then he was killed by the UT. There has to be an explanation and it has to be delivered fast. No, I don't want to go to war over it, but we have to know what happened. For God's sake, she *what*? Left without seeing the body? She what? General Thundertalk? I really don't think I know... Well, let the agent and her pilot stay there until we hear from Nakasone. We demand an apology...make threatening gestures, but nothing that can be construed as serious."

Stimson listened, barked once more into the receiver, and hung up the phone. War? Good God. Could it really come to that? America hadn't been involved in a war for nearly a hundred years. He quickly reviewed the country's state of preparedness for actual conflict. Not very. The point had been to remain out of Europe's filthy squabbles and to maintain a state of peace at home—surrounded as they were on all three borders, although not by out-and-out foes. A policy of accommodation had been in place since...since the founding of the nation, really. But if Hoover had been murdered on a mission to the UT, this would be considered a serious matter, indeed.

The Americans could demand reparations, but what if those weren't forthcoming? This was a mess and a half, wasn't it? Time to call the president. Let any repercussions fall on her head, not his.

"What do you think, dear?" Eleanor asked her husband at their luncheon table. She tried to make it back into their quarters for lunch most days. "Would you like to put the lap rug on and go out for a while? It seems nice enough today. Almost mild."

"It's such an effort," Franklin replied. "And the photographers always seem posted around the back lawn waiting to snap my picture." He stroked the little black cocker spaniel seated across his crippled legs.

"Ah, yes." Eleanor nodded. "We live too public a life. But you can't stay inside all the time, now can you?"

"So long as it's turning nice, maybe I'll fly up to Hyde Park for a few weeks."

"Whatever you say, dear," answered Eleanor, finishing her consommé and cutting into her baked halibut. On the coast as their country was, and with limited space, seafood was the most prevalent protein. Cattle country was across the border and the price of imported beef and mutton was often high—an artificially inflated value.

Her mind drifted off to the topic of the starving

Mexicans. A long drought followed by floods had meant little food for that country's entire population, with only some produce available from the San Fernando Valley. Of course, the decimation of Francspanic livestock had meant no meat for the Americans, either, except for bison brought across the range from Wyoming territory by a few enterprising Cheyenne ranchers. But the UT weren't very focused on external trade, and most of what little trade they did, they engaged in with Japan's Outer East Tokyo "Hawaiian" Islands.

Franklin was looking at her, waiting for a response, Eleanor suddenly realized with a guilty start. She gave him a kind smile. Perhaps the trip would be for the best. After all, if he was to go up to Hyde Park for a while, that would leave her some time to see her long-time lover, a major in the Air Force. She wasn't sure what Franklin hoped for her to say and was grateful when the telephone rang, sparing her the necessity of acknowledgment.

"Hello," she said sweetly into the phone. "Oh, Harry, is Adger back yet?" She listened for a moment and then paled. "What? Damn. I'll call a meeting of the cabinet, but let's not be overhasty. Surely we have a considerable number of options. Nakasone can't be any more eager for a falling out than we are. Any word from our underground agents there?"

Hanging up the phone, Eleanor pushed herself away from the table. "They say Hoover is dead," she announced crisply to Franklin. "I'll make arrangements for your flight to Hyde Park this afternoon." Fowler sprang off his master's lap and trotted after Eleanor, who strode to the door. "Stay with daddy," Eleanor instructed the dog. "Franklin, call him." She was already halfway to the Oval Office.

Finally seated in what the girl had referred to as "lawn" chairs—a flimsy type of construction—the three UT men talked quietly among themselves. The woman sat apart, as was proper, but no doubt she could speak UTlingo, so they kept their voices down. Hitachi reflexively fingered the material of the stiff military shirt he now wore. Examining it, Anjo believed that it was as unnatural as the webbing of the chair he sat upon. All their own synthetics were used only as medical equipment or for other specialized purposes, not for common clothes. How far the UT science was from the American. Should he be envious? No, he felt proud.

"We're in a bind of the worst sort here," said Thundertalk, all serious general, at last. "Obviously these events were a matter of a long-planned coup, but I've turned it over and over in my head and I can't see who benefits. Someone might kill Nakasone and Hoover, then take over, yes. Our history is filled with such unpleasant incidents. But if anyone were to have been in a position to execute such a strategy, it would have been me, and I can assure you, I did no such thing. I wouldn't have run with the two of you if I had. I'd be at headquarters purging my enemies."

So, Thundertalk and Hitachi hadn't murdered Nakasone, as Anjo had half suspected.

"Then whose adversaries are *we*, that they had wanted

to get rid of *us*?" asked Hitachi.

Anjo looked expectantly at each man in turn, for this higher type of politics was out of his realm entirely.

Thundertalk's face was one of blank contemplation, then his expression shifted into a dark region where his companions might not follow. "My children at home..." he began, despairingly, but couldn't quite continue.

Whoever had killed Nakasone in order to promote himself into the chief's position was certain to wipe out Thundertalk's whole family. For once in his life, Anjo was glad that he hadn't yet met his mate.

Unconsciously, he turned to observe the American female. She was an odd type, really, wearing a man's outfit complete with gunbelt, but made up like a geisha. And she wasn't blonde, the way he expected the American women to be. Her complexion was dark, while her skin was as smooth as the back of a doe, her features refined, her dark eyes bright. For a moment he imagined that he looked at a maiden of his own tribe. He blinked, and saw her for who she was once again. She was on the telephone, speaking softly herself and glancing over to see if she was being heard and understood.

She hung up and stared at the three men hard. "Let's take it from the top," she demanded in a voice as devoid of warmth as a winter's night on Devil's Lake. "Tell me what happened."

What had happened, Anjo could only recall from

his own point of view. He had been singing the morning songs in his own quarters, puzzling over the growing of Manchild's leg, which, when he had last checked before going to bed, was three inches longer than a mere couple of hours before. Why so fast? Was it healthy? He hoped that no out-of-control growth had been spurred. If that were the case, he wouldn't have a reference point for it, and few resources to call on, as contact with Honolulu was never certain.

Nakasone's Samurai bodyguard had run in suddenly without knocking. Anjo only recognized the man because he had been there in the sweat lodge the previous night and Anjo had studied his tattoo at length, choosing it as a least-distracting frame of reference for the surface of his mind. The design itself was a hypnotic one, beautiful: Hiroshige's wild sea, with Mount Fuji in the background. Anjo admired the Japanese for their artistry, although, as a healer, he deplored the tattooing process, which sickened the recipient. Anjo believed that ultimately it lowered the person's future resistance to serious infection and shortened his life.

"Something wrong?" he asked at once.

"No, just that the chief wants you to come. I'm to fetch General Thundertalk, too. The chief is in the American ambassador's quarters. Please go there now."

The man turned to leave and Anjo saw with a jolt the landscape that was depicted perfectly across his back: Hiroshige as well, the Kannon Temple perched atop a nightmarishly high embankment. The splendid sight practically took Anjo's breath away.

Called by the chief, there was no question but that

Anjo would go, yet first he had to finish his prayers and ablutions. He was a shaman who obeyed only the Holy People, not a military man to be ordered about.

Admittedly, Anjo concluded his dressing with some haste, but Thundertalk was already in Hoover's room when he arrived, and the general pulled the curtain tight again after Anjo stepped in. Their chief lay lifeless on the floor. Hitachi was there as well, his hand on the hilt of his sword, waiting for Anjo's reaction and seemingly the possibility that he might have to cut the shaman down.

Anjo inhaled. Thundertalk had killed Nakasone and there was a great deal of blood over the floor and walls, as well as a carmine pool at their three pairs of feet. Anjo could hardly blame them for having done away with their fearsome leader; Nakasone would have won no popularity awards. If anyone cared for him or his policies, Anjo had not yet met that man. He nodded his head to himself almost imperceptibly. He hadn't sought this out, but his life, more than others (who might not believe), was led entirely by the whim of the Great Spirit. He would go as he was shown.

He didn't have long to wait for an indication. Thundertalk signaled without speech that they had better leave immediately. They stepped out the door and Hitachi killed Nakasone's guard with a single stroke. What a shame! God's creation, man, laid waste so carelessly, and man's great creation on the canvas of another man's skin destroyed. The dreadful sound of the blade through human bone echoed in Anjo's head and its memory made him, inside the airplane hangar, shiver.

They had run.

The story that Thundertalk told was quite similar to what Anjo had just related. Early that morning as he had walked through the camp checking the state of his on-duty warriors, he had been called to attend the chief in the guest's quarters. Hitachi had joined him.

The evening before in the sweat lodge, Nakasone's vision had been clear. The Francspanics were not to be aided by the Americans; that was the law, and a startling revelation at that. Thundertalk, although not quite easy with that pronouncement, expected Nakasone to ask him now to verify to Hoover their current state of preparedness for war.

Thundertalk would convey the determination of the United Tribesmen to oppose American mercy to the Mexican nation, and then he would withdraw for home, ostensibly to bid his wife and children goodbye prior to preparation for a battle. In reality, he intended to overthrow Nakasone. So it was a great surprise to him when he entered Hoover's lodgings to find the chief already dead, and the foreigner gone. Hoover had killed Nakasone in a rage over his decision, Thundertalk concluded then. Now, he wasn't quite so sure.

"Why did you tell me Hoover was dead?" demanded the American woman, Ulah—almost an Indian-sounding name, Anjo thought.

"The Samurai Guards were following after us. None

of us could have survived their onslaught. Believe me. In the heat of the fight, they wouldn't have spared any of us, not even a female," Thundertalk answered.

Ulah frowned as if she found the concept of sparing a woman completely absurd. "You lied," she muttered.

She glared at the three of them and Anjo almost wished to divorce himself from the soldiers and explain his own position to her. But he kept silent, unwilling to deny his fellow UT.

"I could have rescued Hoover," she added sternly, as if they might care. "According to my superiors, he's been captured by a group of insurgent Tribesmen from Las Cruces. They're demanding a large ransom or Hoover will be killed."

Claude hadn't intended to lose Hoover, but lose him he had. Damn the man for being so unfit. If they had been making better time on the trail, they wouldn't have missed the rendezvous. And Hoover wouldn't have been taken by a bunch of Sagebrush Navajo.

He had tried to prod the man into ducking away before their convergence with the Indians on their lean, hard-driven ponies, but Hoover wouldn't cooperate. Claude had the impression that Hoover wanted to be taken, that he thought the renegades were UT-supporters. Hell, the Americans seemed to think the UT regions were entirely united. Then again, that was what the UT wanted them to think.

Punching in some numbers on a global tracking system that would enable a second rescue team to find him at the fallback hour, Claude mused over the changing situation. He shrugged. Maybe it wasn't so bad this way. If he didn't have Hoover, the Francspanics didn't have to go to the trouble of returning him. The explanation would have been a tricky one. Then Hoover, if he survived, wouldn't actually know who Claude was or his motives in killing Nakasone. And if the man died…well, no harm, no foul, so long as he hadn't died in Francspanic hands.

Not such a bad day's work, after all. Claude had eliminated Nakasone and had gotten away with it. And, one way or the other, he had removed Hoover from the scene.

Aside from the usual trials and tribulations of a government of the people, by the influence-peddling politicos, and for their special-interest constituents, the American government had not gone into any crisis of this magnitude since the Civil War. Hoover's kidnapping and the subsequent ransom demands had Potomac City all atwitter. The town was filled with politicians from all the parties, and they liked to do nothing so much as gossip and find fault with those who opposed them. The taking of Hoover made everyone in P.C. both nervous and rather satisfied with life. At last, something to take up arms about—not literally, Allah forbid—but it was a damn good reason to fret amiably at all the fashionable bars along the river locks.

Having gotten Franklin off in Air Force One, Eleanor had requested that her driver take her to the Pentagon's officer quarters, where she could meet with a senior officer of the armed forces, one Major Jim Doolittle.

"I'm worried about Adger," Eleanor said. "To tell you the truth, I thought I had found the perfect assignment for him—out of P.C. and out of my hair—but now he's gotten himself in the worst possible mess, one that might drag us all down with him. Oh, I shouldn't blame Adger in all fairness, I suppose, but I can't imagine it happening to any other ambassador, really, can you?" She paused and laughed in genuine amusement. "Oh, I'm terrible. What are your thoughts on the matter, Jim?"

She didn't wait for the major to answer her. "We can't hand anything over to some backwater faction and lose face. You know what our forefathers used to say, `Millions for defense, not one cent for tribute.'" She laughed again and looked in the mirror while brushing her long hair.

"I think that a few of us should form a raiding party," commented Doolittle when he could get a word in edgewise. "We'll fly in and retrieve Hoover, settle the score with the infidel."

"That's sweet," said Eleanor absentmindedly. "Maybe I can send in my Secret Service aide. Ulah Whitney. She's one of the Rhode Island Whitneys, you know—a bright girl."

"Damn it, Eleanor, you never take me seriously," complained Doolittle. "You don't have any respect for me, do you?"

President Roosevelt turned wide-eyed away from the

mirror. "Of course I do, honey. You're the best damn flyboy I know." She approached the bed where Doolittle still sat semi-dressed, and leaned over to kiss the major one—well, maybe more than one—more time.

Anjo gave Ulah a stiff smile. "Those are my people," he announced in a voice louder than he had anticipated. "My tribe and my clan."

Now the girl's glare shined solely on him and he felt unusually uncomfortable. It was warm out here in the hanger, it seemed. Anjo grabbed at the cold drink the American flyers had finally passed around and swallowed deeply right from the bottle. (How the devil did they make peculiar materials like these?)

"You bastard," she growled, then flushed. "You're in on it!"

Anjo placed the bottle down on the tray that had ferried the drinks here and gave her a look of strenuous objection. "I'm a loyal member of the Union," he declared. "I can't be held responsible for the actions of the Dog Soldiers." He wiped his mouth with the back of his hand. Whatever the technological wonders behind the bottle, its contents tasted exactly like poison. But the girl—Agent Ulah Whitney, she had called herself to one of the military officers—had gulped her refreshment down as if it were pleasing to her. Maybe the Americans had no pure water, then. Whatever the liquid was, it had a sharp, biting...well, fizz. The damn stuff stung his throat and tongue.

General Thundertalk laughed heartily. "A loyal member of the Union?" he commented. "What Union is that? The Union under Chief Nakasone? Or the Union under—who will it be, Nakasone's brainless son Running Shadow?"

Anjo was taken aback. The fact had been put before him starkly. Things had changed. But naturally he would support the Union, regardless. For the Tribes, what were the options? His next words were probably ill-considered. Certainly they were impulsive. "I'll help you get back Ambassador Hoover. I can reason with the so-called Sagebrush Navajo. I'm a shaman and they'll listen to me."

Ulah appeared more than a little suspicious. "I'd have my hands full looking after you, even if my superiors were to permit such a thing," she argued.

"Hitachi and I will come with you two," interrupted Thundertalk. "We'll watch out for the shaman, if you like. It's my duty to return to the UT and to wrest control from whoever the traitors are. It's my place to lead the United Tribes with Nakasone gone. But first we'll restore Ambassador Hoover to you."

"I take it you didn't understand my original point," replied Ulah sternly. "I'm not going on a mission dragging prisoners with me."

"There's an idea in there somewhere." Ulah's superior, Dinah Morrow, breezed in, no doubt directly off a flight from P.C.

Startled, Ulah's words froze in her throat. Morrow hadn't bothered to inform her that she would be arriving today in Little Rock. Ulah fell back into her chair, mulishly, without even kissing Dinah hello.

"Well, it wasn't my idea," said Dinah in good-natured protest, after registering her subordinate's reaction. "The president wanted me to come. Her plan is to send a group of raiders in to get Hoover out. What would you call it, an extraction team?"

"*Teishin hik ch taie,*" remarked Hitachi, helpfully.

"I'm sorry," said Dinah. "I don't understand. Haven't they given you people lunch?" She glanced around as if seeking a waiter, then threw up her hands. "Well, at least you have drinks. I'm sure they'll feed you, if a tiny bit late." She checked the time on her watch. "I deplore changing time zones," she told no one in particular.

Ulah rose to her feet once again. "I'll go into UT territory to get Hoover, ma'am," she said. "It's my duty to get him out of there. I know I messed up. But I'm going alone. Unless Bob wants to come with me."

"Peterson's already halfway back to P.C.," Morrow informed her. "On the plane I flew in on. You and I are both going to rescue Hoover. And I've been instructed to return the prisoners to their own authorities." She pointed at the men. "We won't want any trouble over them!"

She checked the time again. "We'll go in after dark. Since there are no landing fields that we can discern, we'll have to parachute in. As to how we'll get out, well, that will eventually be decided." Striding over to where Ulah now stood, Dinah kissed the girl firmly on the cheek, while Ulah grabbed her supervisor's arms and responded in kind.

Finding Nakasone's sentinel lying in a pool of his own blood, and then Nakasone in a somewhat similar posture with his throat cut sent the Samurai Guards into a whirlwind of activity. An alert blared over the loudspeaker system. Swordsmen sprinted in all directions and a few Tribesmen who were awake and starting their day's activities pointed them every which way, remarking excitedly that they had personally seen some runners escaping.

Coincidentally, out of all these eager witnesses, one had actually spotted General Thundertalk and his two fellows headed for the airstrip. Seven of the warrior elite, swords drawn, bolted after the alleged assassins. Reaching the airfield, the Samurai raced toward the single American transport that rested on the runway. Nearly at their destination, the pursuers heard the engines rev and were forced to back out of the way as the heavy airship taxied in a full circle before speeding down the tarmac and lifting off. One or two of the soldiers shouted in frustration after the big bird before returning dispirited to their base of operations.

Frenzied gossip and exhausting confusion followed, until the head of the Samurai Guard, Angel Whiskers, arrived and barked at his men to shut their chatter and report in. Nakasone's alleged killers—General Thundertalk, Lieutenant Kenzo Hitachi, and Anjo Black Wolf, who had conspired with J. Adger Hoover on behalf of the Americans—had escaped.

Nakasone's son and heir apparent, Running Shadow, when he arrived presently—out of breath because he usually didn't walk, preferring to be carried here and there in a sedan chair by his servants—demonstrated the great esteem in which he had held his suddenly departed parent by having an hysterical fit. This, for Running Shadow, was not an unusual event. After petulantly demanding that the guards search the Indian Continent from end to end until they found his father's killers, he clarified his position by proclaiming himself chief and ordering Angel Whiskers to arrange for his father's funeral.

"I want to see General Thundertalk roasted alive," Running Shadow pronounced languidly at the end of this oration; his extreme emotionalism was spent for the time being and he appeared to be headed for a snack and a nap. "Someone send off an immediate radio message to the Americans, letting them know of my demands. Angel Whiskers! I order it." Running Shadow swept out and searched around for his bearers, swearing when he saw they hadn't predicted his whereabouts in order to fetch him back to his quarters.

Watching the new chief go, SG Captain Angel Whiskers felt seriously aggrieved. He was hardly the one to make funeral arrangements. Nor was he the person who ought to be insisting that the Americans return the assassins for a trial. Unless he were to make the request in his own name, of course. Dare he? If that were to happen, now would have to be the moment. A nervous excitement took hold of him. He struggled between the idea of seizing power and the more comfortable notion of accepting Running Shadow as his leader and watching someone else seize the initiative, thereafter, to take the reins. Running Shadow would simply never hold the nation. The man had no focus. He was lazy and could garner no allies. But did Angel Whiskers have the nerve?

He turned to his men and saw them staring at him, awaiting instruction. They were uneasy, as if they had just seen a foul vision of the future. Before speaking, Angel Whiskers wrinkled his face with the effort of decision. "Running Shadow is not a fit leader," he declared. "I, Angel Whiskers, a descendent of the great Chief Black Elk, am the new UT chief." The die was cast, as one of the old Romans he had read about in the American books had said. The die—whatever that was—was cast and then Julius Caesar had crossed the...Delaware?

Finally back in Mexico City, Claude reported at once to the head of the Intelligence Agency. He decided to omit all references to Ambassador Hoover, as losing the man would not seem overly professional. He simply described his slitting Nakasone's throat when Hoover was away in the outhouse. That made a lot of sense to him and he felt his recitation went over well. Finally, he was given a chit that entitled him to buy an extra loaf of bread for the week. That was just his bonus, though. His regular pay included stamps for various commodities. Working for the government—especially in a quasi-military capacity—meant that he and his family would survive.

The problem was that when he entered the bakery and handed over his coupon, the woman shook her head in resigned regret. "No bread no more," she told him in her tangled Francspanic—she spoke fluently only her native Indian tongue. "They give us no flour."

"*Ay, conyo*," he swore, walking out of the shop. "*Merde!*"

It occurred to him that he could fly back to UT territory in a "borrowed" rotary. He had, after all, begun his military career as a pilot, and could manage to catch on to the newer refinements of the hovercraft.

Say he returned to the spot where the ambassador had been taken, recaptured the man—who, by now, would be eager to end his stay with the Sagebrush Navajo— and flew Hoover on to America. Surely Claude would be rewarded quite significantly. It even occurred to him that he, Carlitta, and their son, Manuel, could take refuge in America then. He might be useful doing intelligence for the Americans within Mexico itself. As much as he despised the UT under Nakasone, he had no such qualms about the Roosevelt Administration.

Claude was a man of action. He was hardly one to wait and see if he would starve to death.

Eleanor Roosevelt was swearing like a Potomac trucker. She had just read a copy of the incoming UT radiowave that carried Angel Whiskers's accusation and demands. "Those idiot Tribesmen," she said at last, somewhat more calmly. She looked to her secretary of state, Cornell Hull, who was now seated across the table reading the stock market listings in *The Washington Post.*

Sensing the president's focus on him, Hull glanced over. "Whiskey futures are up," he noted, no doubt in an effort to sidetrack the conversation.

"Whiskey futures are always up." She shook her head as if too overwhelmed by her frustration with him to continue, then went on. "I'll contact Stimson. We'll have to mass some troops on the border, if only for show. The UT are being the UT, I guess. Nakasone's dead—murdered—maybe I should say assassinated, since he was the head of state..." She looked as if she were about to spit. "They think we had something to do with it because Hoover disappeared at the same time. Obviously, it was the Sagebrush Navajo who killed Nakasone. They're the ones who have Hoover, after all."

Hull turned the pages of his newspaper, but kept his focus on the president. "I wonder what's playing this weekend at Ford's Theater?" he said. "I think they have a group of Restoration comedies in repertory. Want to go?"

"Cornell, really!" Eleanor was truly exasperated. "We're in the middle of a major international incident. Besides which, you know I don't care for those tedious old plays."

"I wonder if we really should try to get Hoover back," Hull went on as if he hadn't heard a word the president had said. "He's really...irritating. I'd like to go through his office while he's away—trying to find some 'clues' to the kidnapping, we could say. We don't have to release the demands made by the Navajo. We could say that the UT are holding him hostage...and I can't think of anything after that bit, can you? Maybe it's time we had a little border skirmish..."

"Cornell, sometimes you're an idiot," snapped Eleanor. "There's no sense in getting involved in any actual fighting with the Tribesmen. Not until we're a little closer to the election, anyway."

Ulah couldn't eat her meal without first bowing to Mecca and saying a prayer on the bit of carpet she carried with her. But many cultures give thanks before they eat the food offered to them by the grace of the Divine, and the Navajo were no exception, it seemed. Before tucking in to the American Air Force rations, Anjo chanted an invocation.

Ulah found Anjo's supplications quite distracting, although she tried to concentrate on her own special pleas to Allah. The little noises that the Indian made riled this good Moslem and she sped through her prayers, stood, then walked over to the mess table where the shaman still praised Corn Boy for giving them food.

She was sorely tempted to ask the man to cease and desist. Other people, notably those who found their solace in Islam, were able to thank God without stirring up such a fuss. Yet all the while she was thinking this, she held her tongue. She was well aware how ridiculous she was being. If what he was doing was praying to his God, then it was to the God *she* perceived as well that he delivered his prayers. For her God stood as the only One, indivisible; there was none other. It wasn't the man's singing that bothered her, anyway—it was simply that her nerves were stretched thin.

Ulah took her prayer beads from her pocket and held them on her lap with her left hand as she ate with her right. She wasn't right-handed, but her cultural bias was to eat with the right hand—a peculiarity remaining from ages ago, when a person's hands could not be washed so assiduously as in the contemporary age. She prayed as she chewed and prepared to mentally block out the dinner chatter, but there was none. The UT, a male-dominated society, wasn't oriented much to conversation, and certainly not at meal times—unless a leader chose to pontificate, or strategy for one endeavor or another had to be discussed.

The Japanese barbarian kept eyeing her and Dinah strangely throughout their meal, until he finally blurted out at the end in his fractured English, "You American women are unbelievable. Where are your husbands? Can't they keep you in check?"

Stimson came to Eleanor personally with a copy of the message he had sent Angel Whiskers, the man who had declared himself the new head of the UT. Stimson had used as much lawyerly language as possible, hoping that this new chief would take long enough to decode it to give the Americans a chance to think through the situation.

Eleanor was in her living quarters, brushing her hair and preparing for bed. She read the sheet that Harry Stimson handed her and gave it back without comment. "It's time for another one of my Fireside Chats," she said. "I'll give one tomorrow."

Stimson mumbled a miserly concurrence with her idea. He was irked that she hadn't given a tad bit of praise for his own efforts on behalf of the country, their party, and the two of them (with an eye to the upcoming elections, of course).

"I'll reassure the citizens after stressing the great threat to our nation," Eleanor said. "I'll explain that we don't want to become embroiled in the kind of fiasco that the Europeans have gotten themselves involved in again."

Stimson made the sign of the cross over his chest, as if trying to ward off a vast conflict of that nature. "How are things on that front? I haven't read the papers today."

"It's terrible, really," said Eleanor. "We must pray for them."

"That's all we can do," agreed Stimson absentmindedly. "Although we might send a comforting telegram to Winston regarding the recent bombings of London."

"It's an outrage," Eleanor spat fiercely. "But that's the Spanish for you, I guess. Remember, these are the same people who forced your ancestors, the Holy Roman Catholics, from their own country during the Inquisition. I can't say I'm exactly surprised."

"True. The Spanish need to be taken down a peg or three. I hope the Germans find the wherewithal to do it.

But on to our own situation. What do you think?"

What Eleanor Roosevelt, the duly elected 22nd American president, thought was not really what concerned Chief Angel Whiskers, self-declared head of the UT, at the moment. Angel Whiskers had a vastly different agenda on his mind. He had to press ahead with the coup that he had begun by declaring himself to his men and then, in the radiowave, to the Americans. He would somehow have to let Running Shadow know that after about two minutes of power, he had been deposed. And he would probably have to take Running Shadow's head.

He had committed himself in one way, but in another, was hesitant to follow up with the final, irrevocable step. So instead, he thought up a maneuver for dealing with the current problem. "You can get what you want more easily by stealth than you can by grabbing for it," an uncle of his used to tell Angel Whiskers when he was a child. He had always tried to live by that rule and found that generally it worked well for him.

The beginnings of an idea formed, and he strode directly to Running Shadow's teepee. It always amazed him how these Comanche lived. They were not nearly so civilized as his people, the Hopi.

Angel Whiskers called in a greeting to Running Shadow and entered the luxurious structure with a servile posture. Running Shadow lay on a soft pallet in the middle of the floor–sleeping–while his attendants were occupied with various quiet tasks. Angel Whiskers contemplated the unconscious form and wondered if Running Shadow could be roused to the action he contemplated for the young man. Ah well.

"Great Chief," he called in a loud voice to the comatose figure. "Rise up to your greater glory. You must take care immediately."

Running Shadow opened one sleepy eye. "Why are you bellowing? First I am awakened early with news of my father's death, now this?"

"Oh Great Chief Running Shadow, the Americans have responded to our message. They say that they had no part in the murder of Chief Nakasone. They accuse the Dog Soldiers in Navajo country of taking Ambassador Hoover hostage. The Dog Soldiers are the true assassins of your father, I fear. A war party can be led out to eliminate them, at your insistence."

"Without a doubt, I insist." Thus inspired, Running Shadow grabbed at a bowl of dried dates set conveniently close to his mattress. He popped one into his mouth and chewed.

"I will lead them for you," Angel Whiskers said. "But I fear that this will put me too much in the public eye." He sighed after a moment's pause. "I will gain too large a stature that rightly should be yours. Most certainly, you are a great warrior, as everybody knows. Surely now would be the time to display your martial spirit yet again and to set right a wrong grievously done your father. I don't mind going, though. It's such an easy victory, a brief afternoon's work and then home for supper. What a shame if the honor should be mine, however. And I wonder what the menu for a celebration feast might be."

Running Shadow dragged himself to his feet and picked up a mirror from his dressing table. "See how red my eyes are. Lack of sleep and grief have nearly done me in." He shook his head.

"You are known for your courage," added Angel Whiskers. "No more than twenty warriors and a hop over in a helicopter, a few shots fired. You're a legend in your own time."

"I'll lead the Samurai Guard into battle," agreed Running Shadow, inspired at last.

"Not the Samurai Guard. That would be ill-advised," said Angel Whiskers. Take his battalion? That wouldn't do. He leaned toward Nakasone's son and whispered: "After their failure to protect your father's life."

"True," Running Shadow murmured. "I'll take my own men. They know me and they love me."

"Yes," said Angel Whiskers, with a burst of enthusiasm. "And you'll wear war paint, absolutely."

"Oh, do you think I ought to? Isn't that a little...old fashioned?"

"No, you'll look splendid. And your grandfather's war bonnet."

"It's so heavy, though."

"It will give you great dignity..." Angel Whiskers wasn't going to take one step away from Running Shadow's side until he had him and about twenty armed warriors packed in the Apache whirlybird. Then it was up to the Dog Soldiers to shoot down the whole lot of them. As spies had informed Angel Whiskers, the Dog Soldiers had amassed machine guns, flamethrowers, and all sorts of machinery for going to war.

Well, now they were going to war a little bit before they had anticipated it. Two problems could be solved at once, Angel Whiskers reflected—well, three. This would be farewell to Running Shadows, and the forces of the Dog Soldiers would no doubt be reduced in the meantime. And Hoover—Hoover would probably be eliminated during the firefight. Angel Whiskers would then inform the Americans that his people had tried to rescue the ambassador, and the UT/American relationship would return to the status quo.

J. Adger Hoover had been the bedraggled object of the Dog Soldiers' scorn. But alien to his essentially dour inner being, the ambassador now experienced a frisson of delight. They had allowed the American to dress in the long, heavy skirts of a Navajo squaw after one of his captors had looked him over closely and then called Hoover a two-spirit being—something neither exclusively man nor woman, but both at once; a third gender, it seemed.

Once in the comfort of this new outfit, J. Adger merely smiled. He found something delightful in letting the air blow up underneath the flowing garments. He felt oddly vulnerable, yet suddenly free. It was as if the burdensome weight of a life's stringent pretense had been lifted off his shoulders. He presented a meek face to his captors and allowed one of the women to add a drop of carmine to his cheeks.

"You beautiful," she told him in all seriousness.

He believed it.

Everyone was having fun, in short, and there was not the slightest suspicion in the minds of any of the assembled that their party would, before long, be cut short, and their lives endangered.

J. Adger dimly realized the truth of it, however. He understood the machinery of diplomacy. Some political body would demand justification for his disappearance or insist on his return from some secondary party, and that demanded-of constituent, depending on what threatened to be lost or gained, would respond by taking action.

The result of that action would either be J. Adger's return to P.C., or his death. That ought to worry him, shouldn't it? But he had shrugged off his former self with his too-tight pantaloons, and once he was so outfitted, the Tribesmen began to treat him with remarkable respect. The light brush of the cool, colorful cotton swaddling against his legs was as mesmerizing to him as a swami's flute to a cobra. The hell with it, the ambassador decided. If a raiding party descended on them, he was already well disguised. He would run away with the rest of the skirt-wearing females.

"We won't get the whole $30,000 that we've demanded from the Americans," said Barboncito the Fourth. "But maybe we'll get a third of that. Ten thousand. We could..." His voice tailed off. What was it he wanted? All his dreams were in terms of the greater UT world, and he actually longed to travel and study in Outer East Tokyo, which flew in the face of everything he stood for as a Young Navajo.

"What do we want with the white man's money?" Deshna Cley spat—literally.

"We'll buy guns with it," said the third conspirator, Nachez Garcia, the descendent of a Francspanic group of Navajo.

They were boys, really, wearing dirty, half-erased face paint, nineteen and twenty.

"We can hire a shaman to do an Enemy Way sing for us," concluded Barboncito. "That's what we need. We should have an *hitali* hold a chantway for us."

The other two nodded their approval. Not only was Barboncito the leader of the group, what he said made sense. They stood for tradition, and what could be more traditional than a chantway? Yet guns would have been a whole lot more practical for a revolution, Nachez considered, without giving voice to that idea. The purchase of guns would be more concrete and down to earth, but not at all as seemly.

The youngsters, with half an eye out for Hoover's reappearance with the women, turned to discussing a proper *hitali* to hire for the sing. They were uncertain who they could get to perform the long and difficult ceremony; so few knew it any longer—which was their point—and some might refuse to deal with the rebels.

It was about then that all three of the boys became simultaneously aware of a mechanical sound—a humming, a droning, a plane swooping to land across the hills in the one appropriate field for such a venture. The three relaxed. If the pilot knew the airstrip, they could be sure he was a Bitter Water Navajo, and renegade or not, no danger to their cause.

"On the other side of the hill—there!" Anjo pointed, indicating where a long plot of land had been cleared in the typical Tribal way for aircraft to settle on. Unlike in America, there were no paved roads in the UT homelands. But as a consequence, that meant that travel overland was slow and difficult. Therefore, soon after the Wright brothers took their first successful flight at Kitty Hawk, Native innovators began tinkering with motor-driven flying vehicles. Their designs were a flop, but that, ultimately, was for the better, as it initiated a trade for mechanical items with the U.S. From that time on, the nation on the eastern border of the continent stuck to the manufacturing end of things and the Indian Nation began to create in its own mystical spheres.

Yet that spiritual realm didn't always hold sway as the Tribes battled the forces of nature in their agriculture, an endless cycle of droughts and floods, and the raising of sheep and horses to maintain their way of life.

Shamans such as Anjo, however, had a few tricks

up their sleeves that were rumored among the general populace, but seldom revealed.

Anjo pointed again as the runway appeared suddenly over the rise.

"Okay," said the pilot, who didn't like having the Tribesman hovering over his shoulder. "Go strap yourself into your seat."

Anjo gave the man a brief, piercing glance and sat. He didn't buckle up, though, refusing to appear cowardly in front of the two women.

"Lock in your seat belt," said Ulah with a frown.

He did so, as if forced, but the truth was that he wasn't entirely comfortable with automated flight. Sure, flying without an airplane and in the guise of an eagle was within his repertoire, but these metal things with motors didn't seem reliable. In his heart was a chant and he looked to the Holy People to decide his fate now and forever.

The wheels of the plane skipped across the runway, then ran smoothly along its surface. As soon as they halted and the pilot popped open the door, twelve passengers spilled out onto the airstrip. In addition to the Secret Service agents and the three UT refugees, the flight carried a taskforce of seven fully armed soldiers, rifles at the ready in preparation to snatch back Ambassador Hoover. The troops hit the ground running, then had to wait up for the women and UT. Only Anjo knew the probable way to the Dog Soldiers' location—the main reason he and the other two UT were along on this trip—and he was unhappy about the soldiers now beside them. As a doctor, he had seen what bullets did to living organs and he didn't approve.

"Let me go talk to them first," he told Ulah. "They're my people and they'll listen to me."

"No," Dinah said. "There's no reason for us to trust you. You lead us there and then you'll let us do our work."

"If killing is your job, I can't allow it," said Anjo. A flush came into his cheeks, but probably not a single one of them could tell, as their eyes were focused straight ahead.

Claude felt hot and angry. He had taken off his shirt and tied a bandanna around his head to absorb some of the sweat he was generating walking through this godforsaken countryside. Just as well the Indians had this territory. Who the hell else would even want it?

He had obviously landed his helicopter at the wrong spot—nearly crash-landed, to put it bluntly. Perhaps something had gone mushy in his scouting and tracking– and piloting–skills in the last few years. How much longer could he keep this lifestyle up, anyway, especially on short rations?

He stopped and listened and wiped his face with his shirt. He could hear voices over the rise. He crept toward the murmurs.

"...I think I see something up ahead. Ulah, you and I to the rear. Let the soldiers do the heavy lifting."

"But, Dinah. This is my mission, after all..."

English! They were speaking English! Where the hell

was he? Had he even landed in UT territory?

Anjo watched with narrowed eyes as the soldiers fixed bayonets on their rifles. The others in the group continued to bicker.

"If anyone's killed, it will be war with America, I can personally assure you of that," Thundertalk said mildly. "As the new Chief of All the Tribes."

Dinah, Ulah, and Anjo stopped their chatter, turned, and looked at him. He was strapping up his wrists with leather thongs and had the air of a man who already ruled. Hitachi faced away from them, sword drawn, protecting his leader. The sight was impressive. "All right," agreed Dinah, swallowing hard but trying to hide it. "I don't want to go down in history as starting a war."

They agreed that the Airborne Rangers would stand down at the foot of the dune to the left, and the rest of the party would march on to negotiate with the Dog Soldiers. If anything untoward happened during the parlay and their company failed to return, the Rangers would take over the mission, retrieve Hoover, if possible, and return to P.C.

"Our lives are in your hands," Dinah told Anjo.

Death is always a possibility for those who serve the inner machinations of history. The five moved forward under Anjo's direction.

As the oddly assorted team was about to overtake him, Claude popped up, covered with grit. He had his hands overhead, but not too far, showing them to be empty. He could still draw his concealed revolver if he was fast enough. "Thank God," he disingenuously declared in English, "Am I ever glad to see you guys."

One of the women pulled her gun, turning around and around, scanning the horizon, waiting to see if this apparition covered with sweat, sand, and random bits of nature was alone. Apparently, he was.

"Who the hell are you?" she barked, not yet returning her sidearm to its holster.

"I'm lost," said Claude. "Look at me! I don't know where the hell I am. My helicopter went down about five miles back there." He gestured with a thumb.

"And the pilot?" asked Anjo, concerned. Claude recognized him, possibilities blossoming.

"I'm the idiot pilot," said Claude, almost in good humor all of a sudden. His mind sprinted away with possible explanations for his appearance here. He certainly didn't want to take credit for the kidnapping of that ninny Hoover. And he really, really wanted to wind up with his wife and children in Potomac City. As a senator, maybe. Would that be too much to ask?

"Hey, you look familiar," said Hitachi in UTlingo.

"That's right," said Thundertalk. "You're one of Nakasone's servants. What are you doing here?"

"Ah yes," said Claude, reminded of his former role. "I'm Hunting Fortune." He coughed violently, then caught his breath. "I was terrified when Nakasone was killed, you see…”

Hoover and the women stood preparing the evening meal. There was something very satisfying about doing actual, physical labor. He was absolutely not returning to P.C., and he was glad, very glad. He wondered how he had tolerated his old life so long.

“You’re doing it all wrong, Addy,” Meat on Her Bones corrected him. She covered his hand with her own larger one, and showed him the motion. “It’s more like that. Don’t worry, don’t worry. You’re doing just fine. Everything will work out all right. The boys won’t kill you; I’ll see to that. You can come sleep in my hogan tonight, if you want to.” She smiled and showed her three missing teeth.

She was kind, thought Hoover, and very womanly, and yet it was hard to decide if that attracted or repelled him. Wouldn’t it be wonderful to settle down, to take a companion, not worry about strategy so much? On the other hand, as the Dog Soldiers seemed so inept, so disorganized, they could use an advisor, someone with a lot of political savvy. Yes, who better than he?

His explanation to the oddball joint U.S. and UT war party sputtering out, Claude slowly became aware of the *putt putt putt* of a whirring rotator blade. A helicopter made its way over the horizon. Who could that be? It couldn't be a rescue party from America. No, they were already right here in front of his eyes. So it must be some UT. Claude squinted out toward the Rangers, who had been relaxing on the sand, having a smoke. Now the troopers crawled into advantageous positions with their rifles back at the ready.

"Quick, let's get Hoover while they're distracted," one of the women hissed at the shaman.

Claude, relieved of his hard-to-deliver explanation, fell into step behind the main party, which had begun to trot forward. He'd get Hoover out as he'd previously planned and then beg asylum.

When they reached the rocky outcropping where the Dog Soldiers were sitting around, drinking some yucca-root beer, Claude put his arm out and stopped Anjo, who was about to march in alone. "Keep them busy," he said. "I'll go find your man."

Ulah and Dinah gave one another a look. Their eyebrows were raised. Dinah's right cheek followed the eyebrows, indicating to her subordinate that the whole business now was entirely out of her control.

Anjo stepped into the Dog Soldiers' circle and the man who'd appeared out of nowhere now disappeared into the sunset. Somewhere in the distance, Ulah could hear the crack of rifles. She winced.

The Young Navajo didn't seem to notice any of this.

Maybe they were getting drunk.

Anjo's figure showed up dark and looming, and the Dog Soldier boys seemed to be so struck by the image of the holy man, *hitali*, sorcerer, magician, that they simultaneously fell off their perch on a long dead and buried log dug into the sand. Drunk or not, they appeared in awe of Anjo, who swung overhead a twanging bullroarer, made of animal hide and a stick from a lightning-struck tree. They listened as he chanted, and even Ulah, standing beside Dinah in the shadows, shuddered.

An almost habitual look of amusement faded from General Thundertalk's face. Ulah clutched at Dinah's arm as the mysterious song rumbled forth and the magical instrument with appendages of abalone shell and turquoise "roared." The sound reminded Ulah of an oil rigging she'd once visited somewhere off the coast of Maine. It thumped and thumped and the ocean lapped noisily around the base of the platform, so that anything else was hard to hear.

But there *was* something more to hear in this case. Moments later, there came a screeching from the bushes, almost not human, and Ulah pulled out her sidearm for fear of the approach of some hideous animal.

It was merely J. Adger Hoover, however, being dragged by his hair toward the rescue party.

A flash of light seemed to come from the clearing while Ulah's attention was focused on the sight of a rouged and stumbling Hoover in skirts. Then, when heads turned back to catch what had happened, Ulah saw Anjo ambling back to their side, his pupils narrowed down to a pinprick, like a man who had taken a toke on an opium pipe.

Ulah prayed to Allah as she would in the presence of something unholy, while Hoover, oblivious, continued to struggle away from the rescuing party.

"Thank Heaven we've found you," Dinah said. "You're all right, Mr. Hoover. It's us. We're Americans."

Only seconds later, the squad leader trotted up to announce the capture of the UT landing party—one UT slightly wounded and one yowling that he was some high-flying mucketymuck, the new UT chief.

Great Chief Thundertalk stood on the narrow watchtower promenade forty feet in the air, binoculars in hand. He gazed out toward Francspanic territory. All was serenely quiet, as it had been with only brief interruptions for the last one hundred and fifty or so years. He handed the device to Hitachi without comment. "A man ought not to dream of glory," the chief then said abruptly.

"All we are here for is to do our duty," agreed Captain Hitachi somberly.

"Hmm, not always easy to determine what that is, though," said Thundertalk.

"Not that difficult, really." Hitachi shook his head. He'd apparently never had a moment of doubt in his life.

Thank the Great Spirit, the Americans now flew supplies daily to the Franspanics, and while it was too late for many, others would be saved. "If we hadn't allowed their people to be fed, we would have had powerful enemies across that border a few years from now," Thundertalk said.

"Just as well that Nakasone is dead," said Hitachi. "And that Running Shadows was turned back to his tribal lands. I don't think he'll manage to be on top there."

"Just as well," Thundertalk said. "Although I don't see him changing."

The two men descended without speaking; the hike down required more than some breath.

"Odd, those American women," said Thundertalk, swinging off the ladder onto the ground. He suspected Hitachi was partial to the older one and watched from the corner of his eye to see how the captain would take the comment.

Hitachi smiled, his teeth exposed. "Worth a trip to the United States to polish off negotiations, I'd say."

"We'll take the shaman with us to maintain protocol. He seemed impressed by the younger one," Thundertalk added.

Colonel Angel Whiskers approached and saluted. He wanted to report on the readiness of the next meal.

"Splendid," said Thundertalk. "I'm more than a little hungry." He had been up late last night, when his wife and children had arrived from the north.

He allowed Hitachi to take the path in front of him. "And that new spy of ours, Hunting Fortune. Shall we take him along, too? He keeps talking about his dreams of America. Too bad about Ambassador Hoover, though."

"A complete breakdown," concurred Hitachi, somberly. "It's best that he's gone back to his own people now. Quite sad, really. Any man might be broken by being forced into skirts."

Something There Is

BY *C. D. Covington*

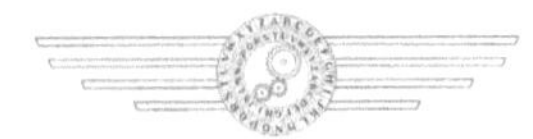

15 June 1961

I had another vision today. During the news, when Secretary Ulbricht said that no one intended to build a wall, I felt a heat as if the air itself were angry and heard a buzzing like a hundred swarms of bees.

"He's lying," I told Papa. I couldn't explain it, but I knew it was a lie. Papa looked at me very strangely then, and my heart started pounding. I thought he might turn me in for sedition. My own father! But all he did was ask me what I meant.

I just said that it was a lie.

I don't know if I should even be writing this. My parents could be Stasi informants, reading my diary, for all I know, but I need to make sense of this.

This isn't the first time something like this has happened. As long as I can remember, I've had experiences I can't explain. I knew where things were that I'd never heard of, or that weren't there anymore. One time I went looking for a bakery that I swore was just up the street, but there was a butcher's shop where I thought it was. We've lived in this apartment my whole life! I know the area, but I was absolutely convinced there was a bakery halfway up the next block. It turned out there'd been one there fifty years ago.

My mother once caught me talking to myself at the train station. She decided I'd made up an imaginary friend, but I was talking to a ghost. There was a little girl, about as old as I was at the time, in a fancy dress and a bonnet waiting beside the tracks. She told me her family was going to Rügen for the week. I told her that's where we were going and that she could come along.

I knew she was a ghost. But I felt like I had to offer her that kindness to let her rest. I found out a few years ago that she'd died of measles two weeks before her family's trip. I was sitting in the park and I suddenly remembered the little girl from the train station. I wondered idly what had happened to her, and I had the urge, the need, to get up and walk to a particular building outside of the area I usually went. When I got there, I touched the tan stone and felt a shock as the memories flooded into me: the little girl, Katrin, playing with her brother and sister; her falling ill; her parents watching over her bedside until she took her last breath.

That wasn't as bad as the time I stumbled onto a house where Jews were murdered. After that, I resolved not to touch buildings unless I had to.

I think the city is trying to tell me something.

5 July 1961

I don't know how to write about today, so I'll start at the beginning. I went to school, like I do every day. I went to my first class and my teacher called me to the front before I could even sit down. Her face was white as a sheet.

"Miss Schneider," she said, "you're wanted in the principal's office."

I had no idea what was going on. I hadn't done anything wrong, not that I could think of. I'm a good student, and I'm a member of the Free German Youth. I had my uniform on for the meeting this afternoon. But as frightened as Ms. Waldemann looked, I was sure I wasn't going to get any commendations when I got there.

As I walked down the hall to the principal's office, I saw my eighth-grade Russian teacher and my ninth-grade math teacher. Neither of them looked me in the eye. I started to get scared; I'd just been nervous before.

I don't know what I was expecting when I got down to Mr. Ackermann's office, but it definitely wasn't Erich Mielke himself. I hadn't done anything to make the Stasi notice me! Had I? I wanted to walk back out the door and run, run as far as I could, but no matter how far I ran, they'd find me. They had their ways.

"Please, Miss Schneider, have a seat," Mr. Mielke said. Mister? Minister. The head of the Ministry for State Security. *Mister* sounds too informal for someone like him.

I sat in the empty chair across from him. Mr. Ackermann was behind his desk and he looked like he wanted to hide under it. I felt a little better that I wasn't the only person in the room intimidated by Minister Mielke.

I waited for him to ask me questions. There was no way I'd be asking him anything! I didn't want to have "impertinence" added to my list of sins, even if I didn't know what the other sins were.

Mielke rested his elbows on his knees and leaned forward. "I hear you've called Secretary Ulbricht a liar."

My heart stopped. I wish it had done so permanently. I wish I could have come up with a better answer than, "Who told you that?"

"A little bird."

I felt like *I* was a little bird, and he was the cat who was going to eat me. I sat there looking at him like a dope. He just sat, too, watching me, waiting for me to make the wrong move. So I waited. Mostly, I was just terrified.

"Why would you call the Secretary a liar?" he asked.

I realized I could try to get away on a technicality. I wasn't sure it would work, but I gave it a go. "I only said that he was lying about one thing, not that he always lies."

Mielke raised an eyebrow. "I hardly see the distinction. You've slandered the Secretary."

My body started shaking. I was going to Hohenschönhausen. I'd never see my friends or family again. Then I felt like the room got cooler, and it smelled like spring in a meadow. It was calming. I looked up at Mielke and said with a confidence I didn't feel, "'No one has the intention to build a wall.' That isn't true."

I wouldn't want to play him at poker. His expression never changed. "What gives you that idea?"

I knew I had to explain it. If I didn't, it would be off to prison. If I did, he'd probably think I was mad and lock me in a mental hospital. I'd rather have the latter. "This is going to sound very strange, but sometimes, I get these feelings. If something is false, the room feels hot, and sometimes there's a noise that goes with it. When I saw the Secretary on the news, I felt like the room was on fire."

He just…*looked* at me, like he was peeling my skin off to find what was underneath. I've always had a healthy fear of the Stasi, but after today, it isn't theoretical anymore. I was willing to confess to anything, just to get him to stop looking at me.

"Interesting, Miss Schneider." He stood up and picked up a pen from Mr. Ackermann's desk. He wrote something on a piece of paper and signed it. "You've been excused from school for the rest of the day. Please come with me."

Mr. Ackermann stared helplessly at the note. There wasn't anything a mere principal could do to stop the head of the Stasi from doing whatever he wanted. He nodded and mumbled something that sounded like "Go with him."

It wasn't as if I had a choice. I picked up my bag, said

goodbye to Mr. Ackermann, and followed Minister Mielke out through the school. Classes had already started, so I didn't run into anyone else in the hall. My whole body shook and I thought my heart was going to beat out of my chest. My legs felt like I'd hiked five kilometers up a mountain and back, all wobbly and exhausted. I started to panic.

I don't remember getting into the car, but I must have done so. I don't remember when I started crying. Would they tell my parents where I was? Was it Papa who'd told them what I'd said, and he already knew what was happening? Minister Mielke sat beside me in the back of the car. He gave me a handkerchief. It was an oddly human gesture.

I knew it would be stupid to say anything unbidden, because he could use my words against me, so I sat silently and watched the city pass by. I thought about jumping out the door while we were stopped at a light, but I knew I wouldn't get far. I resigned myself to my fate. I'd never get to go to Budapest for the Socialist Youth conference. I'd never see my sister or our dog again. How would Mama and Papa explain it to her? "Elisabet said something bad about Secretary Ulbricht, and Minister Mielke took her away." Silke would be extra careful not to say anything bad and be a good little socialist, not like her sister, whom the Stasi took away like the bogeyman.

The driver pulled into the garage. Mielke got out of the car and the driver opened my door. I realized there wasn't a handle on my side. They thought of everything to keep their captives from running.

Mielke told me to follow him. I froze beside the car. I didn't want to go. I think I started crying again. The driver waited behind me, probably making sure I wouldn't run. I couldn't have run if I'd wanted to. I couldn't even *walk*.

"Come, Miss Schneider," Mielke ordered.

I felt a power flowing into my legs and I started walking. It was as if the cement of the garage floor was pressing up against my feet, moving them along. I wasn't doing it myself. Then I felt something like a hug, or a warm, cozy blanket wrapped around my shoulders. The city would protect me.

It seems mad, as I sit here writing this, but I'm sure of it. The city, Berlin herself, wants to keep me safe. I don't understand it, but that's the only explanation I can come up with.

I followed Mielke through the halls of the headquarters and into his office. I slowly realized that this wasn't going to be a regular interrogation. Surely they'd take me to Hohenschönhausen if they wanted to lock me up, not to the minister's private office. Right?

Mielke told his secretary that he was unavailable except for an emergency. Whatever reason I was there, it was important. Maybe they weren't going to lock me up after all?

Mielke sat behind his desk and a pair of officers stood on either side of it. They couldn't consider me a threat to the minister, not after leaving me alone with him so far. Could they? I'm not much of an athlete. I get decent marks in sport, but I'll never make it onto an Olympics team. Surely they'd know that. They knew everything else.

"Have a seat," he said.

There was only one chair, so I sat in it.

"How long have you been having these feelings?"

I knew what he meant without asking him to explain further. "I can't remember not having them."

I swear he looked like a cat who'd stolen a fish as big as himself before he settled his impassive face back on. "Interesting." He made notes in a pad on his desk. "What was the first time?"

I told him about how I got separated from Mama and Papa in the park when I was three or four, and when I got scared, I felt something like a hand on my back, guiding me toward them. He wanted to know how often it happened and I told him it didn't happen all the time, only when something was important. I didn't mention that it's been happening more often recently, and I didn't say anything about what happened in the garage.

"So you can't do it on command," he said. He looked slightly disappointed.

"I'm not sure. I've never tried." The city isn't mine to command. She tells me things when she wants to.

"Let's experiment, then." He motioned to one of the guards, who left for a few minutes, then came back with a man in prisoner's clothes.

The prisoner's eyes were wide.

Mielke asked him who had helped him get across the border.

"There wasn't anyone," the prisoner said.

I didn't feel anything. I concentrated really hard, but there was nothing. Either he was telling the truth, or the city didn't care enough to tell me he was lying. Or maybe she wanted to protect him, too.

"Who sent you the Milka chocolates?" Mielke asked him.

"My mother," the prisoner answered. "It's not a crime for mothers to send their sons chocolate, is it?"

I wished I could have stood up like this prisoner. He was scared; that was obvious. But he'd gotten a gift from his mother. I've never had Milka. You can't buy it here. I wonder what it tastes like.

Mielke looked at me, one eyebrow raised in a question. I'd still felt nothing. I shrugged my shoulders and shook my head.

He looked disappointed again. He waved his hand, and the guard escorted the prisoner out. "Nothing, then, Miss Schneider?"

"I'm sorry, sir."

"You could still be useful to us," he said. "How would you like to be an *inoffizielle Mitarbeiterin?*"

Work for the Stasi? *Me?* Being a member of the Free German Youth was one thing; you go to meetings a few times a month and say slogans and learn about the wonders of socialism, you're allowed to travel to other countries for Party meetings, and you get preferential treatment when it comes to jobs. But spying on my friends and family and reporting them for sedition? I'm not sure about that. I told him so.

"Your position would be somewhat different than the usual IM. You would report directly to me any of these feelings you get that regard the future of the state." He looked at me again, with that expression like he was skinning me. "I'm sure you're looking forward to your trip to Budapest at the end of the month. You don't want your travel permit revoked, do you?"

My stomach clenched. I wanted to go! Marianne and I had been planning it for months and she'd be devastated if I couldn't go. Stefan's going, too.

Mielke was using my trip to get me to agree to work for him! That wasn't fair. But he's the head of the Ministry for State Security and he doesn't have to play fair. I felt the blanket around my shoulders again, comforting, protective. The city would help me. I trusted her.

"I'll do it," I said.

He gave me instructions on how to contact him and had me recite them to make sure I knew them. He gave me a code name: Mayfly. Then he sent me home with the driver who'd picked me up from school.

I still can't believe it. I don't understand it.

I'm working for the *Stasi*.

6 July 1961

At school today, no one said anything about Minister Mielke's visit to the school. It was as if it never happened. Ms. Waldemann asked if I was feeling better today, because I'd looked really ill when I left yesterday. Mr. Ackermann had received a note from my doctor and my absence was excused. I muttered that I felt fine and took my seat.

What happened yesterday? Was it a dream? If it was, it was a very vivid dream. Or a nightmare. No, it has to have been real. Why does everyone else remember something different?

19 July 1961

Marianne, Michael, Stefan, and I went out this evening. We had a picnic dinner beside the Spree, then went bowling. We had a great time.

Except as soon as we got to the bowling alley, I felt like I needed to leave as quickly as possible. I excused myself to the bathroom for a minute to collect myself. On my way, I saw the man who'd driven me to Mielke's office. I stared at him, but he looked away. Were they following me?

I went into a stall and took a few deep breaths. I wished for the blanket-feeling. I wanted to know I was safe. That feeling never came, but the urge to be somewhere, *anywhere* else diminished. I went back to my friends, and we played girls against boys for two rounds. I bowled terribly, and Marianne's score couldn't bring us up to the boys'. Next time!

Stefan walked me home. We talked about our trip—just five more days!—and when we got to the front of my building, he kissed me. I felt like I could fly.

When I got inside, there was a letter for me. I didn't

recognize the sender, and the address was from a suburb. I opened it carefully. There was a typed note that read, "Have you heard anything? I wouldn't want you to miss your trip." And was signed simply "EM." My hands started shaking and Mama asked if I was all right. I told her I was fine, just a little tired, and went back to my room.

I didn't want to make anything up. I could get some poor innocent person thrown into prison. But I had to find something! I couldn't just ask the city to tell me things. I don't think it works that way. I stuck the letter under a pile of papers in my desk and went outside. I took a walk down to the park and sat beneath a tree. The sun was still peeking over the apartment blocks.

I thought back to that day and wished I could take it all back. I wish I'd never said anything to Papa last month. I'd be just another high school student, not an informant for the Stasi. But I can't change the past, so that means I have to live with the consequences.

I leaned into the tree and pressed my palms into the ground, willing the earth to give me something, anything I could take to Mielke.

Nothing came. I'm sending him a note tomorrow morning, saying that I've heard nothing at all. I hope he takes it well.

25 July 1961

Budapest is amazing! Marianne and I are sharing a

hostel room with the girls from Dresden and Leipzig, and the boys are across the hall. There's a common room where we have our breakfast, and out back there's a cute garden with chairs and gorgeous rosebushes. Grandma would love them. We can see Parliament across the river. It's beautiful. It looks like an illustration from a fairy tale.

It's much hotter here than at home. Tomorrow we're getting a tour of the city. I hope I don't pass out!

It's very strange being out of Berlin. As we left, I could feel the city getting further away. I don't just mean in the obvious sense that you're moving in a train. It was like I lost part of my sight and hearing once we got past Schönefeld. I didn't know how strongly I'm connected to the city. We went to Dresden two summers ago to visit Aunt Bertha, and we took that vacation to Rügen when I was seven. I don't remember it being like this. Maybe it's getting stronger now that I'm older, the same way I'm feeling signs more often.

There's a dance tonight for everyone to get to know each other a bit. Ms. Bendtner and Mr. Hagelmann are our chaperones, and they're going to meet us downstairs in an hour. I need to get ready.

—Later—

I met a Hungarian boy who said he can feel Budapest. I went to the dance and while I was getting punch, this boy came up to me and introduced himself. I did the same, figuring he was being friendly and the whole point was to meet the other kids, right? He was kind of cute, too—

light brown hair, grey-green eyes, almost the color of the Danube, actually, square jaw, strong cheekbones. So we talked a little bit–in Russian! I don't speak any Hungarian, and he only speaks a little German–about our favorite subjects in school, what music we listen to, that sort of thing.

Then suddenly he said, "It must be hard for you, being so far from your city."

He could have said "far from home," but he said "your city." My stomach fluttered. I didn't know what to say.

"I've never gone far outside of Budapest," Gregor–that's his name, Gregor–said, "and definitely never outside of Hungary. What's it like?"

I knew he wasn't asking about the fourteen-hour train ride or how it feels to be somewhere you don't speak the language at all. "What do you mean?" He couldn't know about my connection, could he?

He tilted his head and looked like he was asking a question of someone who wasn't there, and he said, "You're definitely the right person, Erzsébet. The city's never lied to me."

My grandmother would have been appalled at my unladylike expression. My mouth hung open like a fish. I closed it and drank my whole glass of punch to give myself a minute to think.

"You don't have to hide it from me," Gregor said. "Do your friends know?"

I shook my head. "They'd think I'm mad." I scooped myself another glass of punch and picked up a piece of cake. It was spongy and had a sort of pudding between the layers.

It was delicious.

Gregor gestured to a few chairs beside the wall. I looked back to where I'd left Stefan. He was talking with Marianne and the girls from Dresden. I was a little jealous, but then, there I was talking with Gregor. I followed him and sat down.

"How does it feel to be this far away?" he asked again.

I explained that it was like I was missing one of my senses, or a limb I didn't even know I had. I asked him if he knew why it happened, what the purpose was.

He shook his head. "All I know is that this city chose me, and yours chose you. There are probably others who've been chosen by their cities, too."

"What's the point?" I leaned toward him and whispered, "The secret police are using me as a spy. The chief thinks I'm useful. I feel dirty."

He put his hand on my shoulder and I felt more than just its warmth. It was a different feeling than at home—older, I think—but still familiar: warm, comforting, solid. "You do what you have to, to survive." He looked back out into the crowd. "I'll let you get back to your friends. See you tomorrow."

As I went back to Stefan and Marianne, I felt odd. I've known them for years, but I've never been able to tell them this one secret. I just met Gregor tonight, and he knew my secret without me telling him. He understands me. Except...he can't move away from here, as much as I can't move away from home. I hope I can get his address so we can write.

3 August 1961

It's good to be home.

I had a great time in Budapest, and I'm glad I met the kids from Dresden and Gregor and everyone else, especially Gregor. But after a few days being away, I felt anxious. It had to be because of my lost connection. I was sleeping when the train crossed into the city, but I felt the link in my dream, like a peg fitting into its slot. It was pure joy.

I hope I can still travel when I'm older. The beach at Rügen is lovely, and I want to see my family that lives in Dresden again.

5 August 1961

I had an unexpected visit today. Minister Mielke sent his driver around to pick me up. He wanted to know about my trip. Specifically, if I'd felt anything while I was there.

I told him I hadn't, that I couldn't feel anything once I'd left the city. He looked disappointed again, probably because that means I can't be sent out to listen in other cities. I'm not going to tell him about Gregor or that there may be others like me throughout the country. If he wants to find out, he can. For all I know, they're reading this diary. I keep it hidden, but they can look everywhere without you even noticing.

He gave me an assignment. He said he got information about a meeting of possible dissidents at a cafe. I just have to go there tomorrow and listen. I'll take a book and have coffee and cake. Maybe two pieces. He gave me ten marks. I can't refuse his blood money, but I can spend it.

6 August 1961

I just wrote my first report to EM. I feel dirty. I'll deliver it in the morning.

I went to the cafe at two. The meeting was supposed to start at half past two and I didn't want to be late. I ordered my coffee and cake and took a seat near a larger table that had a reservation card on it. I opened my book and pretended to read it while I watched for the group to come in. They did, one by one. They acted like any usual *Stammtisch*; each one ordered a coffee and joined his fellows at the table.

They spoke quietly without whispering. It was hard for me to hear them, and I didn't want to move closer. I bought another coffee and sat back down to listen.

I felt sadness envelop me, but then I heard the men's voices as if I was sitting beside them.

They talked about football, their families, and their jobs before turning to more serious topics. People had a right to free speech, they said, and the Stasi went against that. One of them remarked that he'd seen huge shipments of barbed wire and bricks delivered throughout the city. Another talked about packing up his family's belongings and visiting relatives in the west and not coming back. One wanted to have another protest like the 17th of June 1953, but the others said it would just end the same way: Soviet tanks in the streets and martial law.

They went on like that for about twenty minutes, then turned back to safe topics until they left.

After I got home, I took Fritz out for a walk to clear my head. I couldn't shake the sadness around me. After a few rounds of fetch in the park, Fritz dropped the stick by my feet and nuzzled my hand. I patted his head and scratched his ears. He curled up on the ground, so I sat next to him. I buried my fingers in his fur. The dog doesn't care that I'm working for the Stasi. He just wants me to play with him and give him food.

I ran my fingers through the grass and felt the living earth beneath them. "I'm sorry," I whispered. "I don't want to do this, either. I have no choice." A tear dripped from my cheek onto the ground. I don't know how to explain what happened next. I felt reassured, like the city understood. That's why she helped me hear the men in the cafe: she knows that if I don't start giving EM what he wants, I'll be in trouble.

But she doesn't want the Stasi here. She doesn't like them. She doesn't want them to use me as a spy. That's not what she wants me for.

10 August 1961

I've started going out more often. I won't learn anything sitting in the house, and if I can overhear something, maybe EM won't give me assignments. So I wander through the neighborhood, pick up a roll or a sandwich, and head to the park. I haven't overheard anything there yet. I think I'll see if Marianne wants to go window-shopping with me Saturday.

The last few days, I've felt a sort of tingling in my skin, like my arm's gone to sleep but all over, and everything I see is in high contrast. There's a sense of nervous anticipation, sadness, and anger. Something's going to happen soon, but I can't figure what. I dropped another note to EM. He said he wanted to know about any feelings I got; this is one. I hope he doesn't mind that I don't know what it means.

11 August 1961

I can't say my trip to EM's office today was unexpected. There was a different driver this time, but it was the same car. It's less terrifying each time I go there. Today, I was even able to walk into the building under my own power. I never thought I'd get used to going to

Stasi headquarters. I don't really want to be.

He had two guards on either side of him again, and he directed me to the same chair I'd sat in the last time.

"Miss Schneider, please describe in detail the feelings you've had over the last few days," he said.

I hadn't gone into a lot of detail when I wrote the note. "Since Tuesday or Wednesday, I've been feeling like my whole body is tingly, all on pins and needles. Everything is sharp, like I'm looking through a crystal."

"Interesting," he said, making a note. "What does it mean?"

"I'm sorry, all I know is that it's anxiety. I don't know why."

He *looked* at me again. Can he see into me and tell if I'm being honest? I shuddered.

"Fascinating." He gave a slight, ironic smile. "As I've said, contact me with any feelings you get." He shuffled papers on his desk. "Thank you for your report from the weekend. We're following up on it. I'll call on you again if your skills will be useful." He dismissed me with a wave of his hand.

13 August 1961

I had a nightmare last night. I dreamed that my body was being cut in two. I woke with a sense of dread and anger around me. The room felt like it was closing in, and it was hot, almost as hot as Budapest. When I heard that soldiers had built a wall along the border with Berlin-West overnight, I felt that I'd already known. I'd been right back in June: Ulbricht had lied. I penned a quick note to EM, and I told him that the city is angry about the barrier cutting her in two.

I tucked it into an envelope and addressed it like he instructed me to, but I didn't seal it. I slid it under my desk pad. I wasn't sure I wanted to give him a letter that direct. If I didn't change my mind when I got back from my day with Marianne, I'd seal it and drop it off. If I did, I'd write a new one and send that instead.

While I was out with Marianne, we saw the new wall in person. The barbed-wire fence had been replaced by concrete blocks topped with barbed wire. I wished I could tear it down. I'm not strong enough. I'm only one person, one who was scared by the Stasi into working for them. I don't even care so much about contact with the western half of the city; I just want this chain taken off.

Then I felt everything. I felt every brick or concrete slab placed along that arbitrary line, every car driving on every road, every rabbit digging its winter burrow. I was aware in a way I'd never been aware before. I started crying.

Marianne grabbed my shoulder and pulled me away from the wall. "Are you all right?" she asked. "Let's go get something to eat."

I nodded and wiped my cheeks. My mind was reeling and I must have looked like I was drunk walking to the café. I didn't realize until after we'd sat down and Marianne had brought me a cup of hot coffee and a piece of plum cake that it was the café where I'd gone to spy on those men for him. I could still sense everything going on in the city, east and west. I focused on the table in front of me, and that awareness diminished.

I ate my cake and drank my coffee while Marianne and I talked about Stefan and Michael and the next school year, which starts in a few weeks. We'll have to make our career decisions soon. I'm doing well in the sciences, so maybe I can go into chemistry. She's gifted in languages. She'll probably end up as a teacher. She'd be good at it.

We had a leisurely stroll past the shops on our way back home, chatting about everything and nothing. Maybe I should tell her about my gift. I hope she wouldn't think I'm mad or telling fairy stories. I'm pretty sure she wouldn't stop being my friend. I don't think I can tell her about my secret job, though. That would definitely end our friendship.

I went to my room when I got home. As soon as I stopped focusing on something, I was overwhelmed by the sense of *everything* at once. I don't want to spend the rest of my life in a daze, so I need to learn how to control this…whatever this is. I should tell EM, but I'm terrified of how he'll use me once I do.

15 August 1961

I took another trip to EM's office today.

"You say the city is angry," he said. "I'm sure you know what the penalties for seditious statements are, Miss Schneider."

I was scared. He could change my life with a word. Well, change it more than he already had. But I was angry, too. I reached out to the city and asked for support. She gave it to me. "I'm only doing what you told me to," I said. "The feeling I got when I woke up Saturday morning was anger and sadness."

He looked at me with the blandest expression I'd yet seen on his face. "And you're sure it's related to the wall."

I told him about the nightmare I'd had.

"Why didn't you include that in your report?" He *looked* at me again.

"I didn't think it was important."

"I see. You're not holding anything else back because you don't think it's important, are you?"

"No," I answered.

"If you're keeping any secrets from me, I can make your life extremely unpleasant."

"No, of course not." I hoped it didn't come out too shaky.

"Good."

"Minister Mielke," I said, "Do my parents know that I'm working for you? Where do they think I go when I come here?"

His smile chilled me to the bone. "They don't think anything of it."

I stopped myself from shuddering in his office, but once I got home, I couldn't stop. I need to change my hiding place for this journal. I hope they haven't already found it. My friends, especially Gregor, aren't safe if he finds it.

15 September 1961

I went to a football match with Stefan today. We took the tram out to Köpenick to see his beloved Motor play. I'm not much of a fan, but he got us tickets and he was so excited about it that I couldn't say no. He had an extra team scarf that he gave to me so I could support the team. We met some of his friends at the stadium, and we all sat together.

I've gotten used to the newest part of my gift, and it's easier to control. I still have trouble sometimes, though. While Stefan's friends went to get us beer and currywurst, I took my seat and listened. The stadium buzzed with people. The players came onto the pitch to warm up, and I felt them running on the turf, felt the ball rolling. It was beautiful. I almost forgot the constant sense of outrage at the physical reminder of the city's division.

I ate my currywurst, drank my beer, and cheered along with the boys. It was fun and I'm glad I went, even if I overheard things I didn't want to.

During halftime, Stefan's friends talked about heading west, getting emigration permits and jobs. They had cousins in Düsseldorf or Dortmund, they said. There's nothing illegal about that, at least not yet. It's not easy to get emigration permits, but some people manage it.

Then one of them said, "Fuck Ulbricht and the Party."

I don't care much either way about the Party, member of the Free German Youth or not. I'm not happy with them at the moment, since they've built the wall, so I'm inclined somewhat toward "fuck them." But if he said more, I'd have to report him, and I don't want to do that.

"Careful," I said. "You never know who's listening."

He shrugged and drank more beer. "Fucking Stasi. They're everywhere."

He didn't know how right he was. I decided not to say anything to EM about it. He's a high school student; he'd been drinking. He didn't seem much of a threat.

The players came back onto the pitch, and the game continued. I let the sheer joy of this tiny section of my city wash over me, divisions and barriers forgotten.

21 September 1961

Today, while I was playing with Fritz in the park, I took a break under a tree. A group of boys were playing football and one of them missed the friend he was passing to, and the ball rolled straight toward me. Before it could hit me, I moved my hand reflexively to stop it. It stopped, not because it hit my hand, but because it fell into a newly formed hole.

I played with it some more, making little cracks in the dirt and filling them in. I sent a couple pebbles flying. I wanted to see how big a force I could manage, so I found a small tree and thought about shaking it. It moved. I tried a bigger tree, a tall old fir. It wobbled.

This is definitely an interesting development.

EM hasn't contacted me since the wall went up. I don't know if it's because he's so busy dealing with the consequences of building the wall or if he's interrogating new prisoners, or whatever it is he does all day. The border police are sealing the underground rail stations on lines that connect to the west, and where the wall runs into apartment buildings, people are throwing suitcases out the windows and jumping after them to freedom. Somewhere on the western side of the wall, someone is digging a tunnel under it. There is more than one.

I should tell him about it. I don't think I will. This time.

11 October 1961

I sent EM a note yesterday, and today when I got out of school, the car was waiting for me.

"You believe someone is building a tunnel," he said.

I nodded. The tunnel I wrote about last month was finished weeks ago and filled back in. No one ever knew. I've known about three or four others since then, too.

The Stasi would figure out that people were escaping underground eventually, and they'd wonder why I didn't tell them. I could claim that I didn't know, but I don't think they'd believe me. Better to give them something small now. I'm sure people will keep trying to dig under the wall to get out. People who are desperate will try anything.

"Tell me where."

"I'm not sure," I said. "It's started somewhere outside the city limits in the southwest, toward Potsdam."

"How do you know?"

"It was in a dream." It was a good dream, and I'd woken up so happy that I felt awful writing that letter. But I had to do it to protect myself.

"That's an interesting development, and one we can use to our advantage." He smiled a bit absently, like he was thinking about something. All the people he could capture as they tried to escape to freedom, I guess.

"Yes, sir," I said. I tried to sound enthusiastic, or at least agreeable, but I'm not sure I succeeded.

He *looked* at me. I felt the city wrap me in a blanket, or a wall, and he couldn't get past it.

I've figured out what the city wants me to do.

20 December 1961

It worked! I can hardly believe it.

I told my parents I was going to the Christmas market with Marianne. I took as many of my things as I could and packed them in my bag and left. Pictures from Budapest, Dresden, Rügen; pictures of Fritz, Mama, Papa, and Silke.

I left a note where Mama would find it, hopefully before EM gets to them and makes them forget I ever existed. I gave Fritz a hug and scratched his ears. He wagged his tail sadly. He probably knew I wasn't planning to come back. I posted letters to Marianne and Stefan yesterday, telling them what happened. I hope I can see them again someday.

I listened to the earth and found the place where a group of men was building an escape tunnel. They'd almost broken through to the west. They looked at me suspiciously when I knocked on their door. I can't blame them, really—a complete stranger knocks on your door just as you've almost finished the escape tunnel, and you can't be sure they're not Stasi (which, technically, I am, or was...). I told them I needed to get out of the East, too, and begged them to let me go with them.

They asked how I knew about them and I couldn't answer. I just told them I had a feeling. Would they have believed me if I told them the truth? They finally agreed to let me go, but they didn't trust me, so I had to be the first one through. That way I couldn't yell for the police while they crawled to the other side.

I needed them to be on the other side to do what I planned to do. I made my way through the tiny tunnel and waited for the last person to come out. I told them I needed to go back in. The man I'd talked to before stood between me and the tunnel.

I explained that I wasn't going the whole way through, and that they had nothing to fear—I'd even close up their tunnel for them. He looked at me like I'd started speaking

Chinese, so I said, "Watch this," and raised a clod of dirt into my hand. While I was standing.

He backed away. He said he didn't believe in witches. The rest of the group gaped at me.

I told them I had to do one more thing, and that I needed to be in the tunnel for it. I asked one of the women to hold my bag for me. She hesitated, but she took it. I told them to stand back from the wall. They all looked at me like I was mad, or going to go back through and turn them in. I think they were curious about what I was going to do, but I wouldn't have been surprised to find my bag next to someone's front door and them gone. No matter. I had to do it. I went back into the tunnel and listened.

I gathered all the anger and sorrow and rage from the city, from the ground, and pushed. I pushed gently at first, to loosen the foundation like a tooth, then harder, and harder, until the wall fell with a thunderous roar that I felt as much as I heard. The tunnel started to collapse around me, but I cleared it again.

I crawled out, dirt falling from my hair and clothes, and I looked up. The wall had fallen. I was giddy, a mix of my own happiness that I'd succeeded and the city's euphoria that this chain binding her had been shaken off. I walked back toward the group of people I'd escaped with. Two of them had stayed: the man I presumed was the leader and the woman who'd held my bag.

They stared at me in disbelief as I walked toward them. They looked happy, yet nervous. The woman dropped my bag and kicked it toward me, then ran in the opposite direction. The man caught my eyes and gave me a quick nod before he, too, vanished down the alley.

People flowed out of their homes into the street, shouting and crying with joy. I heard many people asking if it had really happened, if the wall had really come down, and how. Some wondered if it had been the Americans who blew it up; others said it could have been the Soviets who did it to blame the Americans.

I had to do something, tell someone that *I'd* done it, before the situation escalated.

Police and soldiers swarmed the area, radios buzzing. I saw East German police and Soviet soldiers across the rubble, talking to each other and radioing. They'd be talking to the police on this side before long.

I walked over to a policeman and told him I needed to speak to someone in charge. He ignored me until I told him I'd made the wall fall. He didn't believe me, so I showed him the trick I'd used with the other men.

After that, I got a ride to the American occupation forces' headquarters. They've given me a room for now, under guard, of course. I expect they'll use me the same way EM did, except I'll feel less dirty about it.

On my way to the tunnel, I'd left a message for EM at the usual drop point. "I did it once. I'll do it as many times as I need to. This wall will not stand. *−Mayfly*"

The Ashkenazi Candidate

by Kaye Chazan

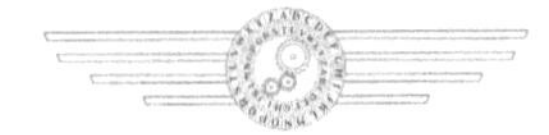

4 January, 1977, 13 Edward IX
Day 1003

I have been spelling with extra Us for the past three years. At this moment, I'm telling my coworker, in writing, that it's been an honor to work with him and that he should get well soon and, God willing, get back in the field, just to spite the Yanks. So I add the extra U in honour, and go on with my sympathies, and sign it, *buck up, Harris.*

Harris Weber-Pritchard is like me: neither slight nor white enough, with a nose the Germans can't look at straight without unspeakable apologies frothing at the corners of their mouths. Forty years old and younger in the face, small eyes, black hair that curls at the ends against the grain of English style. Facility with languages (or so Harris's superiors say), a fair hand at poker, a nearly ideal getaway driver.

I have been Harris Weber-Pritchard for the past three years. Five years ago, I was Steve Wallington, for eighteen months. Before that, David Eisenberg, for eight. They're like me, like Harris is like me, but younger, less facile, like I was. Harris, I think, is more like what I am.

I pass the sympathy card on down the line. My station at SIS Central, 54 Broadway, London, isn't so much an office as a square within three columns of framed blocks, like the chits on a voting ballot. Here, we don't keep secrets from one another, not at Harris's level, so there's no need for any doors but the ones that let us in and out. It feels, more than anything else, like a roomful of accountants toiling at typewriters, generating an incomprehensible stream of numbers. These are the children of the men who revised Enigma for the Germans. I had to be careful not to learn my machine too quickly. Codebreaking hasn't been my specialty since David Eisenberg.

David Eisenberg was my first job, a stint in Copenhagen. Some of my—his—friends were developing the older model of that new Enigma machine. Engineers, not spies, otherwise they would have never talked about it. I'm very good at pretending I don't know what other people are talking about, especially when it has to do with science or art. I did that a lot, growing up. I was always careful not to stick out. The tallest poppy fosters serpents in its shade, and all.

"Mr. Weber-Pritchard," someone says beside my desk. It's Sir Thomas, and that *Sir* is about the only excuse for using a superior's first name in a place like this. And unlike the rest of the Sirs around here, Sir Thomas was knighted publicly, for a different kind of professional pretense than what I do. He was King Edward VIII's favorite actor and he'll have us all know it. I swear he thinks he's Christopher Marlowe.

"Sir Thomas." I smooth a hand over my desk mat, nod in the way that's almost a bow. "Happy Christmas."

"Happier for you, working a gentile's overtime," he says. "For all that we've pricked you, I haven't seen you bleed."

I'd laugh at that joke even if I weren't Harris. It's only polite to think your boss is funny.

He raps his knuckles on my desk. His gloves muffle the impact. They're brown today, matte leather, creased at the knuckles and smooth at the wrist under the bracelets holding them on. "Come."

I remember, and repeat inwardly, that it's all right to be nervous when the supervisors summon you, that sometimes it really does mean your job, that it's fine for Harris to show all concern. Harris can be concerned. It's just that no one can see that *I* am, under here.

They've been planning to move the SIS offices from Broadway since long before I got here, and it hasn't happened yet. (It's difficult to lobby with Parliament for a city block when you don't officially exist. I can't afford to forget that it's not like the CD2 or the KGB here, where the whole point is that everyone knows who's protecting them.) So since we—they—we can't move, the halls are glistening with new wallpaper and glass displays and artifacts that I should probably be spelling with an E, not an I. The top brass lives on the bottom floor, in case they need to survive a nuclear strike. I'd be glad to know I'm so expendable to the CD2 brass back home, but I don't think they know the layout of SIS Central at all.

That's what they sent me here to find out. That, and just how many warheads they have. How they're operated. How fast they'll go. What American cities they'll target. I know it all now.

Sir David's secretary invites us in. Harris admires and fears Sir David a great deal more than I do. That's because Harris doesn't know just how easy it would be to play Sir David. Not that he'd ever tell all under his real name, but when a David J.M. Cornwell treatise hits the ban lists of American booksellers, I won't be surprised.

"Weber-Pritchard," Sir David says, as genuinely pleased to see me as he can convey behind thick glasses, smiling in the glint of the overhead lights. "Please, sit down."

I do, and Sir Thomas remains standing over my right shoulder. I try not to think about that, and say nothing aloud.

"You've made a great effort for us, young man," Sir David says, as much to the files on his desk and the back of his glasses as to me.

"I'm not so young as that," I say. It's true: neither I nor Harris is more than ten years younger than Sir David.

"But you are untried," he says, with a glance at Sir

Thomas, who *is* old enough to call me young and mean it. "And this order comes straight from Sir Vivian, so let me dispatch it in his style. You'll be shipping out, Harris, and God be with you."

Shipping out: unlooked for, but not unhoped for. How many people will I have to be? "Of course, Sir David. And where am I going?"

"The Indies. You touch down in Cuba tomorrow evening—our time, that is, and God willing. Everything you need to know is in this file; if you have any questions, please, don't hesitate to drop by before the end of the day."

It's poor form to read what he hands me while sitting in his chair, so it's not poor form to ask, "Any reason for the sudden vacancy?"

"The Yanks are giving us a few circles of hell," Sir David says. "Not enough to damn us, of course, but you know how Yanks can get. Move one missile silo and they think it's the end of the world."

I laugh because he wants me to. "Of course."

"I'm sure Trevelayn will explain everything when you rendezvous," he says, adjusting his glasses, and for the first time since I landed on English shores, Gabriel Waltman beats against the bars of my chest like a gorilla in a zoo.

Somewhere else, it is 1961, and I have never deciphered a code that wasn't made of lemon juice, and I am sitting in a chair of Trevelayn's design, catty-corner to a table he built to

accommodate the chair's rounded arms instead of our reasonably short torsos. He wasn't Trevelayn then, but still Hugh, Hugh Harrison, and he's sitting with his back against my shins, sketching.

"We can't sit in bowls, Hugh," I tell him.

"Your cosmonauts can," he says, and I think his tempered South London accent is the sexiest, most forbidden thing in the world. "How's your friend in the program?"

"Hell if I know," I say, ignoring the page I have to turn in my law book. "They'd be censoring his letters if he sent them."

"Where was he last?"

"Kamchatka, I think."

"I think the chair should be shaped like an egg," Hugh says. "The kind you can shut yourself back in if the world's too big."

I knee him in the shoulder, not hard, just hard enough. "I think it looks like something out of Disneyland."

He puts down his charcoals. His fingertips are as black as ash. They leave streaks on my ankles, stain my socks so deeply that I'll have to buy new ones. I don't care as much as I should.

I don't know as much as I should.

"Trevelayn," I say, and Harris manages to keep my tremor out of his voice and my larynx safely confined in his throat. "Hugh Trevelayn?"

"You've heard of him," Sir David says, a smile bright across his jaw.

It's a joke. I don't laugh.

"It will be an honor to work under him," I say instead.

"I'm surprised you haven't taken him out of the field yet."

Sir Thomas laughs, but then, Sir Thomas thinks nearly everything is politely humorous. "As the Yanks say, 'If it ain't broke, don't fix it.'" His Tennessee accent is impeccable. It would be. My collar is soaked with sweat.

They're going to shoot my plane down. They're going to send me off with false information and shoot my plane down, and these past three years will have been a shaggy dog story with no punchline in sight. Or worse, they *won't* shoot me down, and I'll make it home with their lies in my ears and then when the day comes, they'll burn everything from D.C. to Disney. They can. They would. I've seen the plans.

"Glad to hear he's still in it, then," I say, and if Harris sounds a fraction of how petrified I am, let the Sirs chalk it up to requisite awe.

They dismiss Harris. I leave.

"It pays to work overtime," Sir Thomas says, on our way out the door, past secretaries with no secrets, not anymore.

"So my mother always said," I say, and it's true for the both of us under my skin.

I read through the file at Harris's station, to the tune of a dozen coded typewriters at a dozen open desks. My Enigma machine is silent, the cover down and drawn.

If I live long enough to make it back to Washington, D.C., I'll build a new one, just so my people can take it apart.

It is Thanksgiving Day, 1962, and I have brought Hugh

down to Savannah to meet my parents. My father thinks we're only roommates; my mother and my sister know at least part of the truth, but say very little about it. It is not Hugh's first Thanksgiving in America, but it's his first Thanksgiving dinner, and he's so impressed with the feast and the spread that I swear they should quote him in Immigration pamphlets, "How To Be a Grateful Expatriate, Win Friends and Influence People."

"I always thought Liberty Cabbage had bacon in it," he says, and it's the first thing that isn't quite a compliment that he's paid to my family all evening.

"You can call it sauerkraut in this house, honey," my mother says, "and yes, it usually does. But it don't taste right, and my parents weren't so assimilated as we are."

"Assimilated?" he asks, as guileless as a golden retriever.

For the first time in our two years together, I explain: "We're Jewish."

"I know," he says. "But all the Jews I knew in England act just like you."

"How's that?" my father asks him.

"You'll pardon the expression, but they work like dogs. Like there's something to prove."

"There is," my father says, and the tone in his voice makes me want to hide my face in the canned cranberry sauce. "We have to prove that it's a bad idea to turn your back on us. And don't tell me England knows that, son."

"They won't know unless Disraeli comes back from the dead like the Son of God," Hugh says.

I don't mean to laugh. Didn't. Don't.

"Your God," my father corrects.

"What I mean to say," Hugh goes on, his smile back in

place, "is that the sauerkraut is excellent."

Harris packs for an extended stay. I pack for a one-way flight. I unplug the electric kettle, clean out the refrigerator, read up on concealment laws in Cuba. I make arrangements to leave my plants with my landlady, Mrs. Yamaguchi, for the next three months, long enough to make her think they're hers. I cancel the newspapers and the cleaning service and arrange for my tabs at the pub and the local currier to be settled through work.

At two in the morning on Day 1004, it is 9 p.m. yesterday in D.C. The hour is crude, and Mrs. Yamaguchi might complain if she didn't know I'm leaving tomorrow, but I play one last old record, turn on Harris's transceiver, and do one false test transmission to Telefunken in Berlin before I unplug the machine for good.

They'll think it's a glitch or a prank, I'm sure. The Fascists don't remember Cole Porter, and if they've heard of Ethel Merman at all, they deserve to catch me.

Do you hear that playin'? she asks in rhythm.
Yes, we hear that playin'! the chorus cheers in response.

Do you know who's playin'?

No, who is that playin'?

Why it's Gabriel, Gabriel playin'!

Gabriel, Gabriel sayin',
"Will you be ready to go when I blow my horn?"
Blow, Gabriel, blow,
Go on and blow, Gabriel, blow!
I was a sinner, I was a scamp,
But now I'm willing to trim my lamp,
So blow, Gabriel, blow!

But even if they don't know Ethel from Adam, there are people in the Abwehr who know what's what, and they'll tell people in Russia, and Russia will bring the news right along home to the top of the Chrysler Building.

Information travels faster than British warheads. It's about the only thing that does.

It will take approximately thirty minutes for the song to reach the desks of my supervisors in CD2 Central, down in Washington, D.C. I only hope they remember me. It's been so long, after all. I don't remember me either.

There's no clean way to dispose of the magnetape. I record hours of silence over it instead.

It is almost the end of 1960, and I have decided to drop my application off at George Washington University Office of Admissions myself, instead of entrusting it to the postal system this time. I'm already a year late for law school as far as I'm concerned, and my reapplication for subsidized student housing has already been rejected for the rest of the year because I'm no

longer a student, and you can't cheat the law in D.C. I know. I've tried.

Hugh, who I don't know is Hugh yet, is sitting on the steps of the Eisner building, sketching University Yard. I trip over him on the way in, scatter his charcoals. No, he doesn't go here. No, he's not faking the accent. Yes, he's sorry if it makes me uncomfortable. It does, but it does the way a charismatic villain in the movies does, like Burt Lancaster in The Longest Border, *or Jude Rawlins as the Devil in* The Master and Margarita. *He has broad shoulders and smoker's gloves and a crewcut and better teeth than I've seen on any other Englishman before or since. He credits socialized medicine and I can hear him try to pronounce it with a Z.*

We agree to go for coffee once I'm done inside.

We agree to go to his house in Crystal City once we're done with coffee.

I don't bother reapplying for student housing.

5 January, 1977, 13 Edward IX
Day 1004

There are layovers in Tangier and Bermuda on the way, or lays-over, and I don't know which is which at this point. Either way, it's going to be hell on Harris's luggage.

But say what you will about fascists: their public transportation is always on time.

Harris Weber-Pritchard is traveling as himself, but winter has given me another layer of homburg hats and lined gloves for me to bury myself beneath. Epiphany is dreary and cold in Heathrow, but it won't be in Morocco, and by the time I get to Cuba, it will be a blazing January afternoon, well past the requisite rain. I'll probably regret the winter coat. It makes me look Orthodox.

At Heathrow, at seven-thirty in the morning, a security steward hangs my coat on a rack for me while two airport police in Italian-designed black uniforms interview Harris and rifle through his briefcase and ask his business in Morocco. I tell them I have no business in Morocco. They laugh. They stamp the permit on my gun. We all bemoan the lack of direct flights and damn the Yankees and they tell Harris not to get lost in the Bermuda Triangle.

It's the first plane to Tangier of the day. The captain has time to finish his tea and shake a few hands before he boards. The co-captain is one of Sir Thomas's eyes-and-ears in the *Kempeitai*, Taro Iwamura. It was in the file. I expected it. He recognizes Harris. I let him, as long as he's quiet about it.

I don't sleep on the plane.

It is 1966, and I am in a windowless room in CD2 Central. It's right out of the movies, but the cameras in the corner are closed-circuit and the only men behind them are two rooms away. The women in front of me have copies of every federal document I've ever been issued and are poring through them like my mother used to pore through the coupon section of Stars and Stamps Forever.

"Gabriel Waltman," one of them reads as the other takes notes, "Savannah, Georgia, born 1938—oh, you just missed the last of the draft, didn't you?"

"Yes, ma'am. And I would have signed up after college if we were still at war," I tell them. It's true. It's truer now than it was then.

"Good, good," she says, and goes on, "W&M for undergrad, GW Law. Are you looking to join the legal teams, Mr. Waltman?"

"No, ma'am. I intend to become a field agent."

"And you planned on this before law school?"

"No, ma'am. Joining the CD2 didn't factor into my plans until recently."

"And why do you want to join now?" the other interviewer asks, her pen already poised to immortalize my answer.

I don't tell them that it's because I know, firsthand, the damage that the English spies can do. Have done. Did, to me, for nearly six years.

"Because I want to bring them down from the inside," I say, "like they've tried to do to us since we broke away."

Two hours out of Morocco, a cabin boy brings a warm airplane bento and sets it in front of me. The bento is wrapped in a souvenir cloth printed in silver with the *de Haviland* logo, *1920-1977,* and the cloth fans down over the edges of the tray, a personal placemat. I pocket it. I didn't pay extra for food, but the cabin boy says I'm on the list, and I would check the file in my briefcase, but that's just asking for trouble. No one expects a passenger to turn down free food. Not in this economy.

I haven't eaten or drank since the airport.

They wouldn't poison it. They wouldn't chance me handing off a bite to the person next to me, who brought nothing and looks at my curry with the corner of his mouth watering enough to cool his tea. Would they? Iwamura's the co-pilot. The *Kempeitai* would take this whole plane down just to get me, if they didn't want me alive. They've done it before.

Or they'll keep me aloft until I don't have a place to land. It's a perfect Shakespearean tragedy: the failure of the messenger leads to mutually assured destruction.

I still don't eat much. I've never developed a taste for Japanese food. I could be the only person on this earth who thinks that British food is better than something.

They might kill me back home for saying that. We're supposed to hate the Limeys and the Japs equally.

The churning in my stomach had better not be poison.

I still let the man sitting next to me finish the *onigiri,* and spend the rest of the flight waiting for one of us to choke.

It is 1974, and Jerry Burr has called me into his office. It's the fifth time. He didn't fire me any of the other four, but Mr. Burr is not the type to make his subordinates optimistic.

"Sit down," he says, and indicates his long, low, brown leather couch.

I obey. There's a window in this office, behind Mr. Burr's desk. The sun passes just above my eyes when I lean back into the cushions, like it was expecting someone taller.

"How long's it been since Port Darwin?" he asks, pouring me a glass of water.

I say, "Five months, I think." Port Darwin was Steve Wallington, eighteen months as a citizen of the Great Dominion and de facto Penal Colony of Australia. Port Darwin was Steve Wallington keeping track of just how tight the English hold on the Pacific Islands was, is, still is. Port Darwin revealed another Australia silo and plans to hollow out Oahu like a supervillain's lair. Port Darwin was eighteen months in skin I wished the sun would melt off.

Mr. Burr hands me the water and I drink. "Then I hope your apartment isn't under more than a six-month lease. How do you feel about us sending you out again?"

"In a month?" I don't have to consider it. "I'll do it. Australia again?"

"No. If it were Australia again, I wouldn't have told you to sit down." He drinks his own glass in two long pulls, like soldiers drink beer to show off. "We're trying something new, Waltman. We're going straight for the heart this time."

I hold the glass in both hands.

"You accept this mission," Mr. Burr says, "and you'll be working your way into the MI6."

I have nothing to say to that.

"We're talking cover so deep it makes the July Plot look like a game of hide-and-seek," he goes on. "You go there. You get work at SIS Central. Knowing you and knowing them, you probably get work running the codes. You learn the layout, the

operatives, the crack shots, and where's every damn bathroom at 54 Broadway. And once you think the jig is up, you boomerang back home, and maybe keep our side of the Atlantic from frying at their temperature."

I have a lot of things to say to that, but the one that comes out is, "Why me?"

He laughs. "To tell you the truth, you're my second choice. But why you? Leaving aside the fact that I think you won't bungle it up, you hate them. You hate them and you've still worn their skin twice, for longer than anyone else we've got lying around. You hate them so much that you put them on and take 'em off without letting them touch you. And if you accept this mission, we need someone with skin that thick."

The sun dips low. I shut my eyes. "How long?"

"However long it takes," he says. "If you go, you've got the identity, but you still need to make them hire you. At least two years. Probably more."

"How much time do I have to consider?"

"I'll let you sleep on it. Come back on Monday with an answer. The file's already in your office if you want numbers."

"I do, thanks."

He dismisses me with a half-wave, half-shrug. I set my glass down on the end table on the way out.

"Why was I your second choice?" I ask, just before I open the door.

"The Limeys feel sorry for Jews," Mr. Burr says. "They buy you drinks. Hell, they dangle Mandates in front of you. You might get to like it a little too much."

I can't help laughing in his face. "With all due respect, Mr. Burr, there's something you have to learn about Jews."

"And what's that, Waltman?"

"It takes a lot more than pity to make us change sides."

The third plane touches down at *El Rancho Boyeros,* and the world hasn't ended. It's high noon and it feels like dusk, and my overcoat is dead weight draped on my arm. The stairs off the plane take us straight to the concrete tarmac, and it smells like gasoline and asphalt and the sour cigarettes that the ground crew were smoking before they started unloading our luggage. It's American tobacco, strong enough and different enough from what they smoke in England that something snaps in the back of my mind.

Blow, Gabriel, blow, I think, and hope it doesn't whistle out on my breath.

They could snipe me from the command tower. It's in perfect range, and I have to stay still to get Harris's luggage. I hide my face in the shade of my hat, keep it tilted out of the sun.

No one in the line of receiving chauffeurs has my name up. I squint for Harris's instead and don't find it, either, until one larger man lets down his sign and the man behind him brandishes H W-P. I catch his eye, wait for him to shoot or stab me through the cardboard.

"Welcome to Havana, Mr. Weber-Pritchard." The driver is a local, or meant to look like one. He takes my suitcase, ushers me toward the sidewalk, toward a sedan parked under the arch of a palm tree. The car's badges and decals are falsified: I'd know a Nissan anywhere, even under a Ford's shell. "They are expecting you at the Hotel Nacional."

So either my message hasn't made it to the CD2, or the CD2 hasn't made it here. I can wait. I have to wait.

If the driver hadn't called me by that name, I wouldn't know whose voice to use. "Then let us be off," I say, and stow my overcoat in the trunk of the cab, right next to the suitcase.

Driving, he asks if I mind, then turns the radio on. The Spanish broadcasting flies by too quickly for me to follow anything but the songs and the gist of what the commercials are selling. My eyelids sag, but I don't let myself sleep. There's a glass panel between the driver's section and the backseat. He could gas me in the car. Come to think of it, he could do that with me awake. I still don't sleep.

The sun won't set for hours, but it creeps down behind the massive white stone buildings like a child playing hide-and-seek. The noises of the street oversaturate the outside of the car and thrum through the windows, undaunted by the radio and my headache. By the time we reach the forked driveway of the Hotel Nacional, any sensible Englishman would want a cup of tea.

Whether I remain a sensible Englishman remains to be seen.

Instead, they offer me iced coffee, nearly as soon as I'm in the door. A concierge takes my overcoat and suitcase, gives me a room number, addresses me as "Mr. Weber-Pritchard" throughout. An American man would never, but I err on the side of tipping the driver. The concierge, though, I may never see again, never mind Harris's luggage.

Inside the hotel, there is live music in every bar and every lounge, and the two guitarists in the lobby are dressed the part, wearing the homely hats and fringed coats of itinerant musicians who make half as much in a year as these two do in a week. As I check in, they play habaneras I don't recognize, in tempo after tempo, key after key. I drink the iced coffee as if I haven't had coffee in three years, which is true, for me at least. Harris may have waited even longer.

"Your business associate will meet you in the *Comedor de Aguiar*," the receptionist tells me. "He is running late, if you would like to go upstairs and rest."

Even if I wanted to, I couldn't. "Just to the WC to freshen up, I think," I say, and they point me to the nearest one.

Inside, closed-circuit cameras or no, I take my gun and its permit out of my briefcase, holster it over my shoulder. This will, I hope, be the last time I have to carry an Enfield. They won't pat me down, not in this hotel: the American and Russian mafiosos have been bankrolling it for years. But concealing a Limey gun on my person, on American turf, I feel the way fairies must feel at the touch of iron and the thought is so disgustingly English that I nearly retch up the coffee.

I have arrived in America in a three-piece English-cut suit. The lines follow my torso almost too closely to conceal the gun at all. The legs are too thin. The waistcoat is a waistcoat, not a vest.

And my bile tastes like coffee and Japanese rice.

It is New Year's Eve, and it will be 1961 in a matter of minutes. They've brought back the Times Square ball for the first time since 1943, but it doesn't matter because Hugh doesn't have a television, and apparently we're spending New Years Eve in bed. I don't mind.

I don't check the clock between 11:48 and 12:16. Considering the reason for my distraction, I don't mind as much as I thought I would. Hugh laughs at me, throws out the condom and makes a joke about dropping balls. I hurl one of the pillows at him. I don't check the clock again until almost one.

"I guess the world hasn't ended," Hugh says.

As far as "things to say after an hour or so of sex" go, this is startling enough to be funny. "Guess not," I say, snickering into the corner of the nearest disarrayed pillow. "Why, were they planning to invade us on New Year's?"

"It wouldn't work twice," Hugh says. "And even then, they waited until January second."

"It's not New Year's yet in the Pacific." I count ahead. "Two more hours for California." And in that case, it's nineteen years, minus one day, since the Japanese took Hawaii, back when it was almost American soil.

Hugh laughs. "They wouldn't invade California. Didn't work the last time, won't work this time. If they haven't struck D.C. and New York from the sea, they won't strike at all. Not today."

"How are you so sure?"

He stretches, folds his hands behind his head, works a crack out of his jaw that the sheets don't muffle. "The cease-fire's only six months old. England's as tired of this as you are, and likes a stalemate even less. It would be a weapons strike, not an attempt at invasion—and the objective would be annihilation, not subjugation. America doesn't have anything Great Britain wants anymore. Just a lot of things it doesn't want."

In the apartment beneath ours, a cheer goes up, as 1961 descends on another timezone.

"Every time so far that the British Empire has gone to war with America, it's been misguided." The way Hugh sighs and smiles, like a cat settling down in just the wrong spot on the couch, makes me nearly miss the words for the delivery. "First, we tried to lay claim to a land that had never been ours in the first place. Then we tried to tax its people blind, never mind that they'd already become expatriates. Then we tried to pretend that your people were our allies against France. And on, and on, and on, until the last. We can't win a land war against you, no more than we could win a land war in Asia. We've just finally gotten it into our heads that there's no sense in conquering something that can't be taken without a certain degree of mutually assured destruction."

I open my eyes in the bathroom mirror, and all those *We* and *You* and *Ours* echo in my sinuses, sixteen years later.

After hours of airports and ocean and sun, the *Comedor de Aguiar*, with its tall yellow archways and its art deco ceiling, is like a nightmare. Harris Weber-Pritchard is expected here. The host, who isn't a *maitre d'* on this side of the Atlantic, escorts me to a table, not quite in the corner. I haven't changed out of my traveling suit, but it's black and tailored too closely to wrinkle, and no one bats an eye. They're too polite.

The waiter asks, in Spanish, if I will only drink a clean Jewish wine. It isn't code, or if it is I don't know it, and I tell him no. He says, "Good, good," and fetches a drink menu. I try not to hide behind it.

Enormous bay windows flood with the sun to my left. Winter or not, there's another hour before it touches the horizon, and another hour after that before it sets. I've taken the seat closer to the wall. Whether Harris's name is on the list because of Harris or because of me, I want the advantage of a wall at my back. The bandstand is across from me, and the jazz singer at the head of the four-piece catches my eye as she slips some American words into her Spanish song. "You can tell President Calvert every darned thing that I do," she sings. "You can tear me to rags as I pack my bags, but you can't stop me from loving you!"

A curl of cold shock runs down my spine. I may not be concealing myself with the wine list, but I can't help reading it. California wines, not Australian, rums instead of brandies, whiskeys that aren't scotch. America is a matter of miles away. Desperate West Indians have made the crossing on rafts. They still do it, from British-controlled

Haiti. England is an ocean gone and I am still wearing an English-cut suit and a Britisher's skin.

I need a drink.

I don't know whether Harris is placing the order, or I am.

"Harris Weber-Pritchard," Hugh says on the other side of the drink menu. "You son of a bitch, it's been years."

Somehow, between Harris's dinner gloves and the reflexive tightening of my fists, I don't drop the menu. Then again, I don't throw it in his face either. *One mistake,* I think, so clearly he must see it in my eyes. *One mistake and it means the world.* "Hugh Trevelayn," I say, and manage not to choke on it.

He looks good, for his age. His hair is still short: grey, now, with the light behind him. His shoulders are still broad, broader in a cream linen suit that no Continental would wear. His teeth have still benefited from American socialized medicine.

But his voice doesn't make me weak in the knees anymore. I've heard far too many English accents for that.

I stand up. We shake hands with the table between us. His suit is cream but his gloves are brown. I remember when his hands smelt like charcoal and tobacco.

Smelled.

Smelt.

Smelled.

"I trust your flight was smooth?" he asks as we sit back down. He's armed; I can see it through the line of his clothes, nestled under his arm like a parasite, like mine. His gun is American.

"Flights," I correct, in Harris's voice, "but yes."

"Guess that's one thing the fascists have going for them," he laughs. "The public transportation is always on time."

The, he said, not *their* or *our.* I run with it. "No," I say, "but the communists give you much better accommodations, if you know how to weave the red tape."

He's already laughed twice, and the most traitorous parts of me still miss the sound. "I'll bet you could fashion a pretty hammock out of that, with pillows to match."

"You'd know better than I," I say.

The waiter comes again. Hugh orders a pitcher of sangria for the both of us without asking what I want, and keeps his eyes on me the whole way through, curling his tongue around the consonants he uses to thank the help. There's no time to reach for my gun. I would. I want to. I want his blood all over that cream linen suit.

But if I kill him, America may never know just what British Intelligence has.

"Sangria," I say.

He cracks his neck to the side. "I assumed."

"You did," I agree.

"It's cheaper that way," he says. "The man I remember used to care so much about that."

"The man you remember was on a budget."

"And the man you remember was still learning just how things worked, over here." He drawls, traces the rim of his bread dish with the tip of a gloved finger. "Why, if I had a quarter for every time I accidentally tipped a communist waiter, I'd be able to eat out more often. Funny, how the years change these things. How long *has* it been, since you last reminded me?"

There's an answer. Harris doesn't know it. I'm not sure I should.

The band finishes its song, and the applause excuses my silence. The singer takes it, tucks her hair behind the flower over her ear and turns to the rest of the band. There's a bassist, a pianist, a trumpeter, a drummer. The trumpeter sets down his mute.

Hugh catches my eyes again, prompts me for an answer with a flick of his greying eyebrow.

"You tell me," I say.

The trumpet rings out.

Do you hear that playin'?, the singer asks in rhythm.

It rings out again.

Yes, we hear that playin'! the rest of the band choruses.

The waiter brings our sangria.

Do you know who's playin'?

He picks up my glass first, and pours, and Hugh's Cheshire-cat smile widens across his jaw.

No, who is that playin'?

Why it's Gabriel, Gabriel playin'!
Gabriel, Gabriel sayin'—

"Oh, look, they're playing your song," Hugh says as he stands up and shoots me.

It is 1966, and I want to set the house on fire.

My name isn't on the lease. My SSN isn't on any of the bills. All of the furniture in the house is Hugh's—hell, half of it he designed himself, and built, out of resin and wood and plastic and varnish, and wire-taps and transmitters to spy on the D.C. elite. Half of the clothes are his, half of the books, half of the posters on the wall. The bedspread. The plants. The papers.

They'll blame it all on me if I stay. The taps. The papers. The secrets that have slipped to the other side of the Atlantic Ocean. All of it. They'll blame me.

I'll blame me.

And they'll find me whether I blame myself or not.

His name's on the lease, not mine; the only thing I pay for is one car in the driveway. I pack everything I can of mine into the trunk, and leave, and pray that only the British have watched this place.

It takes every bit of concentration I have to keep my hands on the wheel, and to remind myself that I need all that gasoline to get me to Savannah.

And all I'll ever say, aloud, to the few people who know, is that Hugh and I had a falling-out.

I've never been shot before. Now, having been shot, that's the only clear thought I have; that this has never happened to me before, never mind who did it and how it was done. Where I am, what I am, none of that matters. I'm not even sure it hurts yet. Something tells me it will.

Dimly, like a silent film, just barely black and white,

I see a giant double bass swing through the air like it's Mike Epstein going for a home run all the way to Yekaterinburg. I duck on instinct, whether it's meant for me or not, and wind up under the table. Sangria drips down the cloth onto my head. At least, I think it's sangria. I shouldn't be bleeding that much if it isn't.

And I don't think there have been any other gunshots.

"Get him!" someone yells in American, and sure enough, they get me.

Now it starts to hurt. Whatever they've done to me might as well have ripped my left arm out of its socket. I probably scream. I wonder if I scream in English or American. I shouldn't laugh at that, but I do. That hurts, too. Harris's suit is too tight for this. Harris's skin is too tight for this. That must be why it's letting me out. That's also funny.

Someone half-runs, half-drags me through a door that opens both ways. White light and shining silver reflect an assault of brightness into my eyes. A kitchen, I think. I hope it's clean.

That same someone grabs my chin. She's black. She's very pretty, though through these tears and this haze anyone might be pretty. She's the singer from the band. I recognize the flower in her hair. It's a Cherokee rose. I think I'm going to be sick. "Still with us?"

"Don't know," I choke. "Who's us?"

She reaches down the front of her dress to where a shoulder holster would be if it could be concealed. "Andrea Peraza, CD2. We're here to take you home."

That's funny. That's even funnier than not knowing

where I'd be coming home from.

I don't think laughing makes it any easier for her to get me out of Harris's jacket and waistcoat, vest, whichever. The wound's in my left shoulder. My holster is hanging on by a thread. She snaps it, puts the gun in my hand.

"No exit wound. I'll do what I can here, but they'll treat you on the helicopter."

"But Hugh–" I cut myself off coughing, once the laughter dies down.

Agent Peraza shoves a gauze pad onto my shoulder, which hurts like hell, and wraps it into place. "But I what?"

"Hugh, not you." That isn't funny at all. "He's out there."

"The others'll hold him off. We have to get to the roof. Start walking, now, before the shock catches up with you."

And that is the funniest thing yet.

We plow through the kitchen toward the service elevator, scatter what few idiots remained after the firefight began. She charges and I stagger, and some part of me thanks God with a thousand *shehecheyanu*s that she's wearing sensible shoes. Just like Madame President, I think, and wouldn't she be proud, as proud as she'll be of me if I survive and it isn't already too late.

I should have killed Hugh before he sat down. I think he must have expected me to.

Agent Peraza presses the call button for the service elevator just as the entire hotel blacks out. At least, I think it's the hotel. There shouldn't be any red exit signs if I'm in shock.

It is 1960, and there have been changes to the procedure for air-raid drills. Hugh and I are sitting under the kitchen table with the curtains drawn, and the radio tells us we should have been at the local CD2 shelter long ago. But Hugh says they'd never let him in, even for a drill, and I believe him.

"You don't even have a basement?"

"It's an old house," he says. "I never thought to ask."

I've been sick of air-raid drills for years. I'll read up on the changes in the procedure later. I'm sure the radio won't stop talking about it every half hour for weeks. "Don't they have basements in England?"

"Cellars," he corrects, "and no, not terribly often. Rich people have them. I never had one."

I lean a little closer to him, get more of us both under his table. "So where did you used to hide instead?"

He shushes me and doesn't answer. The radio prattles on and on about where America can go to be safe. That really should have been my second clue.

Agent Peraza hauls me up concrete flight after concrete flight. There are eight of them. I don't know how many have passed. I can still feel my feet, can still tense my fingers around the gun in my right hand enough to know it's still an English Enfield, but I can't count.

The stairwell is lit with the emergency reds of one EXIT/ SALIDA sign per floor, and it isn't enough.

"He knows," I tell her, because I'm not sure she does.

She helps me around another turn, under another sign. "Trevelayn?"

I wonder if I've left a trail of blood. I shouldn't look down. "He knows where we'll go. There's nowhere. It's hot. He knows my way out."

"That won't matter if my team kills him."

"They won't."

"Sure they will. If you prick him, doesn't he bleed?"

I throw up down the stairwell. So much for not going into shock.

Agent Peraza lets me finish, holds my hair off my face. "Easy. Two more flights. Nine inches a step. Just count with me, okay? One. There. Two. Three. Don't let go of the gun. I've got your shoulder. Four. Five. Do you remember your numbers?"

I think I say yes. It's parched and awful and my teeth are rotting, but I say it.

"Good. Next step. Next. You're doing fine. What's your SSN?"

I creak out about two digits a stair, three on the last.

"DOB."

The concrete is swimming, red and shadow on grey. I shut my eyes, but I walk, and I tell her.

"License plate. C'mon, just a few more."

I trip, and I think I repeat one of the threes, but she keeps me level.

A bar slams down, a door slams open. Wind beats

me back like garbage on the highway. I used to think the quake and slap of an approaching helicopter was unmistakable, but the way this one blacks out what's left of the sunset, all I hear are sirens and all I see is fire.

"They've lowered a stretcher for you already," Agent Peraza says as we rush across the rooftop. "You made it." She's wrong. I know she's wrong. I try to tell her how wrong she is and then Hugh shoots her.

He was firing into the wind. I think he was aiming for me.

My body isn't quite mine right now. That must explain how it can't move how I want it to, how I can raise the gun but not aim with my eyes, how I can move my lips but shout ultimately nothing—how I can see Hugh in the shadow of the stairwell door, his white suit outlined in red from the overhead signs and an American gun still smoking in his hand, and not feel anything at all.

The stairwell door is like a frame around his body, a target in silhouette. The wind and the sunset are both on my side. Somehow, I exert the right amounts of pressure on the safety and the trigger, twice. Adrenaline throbs in my head like hatred or nicotine, like the chill of a limb falling asleep.

Reading lips, it's impossible to tell English from American.

Hugh tells me, *Thanks, it's been a good run*, and laughs in my face before the bullets hit his.

It is 1966, and I am reading a note, left open on the kitchen table, and there are too many Us and not enough Zs.

My Dear Gabriel, *it reads, in the handwriting that signed the lease of this house and the birthday cards and the checks after dinners out.*

This might come as a shock to you, but I won't be coming home tonight, or any other night for the foreseeable future. I assure you, it's nothing to do with you and everything to do with my occupation. It galls me that I must show my true colours now, and I would have been content to continue using you, but, as your people say, the jig is up.

I am no one's expatriate, and am in fact so loyal to the British Empire that it bestowed on me the honour of dispatching me, in its service, to the United States. I am thankful for our years together, and not only because of the knowledge I have thus imparted to British Intelligence, but because of the welcome you have given me, and your hard-won trust. And I must apologise for the inconvenience this levies upon you, and I assure you it was not my intention that you be taken for an accomplice. I bear you no more ill will than I bear any other Yank, and less than most.

I thank you, Gabriel Waltman, from the bottom of my heart. I'd leave you the house if I could, but I don't suspect you want to be caught, dead or alive, with anything in it.

–Hugh Trevelayn

6 January, 1977, 13 Edward IX

A hospital room could be anywhere until you see the

doctors. I wake up in one, and no one's there at all. Frost fogs the window a dreary, humid grey. It could be ash. The movies always say the ash will block out the sun and it's easier to die by fire. The analog clock beside the door tells me it's nearly six o'clock, but not which six o'clock, or where's.

Just to be safe, I don't reach for the buzzer. I try to swipe my clipboard off the side table, but straining off the pillows makes the entire left side of my chest explode into pain, almost as bad as being shot again. At least it can still feel, I think, and shut my eyes, trying not to think about anything else, anything at all.

It doesn't work. It never works.

An orderly wheels by outside the door. The radio on his cart plays, *Dasvidaniye from afar, my love,*
I can see you from the stars.
When I'm looking for you from above,
We both know the night is ours.

His whistling is off-key. The song is American. When someone asks him if I'm awake yet, and he stops whistling to say, "You can go ahead and check," that's American too. Tears sting the corners of my eyes almost as acutely as the pain.

It turns out I don't mind if Mr. Burr sees me cry.

"Looks like I made the right choice," he says, his smile broad and bright enough for me to see through the growing salt haze.

"Looks like," I say. I'm here. America's here. The past three years haven't been a waste. I'm here, and the

British haven't chased me down with warheads or planes, only Hugh. "I can't do it again."

"I wouldn't ask you to. I'm not sure I'd ask anyone to. The Limeys know you're here. You're never leaving the Forty-Eight States again."

He lets me lie here and thank God until I run out of Hebrew.

When I'm done, he only laughs once, on his breath, like a startled apology. "Save your words. Once I get you back to CD2 Central, I guarantee you you'll be talking to the press, the proles, and the President until you're blue in the face. We'll let them know we know if it's enough to keep the bombs from flying."

"Okay." I sink back into the pillows, wince as the bandages on my shoulder resettle. "Did I get him, too?"

"The Limey? Yeah. He's gone."

Mr. Burr is wrong. I couldn't say that aloud if I tried. Oh, I'm sure Hugh's dead, but *dead* doesn't mean gone. That's how the British work. They persist as long as we do. They made us that way. "Did he–"

"Peraza's in the OR. The rest of her unit's still in Cuba. One funeral, two bills, that's all."

That's not what I was going to ask, but I let it go.

It's the price I paid for making it out of England alive.

"Welcome home, Gabe," Mr. Burr says, and claps me on the shoulder that isn't bound up in a sling.

My own name shouldn't sound so foreign.

About the Authors

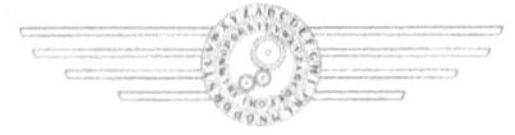

Tyler Bugg

"From Enigma to Paradox" is Tyler Bugg's first published short story, although he has been a fan of alternate history since high school. He is currently studying history at the University of Winnipeg in Canada, and looks forward to writing and publishing more in the future.

Kaye Chazan

Kaye Chazan lives, writes, sings, teaches, and regularly trips over things in New York City. *Substitution Cipher* marks Kaye's first stint as an editor, and "The Ashkenazi Candidate" her third published short story. In all likelihood, her future literary endeavors will involve swords on fire, arranged marriages, punching bouncers in the face, and Freemasons, though not necessarily all at once.

Keep up with her and these projects at @KayeChazan on Twitter.

C. D. Covington

CD Covington's first German textbook had a map with the eastern third shaded dark red and labeled "Deutsche Demokratische Republik." By the time it got to her hands, the vocabulary was long outdated (bell bottoms and reel-to-reels). The map was obsolete shortly thereafter, but the history of divided Germany continues to intrigue her.

There aren't many opportunities to use her German skills in her adopted home in central North Carolina, but she keeps them up by visiting Germany, watching Bundesliga matches, or reading news sites.

She has reviewed books for *Bull Spec*, and she blogs occasionally for BundesligaFanatic.com. You can find her fiction and her blog at cdcovington.com, and follow her on Twitter @exaggerated.

M. Fenn

M. Fenn lives in the mountains of southern Vermont with her husband and a clowder of ghost cats. She blogs spasmodically at mfennwrites.wordpress.com.

G. Miki Hayden

G. Miki Hayden, a long-time instructor at Writer's Digest University, received an Edgar award in 2004 for her short story, "The Maids," in Blood on Their Hands (Berkley, editor Lawrence Block), the same year she was nominated for a Macavity for "War Crimes," also published in a Berkley anthology. Miki's first novel, an alternate history work, *Pacific Empire*, appeared on the *New York Times* summer reading list. Her short mysteries have been published in *Ellery Queen Mystery Magazine*, *Alfred Hitchcock Mystery Magazine*, and numerous small press publications. Many of Miki's science fiction stories have also been published in small press magazines and anthologies over the years. Her romantic short stories have appeared in such national magazines as *True Romance* and *True Love*.

In addition to writing fiction, Miki has been a book reviewer, feature writer, and columnist for a number of small press magazines as well as *Writer's Digest*. Miki's how-to *Writing the Mystery* received nominations for several top mystery genre awards and her *The Naked Writer* serves as a comprehensive style and composition guide for both new and sophisticated writers. Miki's ebook on punctuation (*Punctuation*) is available in all formats.

Rebecca Rozakis

Rebecca Rozakis has the amazing superpower of making lab techs say, "I've never seen it do that before."

She started her career with robots and took a swing through dinosaurs, but now works mostly with Photoshop, which seems so much safer, really. She's just waiting for the ninjas to appear, though. She lives in the New York area with her very tolerant husband.